I0573791

Love's Prey

ENVY AUGUSTINE

CRIMSON
ROMANCE
F+W Media, Inc.

This edition published by
Crimson Romance
an imprint of F+W Media, Inc.
10151 Carver Road, Suite 200
Blue Ash, Ohio 45242

www.crimsonromance.com

Copyright © 2012 by Allison Martinez

ISBN 10: 1-4405-5893-0
ISBN 13: 978-1-4405-5893-1
eISBN 10: 1-4405-5894-9
eISBN 13: 978-1-4405-5894-8

This is a work of fiction. Names, characters, corporations, institutions, organizations, events, or locales in this novel are either the product of the author's imagination or, if real, used fictitiously. The resemblance of any character to actual persons (living or dead) is entirely coincidental.

Chapter One

Snow crunched under Isabelle's boots as she trekked to Keene Lodge. The main building had been renovated. Fresh, red timbers paneled the rustic cabin and wood sap gave the air a pleasant tang. A plank and wire pen to the building's right housed an enormous white Samoyed. The dog barked and yipped at her approach, its black eyes sparkling in the gray morning haze.

Isabelle froze. The Samoyed's shrill vocalizations set off an uncomfortable itch beneath her skin.

Come on, Izzy. One foot in front of the other.

Despite the private pep talk, Isabelle stayed put. The shaking started in her knees and traveled up through her shoulders and into her hands. She squeezed her purse strap, tucked her chin to her chest and ground her teeth behind closed lips, willing away the icy burn of adrenaline spreading through her breast.

"Hey! Hey, there!" The lodge's screen door banged shut and a man bounded down the front steps. He trotted to Isabelle as he rubbed his hands together and squinted when he got closer. "Do I know you?" He sniffed and pinched his nose.

Isabelle hadn't seen this man the last time she'd been to the lodge, but that had been four years ago and her memories of that time were foggy.

"You coming inside?" He was huge; tall and bulky with muscle his loose flannel shirt and baggy jeans couldn't conceal. His girth blocked Izzy's view of the dog pen and dampened that awful barking.

"Hello?" He waved a hand in front of her face and smiled. One of his bottom teeth edged out in front of the others, crowding its neighbors.

3

"Yeah, I'm coming in." Isabelle shook herself and took a bold step forward. As soon as the dog sighted her again it went wild, spinning in circles, jumping at the gate and swooshing its tail. She stumbled and would have fallen if the gentleman at her back hadn't caught her.

"Whoa now, careful," he said, bracing her against his wide chest and grasping her shoulders. Lifting her chin, Izzy gazed into the man's face. His brown eyes were touched with warmth and something else, but he broke their staring contest before she could determine what it was.

"You all right?" He stood her up and ushered her toward the lodge.

"Fine," Izzy said, forcing cheer into her voice. The Samoyed yipped and launched itself halfway over the gate when they passed. She stopped short and the man stepped on her heel.

"Oops, Sorry. Can it, Petey," he said and the dog obediently sat. Its tail thumped the well-tracked ground and its mouth spread in a wide doggy grin. "Don't like animals?"

"It's not that." Izzy studiously avoided eye contact with man and beast. "I had a bad experience a few years back."

"Well, no worries. Petey's friendly as they come. I'll introduce you."

Izzy was about to refuse when she remembered her therapist's assignment.

Challenge yourself, Isabelle. Confront your fears.

She doubted Dr. Turner meant returning to Keene Lodge and coming nose to snout with a wolf-sized dog, but Izzy never did anything halfway.

"All right," she said, hoping her smile seemed genuine.

"Great. Wait right there. I'm Curtis Keene, by the way." He offered his hand and Izzy shook it with her left, keeping her right arm tight to her side.

Snow piled in front of the pen's gate and Curtis had to wiggle it open and kick a trough through the powder. Izzy gave a nervous laugh as the white hound sped forward and jumped up, planting his paws on Curtis's chest. A pink tongue washed his master's nose.

"Down, Petey. Sit."

The command in Curtis's voice was so strong Izzy almost popped a squat. Petey did as ordered and his master crouched at his side.

"Come on. I've got him."

The dog didn't look like it was going anywhere, but Izzy didn't budge. She squeezed her eyes shut, urging her feet onward.

This is a domesticated dog, Izzy. Domesticated.

"Hey."

Izzy cracked one eye to see Curtis waving her over. His large hand secured Petey's ruff.

"I've got him. I promise."

With one deep, winter-cold breath, Izzy propelled herself into the open pen. She tucked her stiff right arm over her belly as she approached the pair.

"Pretty lady, come on down," Curtis said in a pitch perfect *Price Is Right* imitation while she stood staring down at them, fiddling with her purse strap.

"Izzy," she said. "My name's Isabelle."

Curtis's eyes crinkled with his smile. "Izzy, this is Petey. Petey, Izzy." He mussed the fur between the Samoyed's ears. Petey gave an appreciative wuff and she flinched. Two sets of eyes, one black, the other brown, focused on her with the same predatory sheen.

"Sudden movements provoke a hunter's instinct," Curtis warned. Though he still smiled, the alien intensity of his gaze was unnerving. Izzy made to retreat, but the expression vanished as quickly as it came. He tugged on her navy pea-coat and reached for the hand wound tight around her purse strap. She gave him what he wanted, shocked at the heat reaching through her glove. If her hands had been naked as his, they'd have been blue with cold. The hand he squeezed was numb despite her thick glove. Relishing his warmth through the leather, she sank to her knees, frigid damp bleeding through her denim.

Curtis guided Izzy's hand between Petey's ears. She curled her black clad fingers into his white fur and offered a tentative pat. The dog stretched its muzzle to her face and sniffed while she tried to keep still.

"You been up here before?" Curtis asked. His nostrils flared. "You seem awful familiar."

"I used to hike the trails here with my brother. We'd get a cabin for a long weekend once a year." A wet nose nuzzled Izzy's cheek. Instinctively, she pushed at the dog's chest. Petey lowered his head and she patted his side. "We haven't been back for years. You either have an excellent memory or you've mistaken me for someone else."

"No mistake," Curtis said as he moved behind Petey. "My memory's pretty good." His body loomed over the animal. Petey wriggled nervously for a moment then settled down. Even if he lunged at her Izzy was sure Curtis could hold him back. She was so wrapped up with the dog, Curtis startled her when he caught her right arm, circling his fingers around the wrist she never let anyone touch.

"His fur is real soft," Curtis said, coaxing the glove from her hand.

"No." Izzy went rigid. If she struggled, who knew what the dog would do?

"He won't bite you, trust me. God, what are you, frozen solid? I can barely move your fingers." He laughed as he tugged off the glove.

The warmth in Curtis's face disappeared when he stared down at her bared hand. Izzy's doll-like prosthetic rested lifeless in his palm, its jointed fingers bent in what she considered a "natural" position. Natural as long as no one looked close. She yanked her right arm to her chest and cradled it with her left and abruptly stood, driving Petey into a barking frenzy.

"Wait, I'm sorry. I . . . I didn't know."

Izzy could tell Curtis wanted to rise, but he had his hands full with the dog she'd excited. Petey's white teeth flashed as he strained against his master's hold. Her heart leapt with every piercing bark.

Without another word, Izzy took off across the lawn, sprinting for her car while Curtis called after her.

*

Thud, thud, thud.

Curtis banged his head on the desk.

"I am a massive idiot. Massive."

"You know, when I say that you get all huffy and defensive." Light from the clunky PC monitor caught in the flyaway strands frizzing out from Melinda's head and gave her a bluish case of St. Elmo's fire. She sat in her usual place behind the front desk and spun in her office-style swivel chair while Curtis berated himself. He'd pulled up one of the two worn, leather armchairs usually situated near the crackling fireplace so he could peer over Melinda's shoulder while she called up all the websites he wanted. Keene Lodge belonged to Curtis, but you'd never know it if he tried to use the main building's computer or phone. All items on the secretarial side of the desk, including the floor, were Melinda's domain, and that domain extended to the stables and nature trails the redhead favored.

Curtis lifted his head and massaged the goose egg his pounding created. "When you say it, it's out of spite and untrue, and, in this case, I really am an idiot. I *knew* she smelled familiar."

Isabelle Tunskill stared back at him from the computer screen. Even the harsh, digital photo couldn't diminish the ethereal quality of her delicate features. Pale and slender, she'd appeared like a breathtaking phantom gliding over Curtis's front lawn and he, brute that he was, had chased her off with his noise and no manners. If he'd just stopped and used his brain, he might not have made such an ass of himself. He squeezed the glove she'd left behind. Haunting, dark eyes chided him from the screen.

"Ah-ahgh," he hid his face in his hands, toughened over the years with work. Why hadn't he recognized her? Izzy Tunskill was, besides his parents and the pack, the most pivotal figure in his thirty-two year existence. And the most tragic.

"Good riddance," Thomas grumbled from the couch. With a Navajo blanket folded under his head like a pillow, he reclined over the couch's expanse, ticking off items on the construction schedule—construction tome, more like—attached to a clipboard near to bursting.

Curtis stifled the growl rumbling up his throat. Of course Thomas maligned Izzy. Curtis had gone against him for her, hadn't he? And he'd never done that before. Not since either. No doubt she stirred unpleasant memories for all the pack, save Melinda, who hadn't joined them until a year after the Tunskill debacle. Keene Lodge took some nasty press, and he and Thomas and Gerome—Curtis begrudgingly acknowledged Gerome—had gone through hell rebuilding their reputation. They'd shut down the grounds for the next couple of months to accommodate all the cabin overhauls. New construction would put the finishing touches on Keene Lodge's new image: family friendly, rustic chic (Melinda's influence), and no killer beasts prowling the nature trails . . . hopefully. They'd never caught Rapid, their old pack member who now lurked somewhere in the Rockies.

"Maybe I could email her?" Curtis brainstormed out loud. Like a shoeshine rag, he held Izzy's glove in two hands and rubbed it back and forth over his thigh.

"Good idea." Melinda toggled from the local newspaper's web-archived copy of one of the bajillion articles on Izzy and Keene Lodge to the Glazier Studio's homepage. "Dear Isabelle, I know you don't know me, but I recognized you by smell and I was wondering if you'd like to go out sometime." Curtis grumbled, but Melinda took no note. "I like long walks on hiking trails, hunting, and peeing with one leg lifted. By the way, I'm a Werewolf, but

I swear I won't chew your furniture or rip out your throat. That thing with Rapid was a huge misunderstanding, honest. Yours truly, Curtis Keene."

"Thanks for that, Lin." Curtis ruffled her curly hair, making a mess of it. "I appreciate your support."

Sees-Through-Clear-Skies, Curtis's wolf spirit, which was currently a blue light within his chest, flared and sparked, the abstract equivalent of a disgruntled bristle. Curtis's agitation had prodded his wolf to wakefulness and his mind momentarily tangled with a surge of raw animalism. When Clear-Skies settled down into his usual steady pulse, Curtis's thoughts grew coherent once more. The more active, or excited, his wolf, the less human his thought process became until beast came first and man second. By then, of course, he'd usually sprouted fangs, claws, and a tail and tacked a couple feet onto his already substantial six foot four frame. It was a careful daily dance living with a wolf spirit, but one he performed well.

"Enough about the prima ballerina," Thomas said. "I need the two of you focused on construction. We have a lot of work coming up on top of the usual pack business."

Melinda saluted their Alpha behind his back and returned to her *ca-chack, ca-chack, ca-chacking* at the keyboard. No pack member could disobey their leader's direct command when he invoked the Alpha's power. Not without enduring a great deal of pain. Curtis knew all about that. The order, a static shock in his brain, prevented further speech about Izzy, but Thomas couldn't regulate Curtis's thoughts and she consumed them. Her face, her body, her smell; he snuck a whiff of her glove. Plastic and vanilla suffused the leather. Vanilla came across strongest. He ran his tongue over his top lip. Did she taste as sweet as she smelled? Probably.

In the newspaper photo, Izzy looked tired and frail, but she'd filled out—as much as a ballerina did—since the accident. Her lanky, athletic build she'd covered in very tight jeans, for which he sang her praises, and a heavy wool coat. Despite her recovered fleshiness and muscle, her slight figure and white skin gave her a spectral appearance. He'd expected her to vanish into the dismal haze when he'd spotted her that morning. Lifting her glove to his face, he took another deep inhale.

A sharp, familiar scent invaded Curtis's nostrils and Clear-Skies went bright and spiky in his chest; he felt like he swallowed a popsicle whole.

Enemy, enemy, enemy, his wolf snarled.

Everyone in the main room focused on the front door. Outside, Petey barked over and over, his vicious warnings echoing in the otherwise quiet evening. The scent weakened and then dissipated entirely.

"Well then," Thomas set down his clipboard. "I believe Isabelle Tunskill might have her uses after all. Night's-Rapid-Water never could leave crippled prey alone."

In wolf form, Curtis's fur would have stood on end and he would have bared his teeth at the man proprietarily seated on *his* couch. But blood lust lit his Alpha's eyes. Curtis saw the wolf in him, Mountain's-Might, gleefully capering behind them. Thomas's next words arced through him like electric current, laced with the Alpha's will.

"I don't care how you do it, but get down to Tavella and bring me Isabelle Tunskill."

Clear-Skies leapt like blue flame at the challenge and Curtis's muscles coiled tight. They were on the hunt, but why, oh why, did it have to be her?

Chapter Two

A mixture of pride and jealousy swelled in Isabelle's throat as she directed the line of lithe bodies at the *barre*. Girls ages ten to twelve, hair pinned in impeccable buns, eyes fixed on their reflections in the mirrored wall, schooled their faces in focused concentration. Pink slippered feet stretched and pointed in *tendu* as the warm-up music garbled into a discordant warble before clearing into the fuzzy thrum of piano keys. The record was ancient—the same one Izzy had warmed up to when she'd been a student at Glazier Studio. Nostalgia made her smile. Nothing in the world smelled like a ballet studio. She inhaled as the girls progressed into the *dégagé* series, lifting their pointed feet off the floor in a sweeping gesture. Leather, hairspray, fresh vinyl, and cold air melded with recollections of dorm life and grueling schedules— which she'd loved—at the School of American Ballet. She cocooned herself in the hazy reminiscence of the best times of her life.

It was a mixed blessing Madame Glazier needed an instructing assistant when Izzy had left New York permanently. She'd never intended to slide on her tights and slippers again after her accident, but the routine of holding class, the familiar positions, steps, jumps, and stretches drew her out of the crushing depression that threatened her each time mind and body went too long unoccupied. All the girls in their black leotards and flimsy waist wraps, all of them had a chance at a future forever closed to Izzy. Sometimes she couldn't help but envy them. Madame Glazier had all but retired within six months of Izzy's acceptance of her teaching position. Izzy ran the studio in her stead.

When the girls took the *barre* with their left hands, Izzy turned their instruction over to her assistant, Claire Monahan. The petite blond counted time and demonstrated proper form when one of the girls got sloppy. Their students needed to see the best form of each step and pose to advance. They couldn't mimic the clumsy movements of Izzy's prosthetic. Not if they wanted to excel. Madame Glazier trusted Izzy with her legacy. Girls who studied at the Glazier Studio often placed in summer classes at the School of American Ballet, SAB for short, and Madame Glazier boasted three soloists in the New York City Ballet and numerous others who went on to prestigious companies throughout the nation. She wouldn't let Madame down, or the students who came to her because they loved dance. Knowing the simple joy of the single perfected steps combined into a fluid grace, she could not deny them that. And some days she was truly happy watching them, knowing she had a hand in their development.

This was the last class of the evening. Anxious parents milled at the ceiling to floor length windows facing the downtown street, watching daughters complete their final stretches and deepen their splits. Izzy cringed. Arty Purcell, one of the city's resident homeless, made his rounds with his outstretched Styrofoam cup. A stained trench coat hung off his spindly frame. When was the last time he'd used any of his panhandled funds for food? Izzy had him picked up a couple times when she couldn't run him off. He'd never tried anything with her or her students, but parents didn't like him hanging around the studio. There was a reason she kept the doors locked all day. It only took one man wandering in off the street "just 'cause" to ruthlessly enforce security precautions. When she gave Arty the eye through the glass, he took the hint and scuttled off.

Izzy chatted with mothers and fathers as they retrieved their daughters, praising their achievements no matter how small. Encouragement was essential for the beginner and intermediate classes. She addressed problems with form and discipline only with those who were ready to dance for a lifetime. With them, she was brutally honest. She never told anyone they couldn't dance. Anyone could. Limitations—height, weight, weak ankles, flat feet, poor footwork—weren't impossibilities, but a dedication to overcoming them was a necessity.

Those limitations were not like Izzy's arm. True, there were handicapped dancers in the world, but none in any company she cared to join. There was nothing wrong with those companies, but no one would suggest a pro football player who'd blown both his knees join a flag football league to boost his spirits. Performance at the highest level was all she tolerated from herself. Having tasted it once, a smaller company would never satisfy and if she didn't feel her best, she couldn't give the *corps* her best.

After the studio emptied, Izzy checked the messages left during classes, changed into street clothes—her left fingers still tripped over buttons—and shoved her gear into her dance bag. She'd had the pink duffle since her inception at SAB. It was falling apart. She'd sewn the strap back on at least ten times. Slinging the worn bag across her chest, she hit the lights, and stepped into the frigid Tavella night.

"Ain't got nothing for me tonight, pretty lady?" Arty fell into step behind Izzy, his stiff legged stride taxed by her loping pace. His tattered trench coat billowed out like a cape. He was too close. She felt his presence behind her and slipped her fingers around the can of mace tucked in her coat pocket.

"Not tonight, Arty." Izzy kept her eyes on the path ahead. She made a beeline for her SUV parked near the curb. Glittering frost dusted the black paint. There hadn't been snowfall for a week, but filthy slush banked against the buildings that lined the wet sidewalk and clogged gutters along the street. Her foot slid in the icy slop, sending her off kilter, and her heart leapt the way it did when she almost fell down a set of stairs. Abandoning the mace, she fumbled for her keys. She should have had them ready before she left the studio. Why didn't she have them ready? Intimidating Arty with a group of protective parents wasn't a problem, but she was all alone here. She fought with the Velcro pocket on the front of her bag, reassured by the jingle of metal.

The duffel strap bit into her neck and chest when Arty yanked on the slack. Izzy stopped so fast she skidded and nearly collapsed. Arty spun her around and clutched at the bag.

"Holding out on me, girl?" A mélange of booze and sweat rolled off Arty. With the man at her back, Izzy had been spared his stench, but facing him she got the full assault. The booze had her worried. The bum was aggravating and off-putting sober. When he'd been at the bottle all day she'd seen him get belligerent. She couldn't believe he put his hands on her and was too pissed to be scared.

"Let go, Arty, or you'll be spending the night in jail." Threatening him with the cops usually cut through his drunken haze. Not tonight.

"My bag, not yours." Arty twisted his mouth in a malicious pout and wound the strap around his fist, tugging Izzy closer. His yellowed eyes were wide and dazed.

Izzy's functional hand closed around the mace in her pocket. "You really want to fuck off now, Arty." She didn't wait for a response or reaction, just whipped the can out of her pocket and nailed him in the face with the chemical spray. He screeched and clawed at his eyes. He hadn't released the strap and Izzy collided with him when he staggered. They both hit the slick pavement in a flailing jumble.

Trying to disentangle herself, Izzy pushed at Arty's chest and he lashed out, swiping her face. A glancing blow, but his chemical covered fingers left searing trails over her neck and cheek. She yelped and was kicking at him ineffectually when strong hands gripped her shoulders and hauled her up. The strap across her chest snapped under the tension and her dance bag whomped onto Arty's chest. He hooted his triumph and, unmindful of his inflamed skin and squinched eyes, wobbled to his feet. He squeezed between two cars at the curb and galloped into the busy street. Tires squealed and horns blared as he blindly cut across traffic.

"Oh, no you don't," someone said over Izzy's head and whoever held her upright let go. She stumbled back and caught herself on the closest building's brick wall.

A very large body pursued Arty. She couldn't see if the interloper caught the bum from her traffic-obscured vantage. Possessions were less important than stemming the licks of fire over her throat and face. The dirty snow appealed and she went on her hands and knees while her eyes watered. Before she scraped up a fistful of the muck, the large someone returned, flung her bag down, and rushed to her side.

"Are you all right?" he asked, reaching for her.

Izzy jerked away from the stranger's hand. She blinked back tears, trying to make out his face. "Burned."

"Burned?"

"Mace."

"Shit. Wait right here, ok?"

Where the hell would she go? Izzy nodded, scooting back against the building. The man sounded so familiar, but he sprinted down the street before her vision cleared. She really wanted to rub and scratch at the prickling heat spreading over her skin, but that would make the burning worse and spread the mace. Every time her left arm shot up to worry her aggravated skin, she knocked it down with her right. Taking stock of the damages to her possessions occupied her antsy appendages.

Ignoring the wet pavement under her butt, she rifled through her bag: pointe shoes, leather flats, footed tights, leotard, chiffon wrap, e-reader, and wallet present. Cell phone and keys? Absent. Along with the busted strap, the side pocket where she kept her need-them-now items flapped from the few threads holding it to the bag. How would she get home? How would she get *in* her home?

Fantastic.

Izzy groaned as her self-appointed savior trotted to her feet and squatted next to her. Getting her first good look at him, she gasped. Her white knight was Curtis Keene, the handsome man from last week with the scary dog. Embarrassment burned hotter than the chemicals on her skin. She was surprised steam didn't curl from the pavement.

"Ok, tilt your head back," he said, unscrewing the cap from a bottle of water he held.

"What are you doing here?" she asked.

"At the moment, trying to get this crap off you." Curtis chucked a finger under her chin and lifted her head. Icy water ran over her cheek and neck and soaked into her coat and the oversized white tunic she wore underneath.

"You should get that wet coat off," Curtis said when the water ran out.

"I'd rather be a little uncomfortable than completely freezing."

"I don't mean the water. You might have gotten some spray-back. That'll make for a nasty surprise if it seeps through the wool or you touch it accidentally."

Izzy shot to her feet and struggled with the large wooden buttons on her pea coat.

"Your bag probably got some, too," Curtis went on while Izzy warred with her garment, "but I didn't notice anything while I had it. A few tumbles in the wash couldn't hurt. Here," he approached her when her frustration mounted, "let me help."

"I got it," Izzy angled away her body.

"Could have fooled me," Curtis said and chuckled.

The laughter set Izzy off. "I'm not some helpless cripple."

Anyone would have thought she'd sucker punched him. Curtis's bright expression closed and he scratched his neck, shooting a sidelong glance down the street. "I didn't say that."

Guilt twanged in her chest like a popped guitar string. Izzy took her aggression out on her buttons. She'd known going back to Keene Lodge had been a huge mistake. Not only had she buckled under her dog phobia, she'd done it in front of a big, strong man. Curtis Keene probably had a good laugh at her last week, too. She gritted her teeth. She could have handled Arty on her own, but she didn't have to snap at the man who'd gotten most of her stuff back and washed the mace off her. Shrugging out of her coat, she shivered and mumbled, "Thank you, by the way."

Some of Curtis's brightness returned with her praise. "Anytime," he said and pulled off the puffy jacket he wore and held it out. "Trade you."

They exchanged garments and Izzy shimmied into Curtis's enormous jacket while he tucked her coat into her duffel. In his outerwear she resembled a big, black marshmallow. A snug, big, black marshmallow.

"So, besides chasing the homeless and treating minor chemical burns, what brings you my way?" She frowned at her puffed figure.

Stripped of his jacket left Curtis with a white, short-sleeved tee and jeans, but he didn't seem cold. He dug in his left pocket, tugged out a piece of cloth and tossed it to Izzy. She caught it and rubbed the supple leather between her thumb and index finger.

"You came all the way from DeConing to return my glove?"

"Why not? Walk you to your car?"

"Can't drive it. No keys," Izzy displayed the torn pocket on her bag. "No cell phone either."

"Well, shit," Curtis said and strained to see over the passing cars. "Help me check over there?" He pointed at the opposite sidewalk.

Izzy agreed and made to cross when Curtis held out his hand. Hesitating, she finally slipped her left hand into his and they trotted across the street at the first break in traffic.

Their search wasn't entirely fruitless. Curtis found Izzy's smashed cell phone in a slush pile. He turned it over guiltily.

Izzy let her head hang back. "Mind if I borrow yours? I need to get hold of a tow truck and, hopefully, my building manager."

The calls took longer than Izzy expected. Curtis had to be the last person on the planet without Internet on his phone. The Stone Age cell flipped open and closed and had a retractable antenna. He didn't have a tow company in his contacts, so she dialed information. Ten minutes later, she hung up and massaged the deep crease in her brow.

There goes a few hundred dollars. Large, unexpected expenses caused Izzy physical pain.

Building managers weren't as easy to get on the phone as grouchy tow truck drivers. After being dumped into voicemail a few times, Izzy left a message, flipped the cell phone shut, and passed it back to Curtis. She thought he'd take off, what with danger thwarted and her glove returned, but he followed her back to her car. He leaned with her on the SUV while they waited on the tow. Passing cars packed with Friday night party boys honked at them and hollered lewd encouragement to Curtis. Izzy hid behind her hand and prayed they went home sans pleasurable company.

"Aren't you cold?" she asked when a particularly nippy breeze rippled Curtis's shirt. His tanned skin wasn't even goose-pimpled.

"Nah. I was worse after taking a plunge into the creek a few weeks back."

"What were you doing?"

"It started off as fishing, but ended up as snorkeling. I tripped over my tackle-box."

Izzy laughed as the tow truck pulled up. She started removing Curtis's jacket while the driver, who was more attractive than he'd sounded over the phone, hitched up her car. The trip home wouldn't be so bad after all. She went for the passenger door when Curtis called to her.

"Want to ride with me?" he asked, eyeing the tow truck owner while that man eyed Izzy. "Figured you might need my phone again. And a drink."

Cocking her head, Izzy considered him. Curtis didn't seem like a psycho stalker, but psycho stalkers never seemed that way, did they? Whenever someone found out their neighbor or spouse killed a bunch of people, they always said the same thing: he was so normal.

Curtis wasn't normal. He was tall, handsome, friendly, and a little pushy. And he waited for her answer with a hopeful glint in his eye. Something else touched his gaze too, that same something she'd spied at the lodge and nearly forgotten, a shadow skimming just below the surface of deep water. She narrowed her eyes, but he spun around and his shoulders slumped in an exaggerated sulk before she figured out what that shadow was.

"I get it. A man knows when he's been turned down."

"I'm not turning you down. I—"

"Great. Be right back." Curtis jogged for his Jeep before Izzy got in another word. He picked her up by her car, popping open the passenger side door. She sidled into the cloth upholstered seat, grateful for the heat he'd turned up. Peeling off his jacket, she tossed it in the back and settled in for the short trip. Evening news hummed from the radio, but he had the volume down, so it wasn't much of a distraction from the prolonged conversational lull. She didn't know Curtis well enough for the silence to be comfortable. She filled the void with chatter.

"I can't believe you came all this way to use my glove as an excuse to ask me out," Izzy said. She'd had guys get her flowers and treat her to dinner and drinks, but Curtis had gone way out of his way for a total stranger. There had to be an angle he played that she didn't see.

"Why not?"

"It's a lot of work for such a little thing."

"Women like gestures and big gestures make big impressions."

"Can't argue with that logic." Izzy stared out the window where the scenery blurred. Curtis's reflection superimposed over the cars and inviting restaurants they passed. He took his eyes from the road for a quick moment, then a longer one.

"I also wanted to apologize," he said.

Izzy faced him and his attention returned to the road. "Apologize?"

"For not recognizing you sooner," he squeezed the steering wheel. "If I would have thought for a second, I wouldn't have been so stupid with Petey."

Oh, it's a guilt thing, Izzy thought. That made sense. If Curtis Keene didn't own Keene Lodge, he was certainly related to whoever did. Of course he'd remember what happened four years ago even if he didn't remember her specifically. People didn't die on their property everyday. She chewed her thumbnail and swallowed back the painful bulge of emotion stuck in her throat. Curtis could deal with his own guilt, however it related to her. She wasn't in the mood to play therapist, especially not when she was still so attached to her own.

"You could have emailed," Izzy said, voice terse.

"Nope. Couldn't have." Curtis inclined his head toward her. "You know what the Chinese say about the life you save. Well, the *Six String Samurai*, at least."

Izzy snorted. "Samurai are Japanese and Arty is many things, but not a killer. You saved me a lot of inconvenience tonight, but not my life."

"I didn't mean tonight."

"Well then what—"

The car jerked to a stop and Curtis pointed out the window. "This your place?"

They parked in front of her building. Curtis switched on his emergency lights and Izzy jumped out of the car to direct the tow truck to her reserved spot. She had no clue what Curtis meant about saving her life, but the whole "the life you save" thing? She knew enough about bad samurai movies to know he felt responsible for her. She'd have to get that idea right out of his head. No one was responsible for Izzy but Izzy. Still, she was curious. When had he saved her life if not tonight? He hadn't been there that day, had he? She couldn't remember. She stared at him as he slapped a beat on his steering wheel. Good thing she needed a drink.

*

The Glo Bar was overpriced, over designed, and snooty, but it was three blocks from Izzy's building so that's where they went. Besides the proximity to home, the indoor koi pond—the monster fish poked their gulping mouths from the lily-padded water whenever anyone passed and begged for treats—was also nice as were the paper lanterns hung overhead. A snaking fence of towering bamboo partitioned tables and booths from the bar. While Curtis braved the three-body-deep rush at the polished counter, Izzy grabbed a two-person table vacated by a couple heading out early. She'd had no luck with her building manager and spun Curtis's phone on the table, glaring at the handwritten menu touting the evening's featured appetizer: lobster ravioli.

"Do you know how much this was?" Curtis asked. Her personal *ronin* plunked down two napkins, a bottle of beer, and a rum and pineapple on their table. He didn't wait for her guess. "Eighteen bucks. Eighteen! That's not including tip. Bartender gave me the hairy eyeball, too."

Somehow, Izzy didn't find that surprising with Curtis's rugged charm. Anyone else at Glo Bar going for the I-don't-care-how-I-look effect did so in a seventy dollar T-shirt and three hundred dollar jeans. Curtis's graying undershirt and Levis probably didn't inspire confidence in a generous tip. Smiling, she pulled the pins from her hair. Her stylishly long bangs and shoulder length tresses fell loose. She didn't wear makeup or jewelry, but her outfit just passed for decent in this place. The long-sleeved wrap draped over her white tunic covered most of her prosthetic and the flesh colored, silicone glove sheathing the false arm made it look almost real.

"Your hair looks nice down like that," Curtis said after swallowing a mouthful of beer. "How come you wear it back?"

"Because it's practical for ballet. Hair away from the face, clothes close to the body."

"That's right, you're a dancer."

"Was," Izzy stirred her sweet, sweet drink, focusing on the swirling ice. "I teach now." She pursed her lips. No more skirting the issue. "What did you mean in the car?"

"What, the glove? I'm trying to get on your good side, obviously." Curtis arched one eyebrow and swigged his beer.

Izzy wished he'd knock it off. She didn't need him pandering to her. "I meant the 'life you save' comment. When did you save my life?"

Joviality blanched from Curtis's face. He tapped the bottom of his brown bottle on the black lacquer table. "I—" he squirmed in his chair. "I was the one who found you. And your brother."

Bar noise, loud enough that they'd semi-shouted at each other, dwindled, or seemed to. Izzy's mouth opened, but she couldn't speak. The most vivid memories of that day rolled through her mind like a silent roll of eight millimeter film.

There went Izzy and Alan leaving their parents in their rented cabin, her mother at the rough wood dining table sipping from a steaming mug of coffee, her father scrambling eggs and burning toast. They took to the trails. Alan ran ahead of her. Sunlight caught golden flecks in his dark hair. They raced to Rock Spout Falls (a trickle through two boulders), their traditional first hike on their annual trip to Keene Lodge.

Shaking her head, Izzy cut the reel and concentrated on the man in front of her, his chin a little grizzled, his brown hair a little long and falling into worried eyes. Her vision wavered with tears she held back.

"You found us?" she asked and her throat clicked when she swallowed. Curtis dropped his chin in affirmation. He studied her reactions, his gaze roving over her face, shoulders, fingers. "I don't remember you."

Izzy remembered Alan's vacant, blue eyes. Red smears on his face. A dark shape worrying his body. Rumbling noises like creeping thunder. Pain and pain and pain. People. Men shouting. Weightlessness, then nothing. Nothing until she woke up in the hospital two weeks later, doped into numb ambivalence, her right arm and her brother gone. She sucked in a sharp breath and loosened her death grip on her sweating glass.

"I didn't expect you'd remember," Curtis said. "You weren't really there. You talked to me, though."

"What did I say?" She sipped her watery drink and tried keeping her hand steady.

"Sang."

Izzy choked on a sliver of ice. "I *sang* to you?"

"Twinkle, Twinkle Little Star. My fault. I wanted to keep you conscious, so I got you singing with me until emergency response came."

"But why didn't the wolf attack you?"

It came out of the woods a mile from the falls. A humongous streak of black fur, yellow eyes, and white teeth. It took Izzy first, bolting from the trees where she wandered and dragged her by her arm. The silence was uncanny. Any wolf attack she imagined was punctuated with snarls and growling barks, stringed instruments too. Silence wasn't right, was it? Something so awful should be noisier, have its own soundtrack. The wolf growled only after Alan came for her.

"I was on the trail with Thomas, a friend of mine. When we found you, the wolf took off. Two big humans were more threatening than two smaller ones." Curtis's lips twisted. "S'all I can think."

Izzy's hands supported her drooping head. "You know I missed Alan's funeral? I was out cold in the hospital when they buried my brother." Her voice broke and she shut her mouth. What was she saying? They were here for drinks and chit chat. Couldn't she save the soul bearing for Dr. Turner? Chewing the insides of her cheeks, she prayed Curtis picked up the conversational slack. If she moved, spoke, looked anywhere but into her drink she'd cry. Moments like these made her glad her bangs obscured her face.

The wolf attack at Keene Lodge had been downright bizarre. In general, wild animals avoided humans. Until Alan Tunskill, there wasn't a single recorded wolf-related death in North American history. And in Colorado of all places. Hunted to near extinction in the 1940s, wolves avoided the land. In 2002, wolf sightings in the Rockies had excited naturalists, but the animals were reluctant to return. Their numbers hovered in the single digits to date. Press on the Keene attack had been massive. An up and coming soloist from the New York City Ballet loses her arm and survives her brother in a freakish, brutal mauling? What wouldn't the media love? Interests in wolves and ballerinas had skyrocketed for months.

"I thought about visiting you in the hospital. Thomas talked me out of it," Curtis said. "I should have gone."

"I doubt I would have seen you. There were a lot of well meaning nut cases wanting to get to me back then." Strangling her rapidly warming glass in her left hand, Izzy fought rising anger. Why had Curtis been spared? Why couldn't he and Thomas or whoever, have gotten to them sooner? Alan might have lived.

It wasn't his fault.

In the beginning, Izzy had blamed everything and everyone for her brother's death, no one more than herself. If she'd kept up with him, if she hadn't gone off the trail.

If, if, if.

Blame ate through her like acid. She hadn't had those sorts of thoughts in a long time, but Curtis opened old wounds that had never properly healed. This was too much baggage all at once.

"I should have gone to a fucking kennel," Izzy muttered and finished off her drink.

"Kennel?"

Slumping in her uncomfortable chair, Izzy said, "My doctor thought it would be good for me to confront some lingering issues I've had since, since everything." She waved her hand, illustrating how trivial that "everything" was. She had it together. Was totally over it. Except for the panic attacks.

"Doctor as in therapist?" Curtis asked.

Izzy shredded her napkin. "Yeah." There was nothing judgmental in Curtis's tone, but she knew what he thought: poor crippled girl can't take care of herself. She squeezed her eyes shut against that critical voice pounding in her skull. It was the same voice that drove her at SAB and later in the NYCB *corps de ballet*, a harsh inner narrator, twisted by trauma, who demanded perfection. That voice wouldn't shut up until she'd

24

achieved perfection, physical and emotional, all on her own without crutches like therapists and other shoulders to cry on that didn't charge by the hour. When she got better, she wouldn't need anyone telling her how "fine" she was.

"Your doctor told you to come back to the lodge?"

"She told me to think about reacquainting myself with animals and fixating less on my old career. Ever since the attack, I can't be around dogs, any big animal, without panicking." Izzy shrugged. "She meant 'get over it already' and I intend to."

Curtis frowned. "Wouldn't she have said that if she meant it?"

"People never say what they mean. Especially not psychoanalysts. How much do you think they'd get paid if they told every neurotic mess that came to them: yep, you're a whack job."

Shaking his near-empty beer bottle, Curtis appeared to mull Izzy's statement over before he said, "I say what I mean all the time."

"You do not."

Curtis's brows shot up. "Do too."

"Fine. What are you thinking right now?"

"That I wish your top was as tight as your jeans."

Izzy couldn't stop her mouth from twitching up.

Curtis winked. "Your building manager ever call back?"

She shook her head.

"Then it'll be a late night for us. You want another one?" Curtis gestured at her glass and Izzy went hunting for her wallet. Gathering their dead soldiers before she got her cash, Curtis said, "Don't even offer. You're not using the money excuse to say this wasn't a date."

*

"I can't believe you pick locks." Izzy steadied herself on Curtis's shoulder, his worn undershirt soft as silk under her palm. A leather case holding his lock picks rested at his knees. Her building manager had never called, but Curtis had kept her more than entertained.

She'd checked her watch once at ten p.m., and the next time she'd glanced it had read one in the morning. Almost everyone had vacated Glo Bar for other frenetic venues. When she'd noticed the time, theirs had been the loudest conversation in the bar. After her first drink, her formidable emotional barriers had melted and she'd grown more susceptible to Curtis's easy, affable way.

Three rum and pineapples had Izzy tipsy. Alcohol made her warm and languid and wobbly and she hadn't minded when Curtis had laced his fingers in hers on the return walk to her complex. He'd stuck with beer. She hadn't kept track of how many he'd had, but his hands were steady while he worked the nicked lock on her apartment's front door.

"The cabins on our grounds are pretty old. Doors get stuck all the time. People lose keys on the trails and in the creeks. We have a master, but this comes in handy." The door snicked open on his last word and he gathered his tools.

Izzy did a spritely step into her apartment, tossed her dance bag into the utility room when she passed it in the front hall, and dove, belly first, onto her couch.

"I've wanted to do this all day," she said into the chenille throw draped over the cushions. She flexed and pointed her aching feet.

The apartment, though Izzy didn't own it, was home. The wood floors squeaked when she walked on them. The kitchen, dining room, and living area was all one space and the walls were thin, but she loved it. At SAB, she'd dormed with dancers and had shared a place after graduation with three of the *corps* members from NYCB. Some people valued privacy and silence. Izzy couldn't sleep without the hum of voices next door or the thump of footsteps overhead. She had enough to swing a mortgage, but she couldn't bring herself to move to a bigger place all on her lonesome. Plus, where would she find a house with a window for an east wall? She flipped on her back. The spectral blur of the moon hazed through the drawn double sheers backing the heavy curtains.

Izzy pushed herself to a sitting position and noticed Curtis hovering in the front door.

"Not coming in?" she asked.

"I didn't want to assume too much," Curtis said and stepped inside, carefully shutting the door behind him.

"I don't know why not. You've been assuming a lot all night."

"This is different. This is your territory."

It certainly was her territory and she didn't allow many in it. Curtis was the first man inside since the accident. Izzy hoisted herself from the couch and went to the kitchen, which was a strip of counter space, appliances, and shelving lining half of the living area's back wall. It wasn't just liquor that had her at ease. Though she and one-night stands weren't unacquainted, she hadn't had one since she left New York. Not for lack of trying. Most guys she wanted just wanted her story. They needed the whys behind her arm and going through it killed sex drives. She didn't get why they asked for answers they couldn't handle or why they needed them at all. You didn't have to know someone to fuck them, just be reasonably sure they wouldn't smother you with a pillow during the afterglow. With Curtis, she didn't have to explain. He'd been there. He knew. That meant he knew her better than most. She rolled back her shoulders. "I don't have any beer, but I can do coffee or open a bottle of wine."

"Coffee's good," Curtis said. He investigated the living area, stopping when something caught his interest like the portable *barre* and triptych mirror next to the living room's entrance. Worn out *pointe* shoes heaped in front of the mirror and bundles of dried flowers hung over it in a precise row. Old as the bouquets were, they retained their dusty perfume. The *pointe* shoes, too. They sighed out lilac scented puffs of air whenever she slid them on, the floral scent from the sachets she kept in her duffel forever stamped on the satin. Izzy couldn't use the old shoes for class, but they were fine for her exercises at home.

At SAB, she'd done her *barre* work *en pointe*, a technique she used with her advanced students.

"You teach from home?" Curtis called over the high buzz and grumble of the coffee grinder. The apartment filled with the rich scent of ground beans.

"That's personal use only," Izzy said as she tapped the dark, fragrant powder into the waiting filter.

"I thought you didn't dance anymore."

"I don't perform, but I like starting the day with stretches and *barre* work. Not doing it felt wrong." Izzy returned to the couch while the coffee brewed.

"Any pictures of you in a tu-tu?" Curtis asked, checking out her many, many framed photos; heavily textured black-and-white prints by a local artist.

"My mom has a bunch in an album. I hate pictures of me." Izzy didn't mention what she couldn't stand was how happy she was in those photos. "The flowers are my mementos."

Mementos formed her solitary ties to her former life. For six months, Izzy endured an endless parade of emails, cards, and letters expressing sorrow for her loss. The worst correspondence came from her former *corps de ballet* members. She knew they didn't mean any harm, but she couldn't stand the well wishes from her former peers who would fill her former roles. She'd changed her email address and had vacated the social network sites.

Staring at the ceiling, Curtis reached for the paper tags dangling from each bundle of dried flowers above the mirror. That he could reach them without a stepstool threw Izzy for a loop. He read her handwriting aloud.

"Rubies in *Jewels*, Odette and Odile in *Swan Lake*, Columbine in *The Nutcracker*?"

"I saved the bouquets from my favorite roles."

Watching Curtis navigate her space was strange. Everything he touched was so delicate, the flowers, slippers, the crystal figures set on her open shelves. He was a giant tip-toeing through a fairy glade. Though he took up way more space than Izzy, he was mindful of his bulk. He curled one thick finger around the satin ribbon of a particularly worn out slipper, its insole detached and hanging like a tongue from its sole.

Would he touch me like that? Izzy wondered and rubbed her rigid prosthetic. *Like something fragile?* The thought made her brows crease.

Curtis strolled to the couch and leaned over the back. "I know *The Nutcracker*, but what's Columbine?"

Izzy squeezed her fake arm. "A doll Herr Drosselmeyer gives Clara."

"I thought he gave her the nutcracker."

"He does, but he gives her three wind-up dolls before that."

Curtis plopped on the couch at Izzy's right. "And the nutcracker is a prince, right? He transforms and saves Clara from evil rats."

"Actually, it's mice and Clara saves the prince. She throws her slipper at the Mouse King and they defeat him together."

"Would you rescue me if I was about to be slain by an evil rodent?"

"Are you a prince in disguise?"

Curtis shrugged. "Kiss me and find out."

Clicking her tongue, Izzy turned away as her cheeks heated. She started to push herself from the couch when Curtis caught her jointed hand before she rose.

"Is it because I'm not on my knees?" Curtis dropped to the floor in front of Izzy, easing up her wrap's gray sleeve. He lifted her mechanical hand to his lips like a gentleman at court. A genteel gesture, but his smoldering eyes held a very ungentlemanly promise.

"Stop!" Izzy ripped her hand from his and hugged her prosthetic.

Curtis sat back on his heels. "It's true. Chivalry is dead."

"It's not that." Hiding under the sofa cushions seemed like a good idea right about now. "I just don't like anyone touching my arm." She shoved off the couch and went to the kitchen counter, pouring fresh, black coffee into two waiting mugs and pulling out cream and sugar.

She hadn't had a serious date since the accident and now that she had one she did everything in her power to make this guy tuck tail and run. Maybe it was a sign. Maybe she wasn't ready.

"Is there anywhere it's ok for me to touch?"

Izzy jumped. Curtis's silent approach spooked her. The couch springs hadn't squeaked nor the cushions whispered when he rose and his heels hadn't knocked the floor. He was a sudden warm presence at her back, his breath a soft breeze over the top of her head. She grabbed the carton of half-n-half, disregarding his inquiry. Hands, rough and callused, snuck beneath her wrap and brushed her shoulders.

"What about here?" Curtis asked and drummed his fingers on the rounded curves of her upper arms. "Is here ok?"

Mouth quirking as she poured cream into her mug, Izzy nodded and stirred the cloudy mixture until the black liquid turned caramel brown. Just like Curtis's skin. His hands trailed over her back and paused above her shoulder blades.

"And here?"

"There's fine," Izzy said, enjoying the gentle massage he gave her, stiffening only when he grazed the straps and harness holding her prosthetic in place. Waiting for her to relax, he kneaded her muscles all the way down to her waist where he circled his arms.

"Here ok, too?" Curtis's chest butted Izzy's head and back when he brought her close. She rocked forward when he inhaled. Loosening one arm, he gathered her hair, swept it over her shoulder, and lowered his face to her ear.

"What about . . . here?" Curtis pressed his lips right beneath Izzy's jaw. A little sigh escaped her when his stubble scratched her cheek and she shivered. Devilish shudders rippled through her stomach. Her left hand shot up and her fingers tangled in his hair, clenching and urging him on. Why the hell had she waited so long for this? She'd wanted him a third of the way through her second drink.

Opening his mouth, Curtis's teeth grazed Izzy's throat, teasing the delicate skin. His hand traveled from her waist to her belly where he pushed, bringing her tight against his hips. The hard ridge of his erection pressed against her rear.

"Oh." Izzy gasped and craned her neck free of his mouth, twisting to meet his half lidded gaze.

"This not ok?" Curtis's voice rasped.

Facing him, Izzy went on her toes and cupped his stubbly cheek. "More than ok." She guided his mouth to hers, taking his lower lip gently with her teeth before kissing him. He was motionless under her attention and she pulled back. Had she somehow misinterpreted his excitement? He was on her the instant she broke contact. His hands cradled her face and he crushed his lips to hers.

The aggressive burst had Izzy clinging to Curtis's shoulder. He parted her lips with his and his tongue stole into her mouth. She accepted him, sucked him into her. Widening her stance, she raised her hips and rubbed herself over the length of his hard cock. The friction made Curtis groan and he drew back, licking his already moistened lips.

"I want you." He gripped her shoulders. Desire clouded his eyes, made them vacant. He shut them and bowed his head. "I want you, but I don't want to drive you off." He glanced at the stiff arm hanging at her right.

Left hand flat on Curtis's chest, Izzy tested the hard planes of muscle veiled by the threadbare cotton of his undershirt. Pushing, she held him at arm's length. "You saw me at the worst, didn't you? You were with me then."

No matter how hard she tried, Izzy couldn't remember Curtis's reassuring presence, his hand around hers, his singing. She wished she could.

"I was," he said.

"Then I'll get over it." Izzy tugged at her wrap. The garment fell away and heaped at her feet. Her sleeveless, white tunic didn't conceal much. Save for the harness fixing the device to her body, which fitted tightly to her back and across her chest, her prosthetic was exposed.

Izzy never did anything halfway.

Chapter Three

Curtis closed the distance between them cautiously. Not knowing when Izzy might clam up and shut down threw him off. Women normally took to his come-on-strong-and-keep-on-coming approach. He chased them down with unrelenting flattery and no one went home disappointed. Not so with this woman. At times, she warmed to him, encouraged him, then he'd go too far, cross some invisible Izzy trip wire for which he'd get an acidic comment and the cold shoulder. It both frustrated and compelled him and now that she beckoned to him with open arms, he didn't want to fuck up.

Since he'd spotted her on the street—his lip involuntarily curled when he recalled the attack—he'd wanted her in his arms, in his bed. Of course, bringing her home dumped a whole new steaming pile of troubles at his feet. Pack business was the last thing he wanted on his mind.

Snaking one hand up Izzy's back, Curtis eased the other around her nape. Pulling her into him, he bent and kissed her, slowly at first, intimately, dusting her cheeks with the lightest brushes of his lips. Impatient, she strained for his mouth and he obliged her. When he fought for restraint, she craved rough handling, but too rough and she disappeared behind her mental fortress. He couldn't read her at all, but the demands her body made of his inflamed his desire.

Bumping against him, Izzy corralled Curtis backward, her hips and lips propelling him. When he butted against the armrest, he sat down and sprawled over the sofa. Like smoke, she slid over him, curled in his hair and stole through his lips, setting him on fire as he breathed in her perfume and powerful sexual musk. Muscles in his thighs and abdomen tensed and a surge of blood raised his aching cock to strain against his jeans. She straddled him, one leg tucked between his body and the couch cushions while the other braced against the floor like a bicycle kick stand.

She tossed back her head and her petal pink tongue wetted her lips. He wanted that tongue. Wanted it.

Curtis moved his hands up Izzy's pelvis. They vanished beneath her tunic. One palm traced a path up her torso, smooth and soft and hot, and up the trough of her breasts then retreated. Enough with the clothes. Snatching her tunic's hem, he pulled her top over her head. He fixated on her breasts, little round curves plumped by a white cotton bra. With her expensive outfit and apartment, he'd anticipated something lacy and complicated and the unexpected simplicity made his dick kick. Nipples like tiny pearls budded through the fabric. He couldn't stop staring. He reached for one of the flushed mounds criss-crossed by the black straps of her prosthetic's harness.

A curtain of shiny, black hair fell over his arm and blocked his view of Izzy's chest. She tucked her chin and he felt her shutter up, close off her heart. Parting her hair, he caught the shimmer of tears in her eyes before they pinched shut.

Fuck.

What had he done? If he made her cry he couldn't take it. He couldn't stand her pained expression. Neither could Clear-Skies who rippled and twisted in his displeasure.

No more pain. No more! The spirit's short communicative bursts were more intuition than telegraphed thought.

Curtis squirmed and calmed his wolf, and himself, with measured breaths and careful consideration of his actions since they'd lain on the couch. Was it the touching? Kissing? She'd started that. Maybe his staring? But how could he not stare? How could anyone? When a beautiful woman sat on top of you in only her bra and jeans and those had to come off and then the harness and . . . ah. *Argh!*

Staring. He'd stared at her breasts and she'd thought he'd ogled her harness. That had to be it, damnit.

"Izzy." Curtis sat up, tried to get her to look at him. "I don't care about this." He fingered the black straps stretched over her chest and back.

"Wait." Izzy caught his hand and rose. "Just give me one minute."

*

Izzy hurried to her bedroom where she plunked on her bed for a few deep breaths. From her night table she retrieved a condom, tearing one from a chain of three, leaving the rest next to her alarm clock. She couldn't believe she had any. She was on the pill, but Curtis's magic hands didn't change the fact that she knew next to nothing about him. That she stalled for time didn't cross her mind until she noticed her alarm clock's minute hand had moved three ticks since she took root on the mattress. She clutched her plum colored comforter and the condom wrapper's toothed edges pierced her palm.

There was still a way out. She could still send him away. The ache that spread through her chest and between her legs at the thought sealed that idea away.

Trailing her fingers absently over the black straps at her chest, Izzy shook her head, casting off the cloud of fear and insecurity fogging about her. She stood like a soldier and strode back into the living room where Curtis waited expectantly on the couch. Seeing her, he smiled, but hesitancy tinged his questioning expression. As she passed, she placed the condom on the coffee table in response. His hand brushed her naked side, but she didn't stop. If she lost momentum, doubt would creep in. Her barriers would shoot up and she'd find the words to send him running.

"Izzy?" Curtis said when she reached the short hallway leading to her front door. She paused next to her mirror and *barre* and switched off the lights. She didn't want an audience when she shed her prosthetic and came before him bereft of the one thing which kept her shape normal.

In the dark, Izzy found the buckles securing her harness and loosened them. She eased out of the contraption, located her heap of *pointe* shoes with her foot, and set her arm atop them. Then she fumbled her way to the couch, groping for the nearest cushiony armrest.

Curtis found her as she flailed and his hands locked around her forearms. Instinct nearly overrode desire when he grasped and stroked her bare, incomplete arm and, for a moment, the urge to flee overwhelmed her. He must have sensed it, felt her go taut all over, for he traced light circles in the sensitive crooks of her elbows, whispered sweet and sensual words like a husky lullaby. She melted into his hold and let him guide her so they were front to front. She hadn't heard him do it, but he'd removed his clothes and, standing there, his bare skin threw off heat like banked coals. His heavy prick thudded against her jeans and the head of his cock nudged her belly just below her navel. Gasping, she reached for his length, but he caught her hand and drew it up. Wet heat engulfed two of her fingers and Curtis's tongue swirled around them, stroking and lapping. The sensation traveled in a direct line to her sex and a slide of moisture wetted her needy entrance. She pressed herself against him, face buried in his warm chest. Her hips moved over his cock. Its tip brushed up and down her stomach leaving a dewy trail over her skin.

Releasing Izzy's fingers in a slow, sucking pull, Curtis settled back on the couch. His palms roved over her body, learning her shape in the dark. Slow fingertips traced the straps and cup-line of her cotton bra, following the curve of her breast. He hooked one finger into the band of her jeans and tugged her gently forward, hands moving down her hips until they met the supple leather of her calf-high boots. He patted the back of her thigh. Lifting her foot, she let him brace her on the couch. He removed one shoe and then the other before tackling her jeans. The confidence of his movements baffled her. Despite the moon and streetlights, she barely made out his form in the dark. He seemed not at all hindered by the gloom and stripped her easily. Cool air on Izzy's already damp thighs provoked the all over tingle of emerging gooseflesh even in the room's comfort.

Standing before Curtis, Izzy heard his weight shift on the couch. For several moments, he did not touch her and she could have sworn he appraised her through the shadows. Something flashed in the dark like the eyes of a cat or raccoon. Her breath caught, but the circles of light vanished when Curtis leaned forward and eased his rough hand between her legs.

*

Darkness didn't hamper Curtis's vision. He didn't mind it. He did mind what the dark implied: Izzy didn't want him seeing her. The gloom didn't assuage her insecurity either. As he sat back on the sofa, her left hand went to her right arm, a half-hearted attempt at concealing the damage. Disregarding the nervous gesture, he let the sight of her imprint itself in his mind like an exposed negative.

Long legs met the slight outward bow of hip and inward dip of waist and torso in a sweeping line. The slender column of her neck twisted as she struggled to discern him and a tendon, a severe diagonal against the otherwise soft angles of her body, caught his attention. He wanted to nip at it and at her breasts.

A sharp breath rasped from Izzy's throat and her eyes trained on his. His eyes often betrayed his wolf. Even the utterly clueless caught glimpses of the inner animal sometimes. Whatever she'd seen would be easily forgotten or explained away.

Reaching out, his hand grazed her inner thigh. His nostrils flared. Arousal made the smooth skin he touched damp and sticky. Curls from a narrowed strip of hair tickled his finger as he parted the delicate lips of her sex. He stroked her languidly and she rewarded him with a moan little more than a ragged whisper. Encouraged, he surged upward and her heated passage enveloped him, closed around his finger like a snug and silken glove. He caressed the sensitive knot of flesh at her apex with the pad of his thumb.

Izzy faltered on unsteady legs and she caught Curtis's shoulder. He smiled. He knew if she let him he could make her forget her pain and feel only ecstasy. Proving it would be his pleasure.

*

Izzy opened for Curtis as he stroked one finger through her wet slit. That thick finger slid inside her and she moaned, letting her head fall back as he thumbed her clit. Her mind buzzed with pleasure and her legs trembled.

Reaching, Izzy found Curtis's shoulder, using him for stability. His breath tickled the fine hairs dusting her stomach. Teeth gripped the tender flesh below her navel and she gasped. Lips kissed the place he'd nibbled and continued up her chest and between her covered breasts. When he sucked her peaked nipple into his mouth through the cotton of her bra, she cried out and clenched around his finger. Easing her bra straps from her shoulders, he pulled down their cups and her breasts spilled free. He squeezed and toyed with them, pinching and brushing her budded nipples, before doing away with the last of her clothing altogether.

"Curtis," her voice was breathy with mounting excitement. With one last tug at her nipple, he withdrew. His absence was an awful jolt. Moving around her, he threaded his arms behind her. His shoulders flexed under her supporting hand and he sat back.

From the crinkle of foil and wet roll of plastic, Izzy knew when Curtis sheathed himself and she pulled her lower lip between her teeth. His hands fixed on her waist and brought her forward. Shins meeting the couch, she bent her knees and crawled astride him, flinching when the blunt head of his cock parted her aching lips.

Holding her, Curtis held still while Izzy impaled herself inch by inch onto his thick shaft. His low moan stuttered as she opened and stretched around him, gripping him in her tight space. She clutched his shoulders and whimpered into his neck. It had been ages since her last partner and Curtis was so long and wide he touched parts of her that were near painful in their intensity. Her body had to adjust.

Curtis petted Izzy until her breathing slowed and her grip on him loosened. When she finally raised her head, he took her face in the vee of his thumb and index finger and stroked her cheek. Leaning into him, she found his mouth and drew on his lips as she rose on her knees. The motion had Curtis groaning into her mouth and when she came back down, their thighs clapping together, he broke away, a low rumble vibrating in the back of his throat. His fingers dug almost cruelly into the soft flesh at her hips and he pumped into her, his ass lifting from the couch.

All Izzy's musings about his touch were answered as his rhythm intensified. He wasn't careful, thank God. He didn't handle her like she might shatter at any moment. He fucked her like he never needed anything more than her body wrapped around his.

Curtis's hands covered her small breasts, kneading as he bucked beneath her. One slid to the hollow above her rear, supporting her as she angled back. This way, her clit rubbed against him, creating delicious friction. Insidious little hooks of pleasure latched inside her belly.

"Oh," she said, actually surprised when the first shiver of impending climax rolled up her spine. She latched onto Curtis's neck and undulated against him, sending herself into a mindless fugue as she came.

Cupping Izzy's ass, Curtis lifted her, giving himself room to drive in and out of her, quickening his thrusts until he released, his cock jerking inside her with each heady spasm. She heard the squeaky grind of his teeth.

Limp against each other, they lay together on the couch until Curtis repositioned himself, drawing out of Izzy—who made a grumbling, discontented noise—and bringing them both on their sides. He kissed her cheeks, eyelids, face, and forehead, letting her tangle her smooth legs around his prickly ones.

"May I use your bathroom?" he asked, nuzzling into her hair. Izzy said he could and told him where to go. His sure steps sounded in the dark room, his feet slapping the hardwood floor. A light flicked on from the hall leading to her bedroom. Nervous, she sat up and hugged a throw pillow to her chest. Would he leave now that they'd finished? The cold heaviness in her gut surprised her as she contemplated this. Many times, she'd hoped her onetime lovers wouldn't make nuisances of themselves after they'd had their fun. She didn't feel that way about Curtis and cringed at her need for him. While he cleaned himself she padded into the bedroom, not bothering with the light. She pulled the covers back in a one-handed tug and tucked herself under them. Chilled sheets felt wonderful over her deliciously sore body. The bathroom light clicked off.

"Izzy?" Curtis called quietly. "Did I hear you come in here?"

"Yes."

Curtis was just visible, one hand scratching his thigh, his cock hanging against his shadowed groin.

"Is it ok with you if I sleep here?" he asked.

Izzy turned into her pillow and smiled. "More than ok," she said into the plush fabric. She didn't see it, but she knew he grinned when he bounded into her bed and his warm weight settled beside her.

Chapter Four

Dull pain in Izzy's stunted arm woke her and the extra weight in her bed jolted her sleep-muddled faculties. Curtis sprawled over the mattress like a starfish, legs spread-eagled, one arm draped across her chest, lips parted as he snored. She snorted and squirmed from under his heavy arm, pausing to see if she roused him. When he took his next thunderous breath, she tiptoed to the bathroom, shutting the door to a crack before she flipped on the light.

Before the accident—Izzy considered it B.A. time and the aftermath A.A., or after the accident time—when dance had been her whole world, mirrors had been invaluable. As a child in the Glazier Studio, she'd watched her little form, jaw set and expression too serious for a six-year-old, repeated over and over in the reflective walls while she learned basic steps and positions. Mirrors had shown her mistakes and had proved her accomplishments. Mirrors were the only gauge of her talent besides the glowing praise of Madame Glazier herself. In their shallow surfaces, she'd trusted. A.A., she knew the truth: mirrors lied.

Izzy blinked as she regarded herself. In the deceitful glass, she was whole. She had two arms, strong, graceful, powerful. Of course, the mirage faded and her right arm vanished two inches below the elbow. When she'd first left the hospital, she'd seen herself complete all the time whether her brain was sleep addled or not. Worse was when phantom pain accompanied the hallucination, but, the pain that had woken her was very real and wasn't a mystery. She inspected the pink and shiny scarred skin at the end of her incomplete limb, already knowing what she'd find.

Deep indents marked where her prosthetic dug into her skin and a reddened patch of oozing flesh showed where the arm cup chafed. Izzy hunted for disinfectant in the cabinet under the sink. When she rose, someone else stood reflected behind her in the mirror and she yelped, dropping the Neosporin.

Curtis looked sheepish and picked up the tube of medicine. "Didn't startle you, did I?" He yawned. "I heard you leave. Usually takes a nuclear device to wake me up."

"I—"

With the lights out in the living room and bedroom, Izzy hadn't had a proper view of naked Curtis. His brawn had been obvious under her hands but seeing him so unexpectedly made her brain mushy. Broad and thick, his arms and face were tan, his torso onward paler where his clothes shielded his skin from the sun. Deep lines on his stomach contoured his abdominals, creating a vee that pointed down to his groin where his softened sex lay against a thick patch of dark hair. His thighs, she knew, were equally sculpted as his torso, but she couldn't pull her attention from his cock.

"Startle me?" Izzy said, her words high pitched and constricted. She cleared her throat. "No. Not too badly." She shut her eyes against the sight of him and instinctively covered her right arm, wincing when her salty fingers brushed the open sore.

"What's wrong?" Curtis asked and came toward her.

Izzy shied away, turning her right side to the sink. "Just some irritation from my prosthetic. Happens a lot. No big deal." She wished he'd go away, but he just kept coming. Seeing her couldn't be half as impressive as seeing him.

Reaching out, Curtis ran his fingers over her shoulders and back where her harness straps had left reddened marks. "May I see?"

No.

No one looked at her arm but her, her doctor, and her physical therapist. Izzy's dark expression likely spoke for itself.

"Please," Curtis said.

Reluctantly, Izzy relinquished her arm. Foreign hands roaming over her skin gave her the shivers and made her nipples taut, achy, points. Curtis didn't seem repulsed by her deformity, but a severe line appeared between his brows and he frowned as he uncapped the Neosporin.

"You wear your harness too tight," he said as he squeezed a

dollop of balm from the tube and dabbed it on her irritated skin. It stung, but Izzy had toughed out far worse. B.A., there'd been ankle injuries, sores from her *pointe* shoes, and split toenails. A.A., there'd been recovery and physical therapy.

"I have to wear it tight," she said. "If I don't, there's a gap between the prosthetic and my arm. My clothes get caught in it and you can see the seam. I hate that." She disentangled her arm from his loose grasp and rooted for a cotton pad and Band-Aids.

"You're hurting yourself," Curtis said.

"Most dancers live with a certain amount of pain."

"Yeah, but your arm has nothing to do with that. Just because you can take the pain doesn't mean you should go looking for it. There isn't some kind of insert you can put in your prosthetic to protect your arm?"

"There are, but those make gaps, too." Inserts also reminded Izzy of the gel cups her younger and non-professional students used to cushion their toes *en pointe*. Dancers at the advanced and professional levels had no business wearing them. They restricted movement and foot expression.

"So there's a gap. Who cares? Hiding who you are all the time is a lot of work, don't you think?"

"You know what I think?" Izzy ripped open a Band-Aid with her teeth and spit out the paper scrap. "I think it's none of your business how I deal with my disability. I don't need another therapist. I need," Izzy stopped short and puckered her lips. She couldn't argue properly when he was all . . . out there.

Curtis raised his brows.

"I need to get back to bed," Izzy finished and brushed past Curtis, jumping when his semi-erect cock grazed her hip.

"That was my plan, too," Curtis said.

"'Bed' as in 'sleep.'" Izzy strode into the bedroom, ignoring the flutter of excitement in her gut and the way her breasts tingled in anticipation as they jiggled. Curtis followed.

"You're ready for bed after chewing me out? All keyed up?" he asked.

"You want to screw after I did?" Izzy belly flopped onto the bed. The dipping mattress and creaking springs announced Curtis's arrival. Crawling over her, the length of his erection brushed her back and his balls lightly smacked her rear.

"Can't help it."

"And why's that?" she asked. Face down in her pillow, the question came out muffled.

Curtis sucked in breath. "You want the PC answer or non PC?"

Flipping over, Izzy saw Curtis boxed her in. His arms caged her head and his knees trapped her lower half. Hairs on his legs tickled her calves. His cock curved toward his belly.

"Both," Izzy said, swallowing. "PC first."

"It turns me on when you get aggressive."

"And?"

"When you challenge me, I want to show you who's boss."

Izzy bent her leg. With her knee, she put gentle but insistent pressure to his balls. "Well, the boss thinks out the door might be the best place for you."

"Putting me in the dog house?" Curtis rubbed against her knee and dipped his head to her face, tracing her lips with his tongue. "Sure that's what you want?"

"I want you to apologize."

"For what? Overstepping personal bounds? Giving a shit that you're hurting yourself? I need you to be specific." He narrowed his eyes and captured her lips in a soft kiss. "I don't want to fuck this up."

Izzy's leg went slack and she pushed up his head. "How about for your completely tactless and sexist comment?"

"Oh," Curtis went back on his heels. "You want me to apologize for being honest when you asked me."

"That's—"

Curtis put his finger to Izzy's lips. "Shh, I want you to watch this. Observe, for I shall withstand your many trials." Izzy rolled her eyes. "I'm going to count to three. If you tell me to fuck off before then, I'll apologize just how you like and leave. If you don't kick me out you'll still get your apology, but I'm doing it my way." He lifted his finger from her lips. "Ready?"

Izzy's eyes slitted as he bent his head to her chest. She should have bit his finger.

"One . . . " Curtis feathered his lips between her breasts.

"Two . . . " He worked himself down Izzy's body, planting kisses on her shuddering stomach and easing her thighs apart with his palms.

"Two and a half . . . " The countdown feint made Izzy start. Curtis glanced up at her and took the flesh of her thigh between his teeth. Holding her breath, she prepared herself for the ominous "three" that never came.

Curtis's head darted between her legs. His hot mouth covered her clit and he fluttered his tongue against her. Startled, she squeaked and bucked up. Without pause in his "apology," he steadied her hips under his hands and pressed her into the mattress, holding her in place. She clenched the rumpled sheets in her fist, furious he hadn't gone to three, but too pleased with the result to make a fuss.

Spreading her wider, Curtis ran his tongue up the length of her slit, bestowing a sucking kiss to her clit before sliding one finger inside her. Izzy let out a panting moan as her climax uncurled from the base of her spine like an eager tendril at first light. The shock of cool air on her wetted sex when he suddenly withheld all contact sent that tendril retreating into a tightly wound bud. He restrained her as she groaned her displeasure.

"You know," Curtis said, looking up at her, "I think I deserve an apology, too." He licked the delicate crease between her thigh and her open sex. "Can you say 'I'm sorry for snapping at you, Curtis?'" Parting his lips over her clit, he warmed her with his breath, but he wouldn't touch her.

"Curtis." Izzy struggled to lift herself to him but he kept her firmly in place.

"That's not how it starts," he chided.

Izzy growled and slammed her head into her pillow, thrashing when he teased her with the lightest flick of his tongue.

"I'm sorry," the word "sorry" pitched high when Curtis closed his mouth on her, rolling his tongue against her clit. "I'm sorry, sorry for . . . "

"Mmmmhmmmm?" Curtis hummed into her and Izzy couldn't get enough air to form the words he wanted. Shivering, gossamer filaments looped her spine and snaked toward her brain, lacing her vision with sparkles of white light. He hesitated at her unintelligible moans and relaxed his grip and her hand shot out, fisting in his hair.

The tip of Curtis's tongue circled her clit. "Greedy," he said and settled between her open lips, pushing two fingers into her pulsing entrance.

Izzy yelped at the sudden pressure and her back arched. The tendrils flirting with her spine constricted and vaulted unbearable ecstasy into her brain, pitching her heavenward.

Waiting until Izzy's spasms weakened, Curtis untangled her clenched fingers from his hair, sheathed himself in one of the condoms from her bedside table, yanked her legs around him, and thrust his cock into her. Her tight space stretched and clamped around him as she trembled with the stoked aftershocks of her climax. With her legs tight around his waist, he wormed his arms under her shoulders and lifted her from the mattress to his mouth. The taste of her sex was on him, strange, but not unpleasant, as her tongue twined with his. She dug her nails into his back as he pounded into her, faster and faster until he gasped, tightening his mouth over hers. Deep grunts punctuated each spurting thrust.

Curtis's arms relaxed around Izzy as his pleasure waned. He eased her back onto the bed before he moved out of her and collapsed at her side, pulling her to his chest. She pounded him with her fist, the playful strike bouncing off his solidity.

"You never said 'three,'" she managed between labored breaths.

"That's ok," Curtis said, stroking her hair. "You never got the whole apology out."

"That doesn't make it ok."

"Yes, it does."

"No, it doesn't."

Curtis sighed in resignation and a passing car from the street below made the only sound besides their slowing breaths for a long time. Izzy snuggled into his side, smug with victory.

"Yes," Curtis snuck in just before she drifted off.

*

In the morning, Curtis was gone, but he hadn't gone far. Izzy smelled fresh coffee. The sound of clanking pots and pans traveled from the living area. Her alarm clock read eight twenty-two a.m.

What could he possibly have found to cook? She hadn't been to the grocery in a week.

Trudging to the bathroom, Izzy rubbed her bleary eyes and started the shower, brushing her teeth while the water heated. Her floss and mouthwash were already out. Curtis must have used them. After completing her morning maintenance, she gathered her damp hair into a neat bun and dressed in her standard warm-up wear: leotard, tights, sweat pants, leather flats.

"You've certainly made yourself comfortable," Izzy said when she found Curtis with his head stuck in her fridge. "What the hell are you doing?"

Curtis stayed wedged in the fridge. "You've got water, fruit, some wilting salad mix, cream, and eggs." He righted himself and stared at her over the fridge door. "How am I supposed to make us scrambled eggs, bacon, and toast when you don't have any bacon? Or bread."

"There's an IHOP right off the service road if you're hungry." Izzy's voice was flat as she headed to the *barre*. She needed her prosthetic for her exercises and considered kicking Curtis out so she could go through her routine in private. She spun around to tell him so and held back. Barefoot and shirtless, wearing only his low slung jeans, he flipped open the egg carton with his back mostly to her. He sniffed the eggs and wrinkled his nose. There was something about his obtrusive presence she enjoyed besides the attractive figure he cut from the back. He seemed natural in her space and, oddly, she didn't want to disturb him as he lifted one pan, then another, comparing the two.

Izzy fastened her harness and tensed and flexed her arm muscles, contracting her body-powered hand's jointed fingers. "Can you poach an egg?" she asked and gripped the *barre* with her left hand, eyes on the chef's bare back. Usually, she began facing the mirror, but didn't feel like conversing with Curtis's reflection. With her right arm out and curved as elegantly as her prosthetic allowed, she bent her knees in the first *plie* series in first position. Her joints creaked and her stiff muscles yawned with a burning ache as they came alive.

"Ah, I can scramble," Curtis said, glancing over his shoulder. "Sometimes I can go sunny side up, but I can't promise I won't break the yolks."

"Breakfast is a grapefruit half with an egg on the side. Try sunny side up if you're set on cooking."

"I'm not banished to IHOP?"

"If you absolutely need bacon and toast that's where you're getting them." Izzy rose into *relevé* and her toes cracked.

"You don't want to come?"

"I can't have all that grease sitting in my stomach while I teach my soloists. I have a private session at the studio at eleven." Curtis appeared to accept this as rational and commenced cooking while Izzy did her warm ups.

The eggs were overdone and salty enough to dry out Izzy's mouth, but the grapefruit was very pink and its meat juicy. She finished both and didn't whisper a word of dissatisfaction. Curtis stuck with coffee, adding so much cream and sugar she thought the mixture might whip into an espresso mousse when he stirred it.

"You see," he said when she set her utensils down, "I can't be sexist. I made breakfast. Watch me clean." Curtis whisked her plate away before Izzy lifted a finger. He smelled like her vanilla bath wash.

"Being barefoot in my kitchen doesn't excuse your behavior last night," she said with a smile she tried to hide.

"My instincts I cannot help," Curtis said, rinsing her plate in the sink. "Only how I respond to them."

Izzy hadn't run her maced dance bag through the wash yet and had to scour her closet for an old backpack. After stuffing what she needed for class into the bag, she threw on a fresh pair of jeans, boots, a low hemmed gray tank top, and her comfy—and snuggly warm—bathrobe style sweater. Retrieving her spare keys from her everything-goes-in-it-drawer out front, she eyed a clothed Curtis who sat spread eagled on her couch, frowning at his phone and tapping something out on its green-lighted buttons.

"I'm heading out," Izzy said.

Shoving his phone in his pocket, Curtis jumped from the couch. "You want to meet for lunch?"

"You're not going back to DeConing?" Izzy asked as she headed to the front door.

"Not 'til tomorrow. There are a few things I need to do in town."

"We could meet for lunch." The acceptance tumbling from Izzy's lips was a shock as was the little flip her stomach performed. "You'll have to meet me at the studio at one. I won't have time to get a new phone until my session's over."

"Great," he said and followed her out of the apartment, beaming all the way.

They parted at the front of the building. Visitor parking was on the opposite side of the complex and Izzy turned down Curtis's escort offer to her car. Clambering into her SUV, she backed from her reserved space and maneuvered to the street. Curtis's Jeep idled by the curb. Exasperated, she clenched the wheel. He wasn't waiting for her, was he?

Izzy squinted. Curtis sat in the driver's seat, phone tucked between his ear and shoulder as he adjusted something on his dash. His face was tight, angry, and his mouth opened wide when he responded to whomever he spoke. His right hand came down in a chopping motion, visually articulating whatever point he made. Abruptly, he flipped his phone shut and hurled it onto the passenger seat. His jaw worked and he ran his hands through his hair. A lightning-strike vein stood out at his temple.

Izzy turned into the street and drove past without making eye contact.

*

Curtis's phone cracked against the door then plopped onto the passenger seat. Not yet. He couldn't bring Izzy to the lodge yet. And not how Thomas wanted.

"You're telling me you can't overpower a hundred and fifteen pound woman?" his Alpha had snarled over the line.

"I'm telling you it doesn't have to be that way," Curtis had shot back. "Do we have to accomplish everything by force?"

"It's easy and efficient."

"It's inhuman."

Neither of them had uttered a word for a good while until Thomas had countered, "I can send Gerome if you're not up to this. I'm sure he'd have fun."

Curtis's blood pressure had skyrocketed and he had to take care not to crush the phone cradled next to his ear.

"Let me do this my way. Give me a week," Curtis had said.

"A we—"

"She'll come to us on her own next weekend. She doesn't have to know what we are and what we're doing. All she has to do is lure Rapid out, right?"

"Correct."

"Then we don't have to hurt her."

"If she's not here by Saturday, I'm sending Gerome after her," the Alpha had said and had hung up.

A week. Curtis bought Izzy one week. He couldn't spend it with her, but he could find a way back into her bed at least for tonight.

"Fuck!" He punched the dash, splitting the plastic casing above his stereo and his knuckles. Clear-Skies arced in a thin, blue line, the wolf spirit goaded out of slumber by his host's fury. The spirit line undulated, tickling Curtis's heart, then contracted into a disgruntled knot.

Drawing back his fist, Curtis scowled at his damaged hand. Blood seeped from his gashed and stinging knuckles. A warm, red trail oozed down his clenched fingers. Surprisingly, Clear-Skies deigned to loosen from his sulk. The wolf spirit shot a tendril from its wispy central mass down Curtis's arm. A tongue of cold fire licked from behind the broken skin of his hand and the wounds sealed.

"I didn't deserve that," Curtis said.

Sees-Through-Clear-Skies collected himself, coiled into a spiral, and retracted back into his sulky knot. Wolf spirits protected their hosts. It was part of whatever bargain whoever had made however many years ago, enabling the spirits to pass into human bodies. Curtis didn't care about the details or the history. He knew what he had to. Clear-Skies had been his father's wolf and Keene Lodge had been his father's land. They were Curtis's responsibility. The pack should have been, too.

Robert Keene had been the pack Alpha, but when he died, that honor passed to Thomas, Robert's business partner and former Beta. Initially, the power transfer pleased Curtis. He could care for the lodge and the land, but other people? No thanks. Lording over everyone wasn't his style. Thomas took to the position well. Too well. Pack and lodge management had slowly merged until one became indistinguishable from the other. As Beta, Curtis couldn't say much about the takeover. Thomas would never own Keene Lodge, but he owned its owner and Curtis liked that less and less.

The last few years were the worst. Thomas wanted arranged matings. He'd nudged Curtis in Melinda's direction with no success. Curtis loved the kid, but not that way. He shuddered. If Thomas chose, he could command the mating and backed with the Alpha's power . . . no. Thomas wouldn't do that. He wasn't that crazy, not even with his recent ramblings about the Werewolves's "true purpose" that Mountain's-Might supposedly divulged to him when he and his wolf spirit communed. The older their Alpha got, the more zealous and closer to his wolf he became, preaching to the pack about a "coming darkness" that only the Werewolves could stand against. Curtis had hovered around his bullshit limit for a while, keeping the peace like a Beta did, but Izzy threw a monkey wrench in all that.

The first woman Curtis wanted as more than a now-and-then playmate and the Alpha pulled her into pack politics. Curtis's wants were so simple. He wanted to keep up the lodge and start a family, eat good food, and keep a roof over his head. That's it. What he wanted with Izzy was also simple. He wanted her with him. They were good together. You didn't need years to figure that crap out. She looked good, smelled good, made him feel good in all the right ways and places. The one thing she wasn't was a Werewolf. Big deal.

Curtis banged his head on the steering wheel. Yes, big deal. Very big deal. After the pack took care of the Rapid problem, he wanted Izzy in his life. If he were careful, she wouldn't ever know what went on next weekend. He could protect her from the rogue wolf and his Alpha and she'd be none the wiser. Then, after a few months, he'd break his nature to her easy.

I like long hikes on nature trails, hunting, and peeing with one leg lifted. By the way, I'm a Werewolf . . .

"I'm a Werewolf, Izzy," he muttered to the steering wheel. "But I'll never hurt you, I swear." He jammed his key into the ignition and fired up the Jeep. There were some wolves in town he had to see. Besides tracking Izzy, he meant to find out if anyone else knew anything about some enemy or "darkness" they were supposedly destined to fight. Thomas might be an asshole, but he wasn't stupid. Dismissing him was a mistake. On the way to the Tavella pack's den, he'd figure out how to keep Izzy close for the rest of the weekend.

Chapter Five

"Travis, what are you doing? You're shrinking. Keep your shoulders up and back. No, not up by your ears. You've done this a hundred times. I know you know how."

Izzy crossed the studio floor to Travis, the young man cast as the Sugar Plum Fairy's Cavalier for the Glazier Studio's production of *The Nutcracker*. Dark haired, fine boned, and broad shouldered already at his age, the boy was the picture of petulant aristocracy in his costume regalia with his black expression and hunched stance. The Sugar Plum Fairy, a particularly talented student called Amanda, went over her solo choreography while her partner sulked. Sunlight shafting through the large windows made her blond hair gleam.

Body curved in on itself, Travis averted his eyes as Izzy approached. She corrected his posture, giving his lower back a gentle swat when it curved outward again.

"Travis—"

"Madame Tunskill?" Amanda's voice quavered.

Izzy looked over at the girl who eyed the studio windows warily.

"I think that man wants to talk to you." Amanda pointed.

Hands pressed to the studio's picture window, a brown bag clutched in one of them, Curtis waited until he had Izzy's attention before mouthing, "Can I come in?"

"One second, guys," Izzy said and trotted to the studio door, waving Curtis over. She was ridiculously happy to see him, which gave her pause. Her mind should have been on Travis and Amanda and it wasn't. The session had been nothing but frustrating and the promise of a lunch date after work further strained her patience. Cold air swirled around her ankles when she let Curtis inside. "Would you please stop scaring my students?" she rebuked him as she shooed him into her office, closing the door most of the way behind them. "You're a little early. I still have half an hour with them and we may need to go over." She checked her watch.

"Problems?" Curtis dropped the paper bag on an uncluttered corner of her desk. Fresh baked fragrances, warmed bread and meat, filled the small room and her stomach growled. "Ham and cheese croissant. Want some?"

"Please," Izzy said and Curtis opened the bag and fished out the butcher paper wrapped pastry. Biting into the savory croissant scalded her tongue. She blew air out of her mouth, cooling the cured ham and Swiss cheese, before chewing and swallowing. "My Cavalier is having performance anxiety and I don't know why. He's been fine until today."

Travis was perfect casting for the Cavalier. Besides ballet, he played baseball and soccer and had a unique level of self confidence for a thirteen-year-old boy; a requirement for any man interested in classical dance. Ballet wasn't Travis's passion, but he'd taken classes with his sister, who had the role of Dewdrop this year, since they were five and Izzy got the impression he stuck it out for her sake. He'd also confided the leg work helped his kicks and control on the pitch. His sudden reticence was a mystery. Maybe it was the dress rehearsals she'd started after their costumes had come in? Travis preferred dancing in shorts and a T-shirt, but he'd done classes in tights.

"Can I watch?" Curtis asked.

Izzy picked at the grease stained butcher paper. Having an audience might give her more trouble with Travis. "That's up to them." Izzy stuck her head out into the studio where Amanda attempted a string of *fouettés* while Travis slouched on the *barre* at the floor's far end. "How do the two of you feel about an audience today?"

With an eager bob of her head, Amanda performed a graceful *arabesque* and went to her starting position in the center of the studio, regal head high, arms floating out and framing her torso in an oval. Her flourish was entirely for the man crowding behind Izzy. Amanda thrived on stage and she clearly enjoyed being the center of Curtis's attention. The same couldn't be said for Travis, who sank further into his slouch and ducked his head. He'd have to get used to an audience or Izzy would have to recast.

"You ok with it, Travis?" she pressed. His body language said "no," but he wouldn't back down from a challenge.

"S'fine," he said, tossing his dark hair out of his stormy eyes. He dragged his feet to Amanda and took her hands.

"All right then." Izzy set up the music and took her place behind the young pair, her back to the frosty window. "From the top." She counted time as the music warbled through the speakers, broken here and there with loud pops. Curtis sat on the stoop separating her office from the studio proper.

Delicate harp strings plinked and Amanda and Travis parted. They made a wide circle and came together again center floor. The *coda* was truncated for the Glazier Studio performance. Izzy had simplified the choreography, taking out most of the lifts and easing the Cavalier's part as much as she could without diminishing Amanda's role. Sugar Plum's solo remained, also simplified, as a showcase of her talent, but Izzy cut Travis's solo altogether. At the stretch of partnered steps preceding the first of two lifts, Travis's shoulders hunched and he went off step, cringing when Amanda stepped in for her assisted *pirouettes*.

"Stop, stop!" Izzy shouted over the music and dashed to shut it off. She returned center floor, massaging her temples. "Travis, are you worried about dropping Amanda? Should I eliminate the lifts?" Originally, she'd removed all lifts from their number. At Amanda's insistence, she'd restored two. The duo had practiced the lifts independent of accompanying choreography, but this was the first time they'd incorporated them into the dance. Could they be the source of Travis's distraction? Amanda's safety hinged on his skill after all.

The suggestion of still more simplifications devastated Amanda, who looked like someone had shot her kitten, and Travis gave a non-committal shake of his head. He wasn't one to admit trepidation, but Izzy didn't think he'd let Amanda fall. A demonstration might bolster his confidence.

"You two, over there." Izzy motioned Amanda and Travis to

the far side of the studio then turned to their audience. "Curtis, would you join me center floor?"

"Sure," Curtis said, bounding up. His shoes squeaked on the vinyl flooring.

Placing him in Travis's position—posture and all—for the lift, Izzy took Amanda's spot. "I'm going to come to you," she told Curtis. "Keep eye contact with me and I'll prompt you when you need to lift me."

"Lift?"

"Lift. Think you can pick me up?"

"I'm sure of it," Curtis said and clapped and rubbed his hands together, shifting his weight side to side like a wrestler ready to grapple his opponent. Amanda giggled and Izzy suddenly doubted the brilliance of her idea.

"You'll have one hand here," Izzy slapped her torso, "and one here." She clapped her thigh. "Pick me up and then turn around while you hold me. I'll take care of the rest." Resetting the record, Izzy returned to her place and awaited the musical cue.

At the rise of strings, Izzy glided into the choreography and danced to Curtis. With her eyes on his, she gave a short nod and leapt into his readied arms. He gripped her so strongly the breath rushed out of her and she almost forgot to position her arms and legs, also made difficult by his supporting hand closer to her knee than its proper place on her upper thigh. They made a wobbly, if firmly secured, turn with Izzy holding her legs in a sort of figure four, her left toe touching her right knee and her right leg extended back and up. Certain they appeared a pair of graceless elephants, Izzy thought she'd made her point. On her feet again she addressed Travis.

"He's never danced. Have you?" she asked Curtis.

"Nope."

"But he caught me and did the turn even with his hands in the wrong place. It's about trust. Trusting yourself enough to know you won't hurt your partner and trusting your partner to know her choreography and cues." Izzy could tell Travis's mind was already elsewhere, like he'd absorbed her advice before she'd uttered a word and already shrugged it off, but she continued anyway. "If you feel off-kilter, forget technique and hold onto her. Amanda, you can brace yourself if you feel like you're going to fall, right?"

"Yep," Amanda answered her teacher though her gaze remained on Curtis.

"Where were my hands supposed to be?" Curtis asked, sounding wounded by the critique.

"Well, the one on my torso was fine, but on my supporting leg you should have been here." Izzy patted her inner thigh. "Otherwise your arms ruin the shape of the ballerina's extension."

Realization widened Curtis's eyes and he suppressed a chuckle behind his hand.

"Yeah," Travis shot at him. "I'd like to see you do it with the *proper* technique in this get up." He gestured at his white tights and military-style jacket complete with gold epaulettes.

Curtis waved the boy over. "Mind if I have a word?" he asked Izzy, who shook her head.

The men had a pow-wow in the corner—Travis gesticulating with sharp motions and Curtis's mannerisms calm and assuring— while Izzy took a seat next to Amanda.

"He's cute," Amanda whispered.

Izzy nodded, concentrated on the pair deep in hushed conversation. "The Cavalier regalia suits Travis. He'll look great onstage."

Amanda made an exasperated noise. "Not Travis, Curtis. He's *very* nice."

Jolted from her inquisitive engrossment, Izzy fixed her student in hard eyes. She didn't mind gossiping with the older girls—some of them spent so much time at the studio they felt more like little sisters than students—but there were a few lines she didn't cross. If Amanda wanted to talk boys, fine, but her own love life was off limits.

"He is," Izzy said, her words clipped and tone final.

Chastised, Amanda toyed with one of her *pointe* shoes' loose ribbons, then fingered the browned edges of the pink satin toe she'd singed with a lighter to break it in.

Curtis apparently absorbed whatever Travis confided in him. The boy had opened up to him in a matter of moments. In all the years she'd known him, Izzy had never seen Travis talk so much. Where had Curtis learned that skill? She'd fallen victim to it herself. It generally took a while for Izzy to drop her guard when she met new people. Her ease around Curtis spoke to weeks of interaction, not days. Subconscious memories of him with her during the worst experience of her life, she'd thought, contributed to her attitude but everyone, it seemed, was drawn to him. She was still shaking her head when Curtis and Travis reached some sort of understanding.

"We good for another twenty minutes?" Izzy asked. "Or do we need to call it a day?"

"I'm good," Amanda said and popped up.

Travis gave a curt nod and joined his partner center floor.

Those twenty minutes went well. Travis corrected his own posture when it slipped and his technique with lifts and assisted turns improved. Izzy finished their work with a little one-on-one time with Amanda, who was accomplished enough to concentrate on portraying character and understanding the nuance of her movement's emotion than with technique.

"Do the solo with me!" Amanda begged while Travis retreated to the dressing rooms. Her excitement was infectious.

"You want to try the full choreography or stick with the truncated version?" Izzy asked.

The challenge had Amanda's eyes sparkling. "Full."

"All right then." Izzy reset the record and stood in position far enough behind Amanda so they wouldn't collide during their dance. Delicate chimes tinkled when the *Dance of the Sugar Plum Fairy* began and their bodies became elastic with movement.

The fairy's solo tempo was *allegro*, light and dainty, and as she danced Izzy imagined herself a pale, gossamer scarf flitting in a breeze. Steps and turns were quick, bouncy, and airy. She couldn't focus on Amanda, but her student appeared poised and spritely. Amanda was a joyful fairy, but the *pas de chat* wore her down.

In three parts, the solo increased in difficulty with each turn of the suite. The first showcased Sugar Plum's character, the dancer enchanting the audience with expressive but simple movements. Part two taxed the dancer with a series of *pas de chat*, cat-like jumps. *Pas de chat* series were strenuous and they came one after another in this choreography in an unrelenting chain. As she went through them, Amanda's endurance faltered. She visibly pushed to launch herself into the air and came down hard. She wouldn't make it through the finale.

Izzy's fingers tingled with adrenaline and sweat beaded at her brow. The *chaîne* at the conclusion of the solo, a dizzying string of turns and *fouettés en tournant*, was exhilarating to perform. As she whipped around and around—the dreamy music fueling her performance—she caught Curtis's rapt expression and nearly fell off *pointe*. She'd forgotten about their audience. This was the first time she'd really danced for someone A.A. An ache stretched in her heart like muscles awakening to morning *barre* work. She missed this. She missed this so much.

Watch me.

Nothing compared to an audience dazzled by a talented soloist. *Watch me, Curtis.*

The end approached and it was abrupt, demandingly precise. When Izzy finished directly from her *fouetté* into fourth position, arms outstretched, her throat tightened. Curtis and Travis, sitting together in street clothes by the studio door, applauded. Izzy made her *reverence*, bowing her head and dipping into a *demi plié*, one foot pointed behind her ankle. Amanda did the same, chest heaving and hands trembling.

"Did you make it through?" Izzy asked, turning to her exhausted student.

Amanda shook her head, her jaw tight. "I had to fall back on the amended choreography."

"You'll get it. We'll work more on endurance after performances.

I have a feeling you'll be in California or New York for the summer intensives this year."

Amanda brightened at that and Izzy sent her to change out.

Parents waited testily outside for their children when the group finally emerged from the studio. Izzy confirmed their next session Thursday afternoon and Curtis accompanied her to her car.

"If it's not a sacred man secret," Izzy said as she munched on what remained of the cold ham and cheese croissant, "what was it you said to Travis? He was much better after your talk."

"I told him there was no reason to feel guilty."

"Guilty?"

"Those lifts of yours put his hands in places boys dream of going but are generally denied."

Izzy inhaled some half-chewed croissant and beat her chest with her fist. She hadn't thought Travis might be uncomfortable. Chemistry between partners often added to a performance, but they were a little young for that.

"After you had me do the lift with you, I figured he might be self-conscious what with the tights and the proximity."

Waving that line of conversation away, Izzy struck her chest a few more times to clear it. The bit of food felt like a pebble lodged between her lungs. "I'll take the lifts out if it's a problem."

"I think acknowledging it would be worse. Let him work through it. Half the problem is he has a girlfriend and he thinks the feelings he gets with Amanda are like cheating."

"And you told him . . . ?"

"That his instincts don't make him a bad person. That he's normal."

They walked without speaking until Izzy broke the silence at her car door. "Thanks for helping."

"No problem," Curtis said, "but you know, you could return the favor."

"How's that?"

"I don't know Tavella as well as you. After we eat and you get a new phone, can you take me to the local animal shelter?"

Chapter Six

On all sides of the kennel, dogs barked and yapped from inside their pens. This wasn't the best place in the world for Izzy. The Tavella shelter kept their dogs and cats housed separately and she'd prepped herself in the cat wing first, feeling gloomy when all the sad and bewildered kitten faces begged for a home she couldn't give them. Their pitiful mews tugged at her heart strings. Challenging her canine phobia had to be better than battling guilt, so she'd headed to the dog wing where she stood now. Barks rattled through her. The cacophony traveled like a concussive wave over her skin and all the little hairs on her body stood on end. Terror mixed with the sour smell of animal and antiseptics made her queasy. She backed from the room of cages and right into Curtis who entered with a volunteer in tow. His hands came down on her shoulders.

"You ok?" Curtis stared down into her face.

"I don't think this is going to work for me." Izzy kept her voice hushed in the volunteer's company and Curtis followed suit.

"You don't?" He gave her a reassuring squeeze and glanced around the room. "All these fellas are behind bars and I really need your help. Petey needs another dog around and if you leave it to me, I'll end up with another spaz-hound. I'm a spaz-hound magnet." When Izzy's expression remained pinched, he said, "Maybe you could wait in the car."

"Excuse me, miss," the volunteer interrupted them. Her light hair was gathered in a short ponytail and her plump cheeks were bright pink, the single points of color painting her otherwise cream and khaki person. "Do you need some water? You look a little pale."

"Sure," Izzy said and stepped out of Curtis's arms. She didn't have to wait in the damn car. One drink, a quick breather, and she'd be fine. "Thanks."

"No problem. Take your time. They're noisy, but they're all sweethearts," the volunteer left for the water, leaving them alone in the kennel.

While Curtis wandered from cage to cage inspecting their occupants, Izzy hung back awaiting the gal's return. After she'd accepted and downed the contents of the waxy paper cup and pretended she had more to drink for a few minutes, she pitched the crumpled cup in the trash and joined Curtis at the back of the kennel where he stooped in front of a large pen. Inside, a wolfish Siberian husky sat against the far wall, sneaking tentative glances at the humans watching him.

The husky's coat was silvery white. Black markings striped over his back, framed his face, and darkened the tips of his ears. His sickle tail tucked under his legs and each time he turned his head, Izzy caught a flash of the most beautiful ice blue eyes.

"How would you say this dog is feeling?" Curtis asked.

"Scared."

"How can you tell?"

Izzy watched the husky back into the corner of his pen, overturning his water dish. "He doesn't want to be anywhere near us. His ears are flat and he keeps looking back and forth like he wants to check that we're still here but not draw any attention."

Nodding, Curtis said, "What about the dog over there?" He indicated one of the large breed pens to their right where a big brown mutt paced and barked at them.

"Angry." Izzy hugged herself. While she couldn't pick out a particular breed for the animal, it was barrel chested with a great big belly and powerful legs. Its huge head came with equally huge jaws that looked strong enough to crush a boulder to powder.

Curtis frowned. "Why angry?"

"He's showing a lot of teeth and making a lot of noise."

"Loud barking doesn't mean angry. If you learn dog behavior, you might be more comfortable around one or two. His teeth are out because he's opening his mouth but he's not purposefully baring them or snarling. He's excited and his ears are a little flat so, wary." Curtis rose and approached the mutt's cage. It went into bark overdrive, then dropped its chest down and wiggled its butt high in the air as it jumped back and forth.

"See," Curtis said, "definitely not angry. Antsy. He's cooped up and wants to play. Probably jealous of the attention we're giving our timid friend. Too bad for him because I think Mr. Shy there is coming home with me." The mutt rolled over on his back. "And that's about as submissive as you get. When a dog shows you its belly and throat, you know for sure you're in charge." To the mutt, he said, "Beg all you want, I'm not letting you out."

While Curtis chatted up the playful mutt, Izzy read the tag fixed to the husky's cage where someone had scrawled information in blue, looping script. The staff had named him Nook and he'd been rescued from an abusive home.

"What do you see?" Curtis rested his chin on her shoulder.

"His former owner was abusive."

"That explains a lot. Let's see if the shelter will let us spend some time with him."

The cheery volunteer brought them to a smaller, quieter room with a bench attached to one wall and a few dog toys—squeaky balls and a length of knotted rope—scattered over the floor. She warned them Nook didn't always take to strangers and not to get discouraged if he wasn't ultra social.

"What did his last owner do to him?" Izzy asked.

Expression shuttering, the girl retrieved a leash hanging from a hook. "Kept him in a tiny, squalid yard tied to a metal stake. The hair around his neck is still thin from straining against the rope. When he'd get loose, he'd dig under the fence to get out, and when his owner found him he'd beat on him. Some new neighbors called animal control. Poor baby had a couple broken ribs when he came to us. He's not the most outgoing little guy, but he's a softy once he gets used to you." The pleading undercurrent was evident in her tone. She really wanted Nook to get a home.

"He bite at all?" Curtis asked.

The volunteer pursed her lips. "He nipped at a few of us at first, but we spent a lot of time with him every day. He hasn't taken a chomp at anyone in a month, but I'll be watching. If he's super skittish I'll take him back."

"Right," Izzy said when the volunteer left the room. "Nook bites." She fretted with the right sleeve of her robe sweater.

"Give him a chance." Curtis took a seat on the built in bench.

The door swung open and Nook padded in, hugging close to the girl's leg and whining. She unhooked him from her lead and gave his ruff a light stroke.

"I'll be right outside," she said and closed them in with Nook, who hunched low to the floor as far from Curtis and Izzy as he could get. There was a clicking noise and the top half of the playroom's door swung inward, creating a window so others could monitor their activity.

Spreading his legs, Curtis slapped the inside of his thigh and whistled. Nook's ears perked and twitched in the sound's direction, but he didn't come. Curtis dropped one hand between his legs and snapped. When the dog didn't budge, he made a low noise in his throat—the sound gave Izzy the chills—he promptly cut off with a shake of his head, but the damage was done. Nook's ears went back and he flattened against the floor, pressing himself to the wall and whimpering when Curtis stood.

"What was that?" Izzy hopped in the space Curtis vacated and tucked her feet onto the seat. Nook wasn't exactly an agro-beast but, a dog was a dog and the more distance between her and him the better.

Curtis pinched his Adam's apple. "Lost patience." His rough voice rumbled like he'd spent a night shooting whiskey over gravel. Already spooked by her surroundings, the sound that had come from Curtis struck Izzy as bestial. It had sounded like he'd growled at Nook, but that wasn't possible. Curtis coughed and cleared his throat and moved to the door. The husky tracked his movements as he exited into the hall and closed the lower half of the partition.

*

What the hell happened?

Curtis hadn't been that out of control of Clear-Skies since he'd first inherited his father's wolf at twenty-five. Usually, the wolf spirit made himself unobtrusive until Curtis needed him. When he did need him, Clear-Skies permeated his being, suffused his bone and tissue with quicksilver spirit and changed him from man into monstrous wolf. Then Curtis became the small flame flickering within the beast, a human soul directing a force of nature. Only twice during the course of their symbiosis had the spirit overcome Curtis's dominance. When the mantle of the wolf descended upon him after his father's death, Curtis lost control. His mind couldn't cope with the spirit's intrusion. The wolf dominated him. Trapped in his bestial form, he raged and attacked his pack mates. Thomas overpowered Curtis and, under threat of death, had his Beta sequestered until he could control his wolf. Curtis mastered the wild spirit. The second lapse in his control occurred when he challenged Thomas for Izzy's life.

Technically, no one could act against the pack leader. The spirit, human souls included, bowed to the Alpha. Personal will determined spiritual dominance. Those most sure of themselves, their position in the world, and their individual power became Alphas. But the position wasn't permanent. If a pack mate's will exceeded their leader's one of three things could happen: the Alpha could peaceably concede the rank; the challenger could split from his or her pack and form a new one; or the Alpha and challenger entered combat and the one left breathing assumed leadership.

Stirrings of discontent in pack hierarchy stirred malcontent in the collective spirit of the pack, and Curtis and Thomas had butted heads for a long time. It made Clear-Skies unruly, so that a frightened hound unheeding of an unfamiliar hand triggered a very wolfish, a very Alpha, dominance display.

Closing his eyes, Curtis thudded his head against the wall. He opposed Thomas and his plan to lure Rapid out, and Curtis's will concerning Izzy was quite strong. Beta or not, he couldn't change the depth and strength of his desire.

The wall propped up Curtis's slumped weight. He waved the volunteer away when she made to approach. He didn't trust himself not to lash out. Not with Clear-Skies a blue wash rippling just below his skin, so close to initiating the change and taking over. Hyper aware of his body, he felt the microscopic expansion of each pore and its accompanying contraction, the currents of circulated air passing through the black hairs covering his arms.

Easy friend, easy, he inwardly addressed his wolf. *There is no danger here to us or Izzy. No enemy. No one challenges our will.*

Even his inner monologue sounded like a burgeoning Alpha's. The Tavella wolves had treated him like one when he'd paid his visit, answering his questions without hesitation and offering their hospitality. They knew nothing of coming enemies or darkness, but they'd heard a rumor or two, mentioned an old wolf in Arizona who rambled to anyone who'd listen about how the wolves had strayed from their duties. Might be worth a trip west when local pack business resolved.

One of the female wolves he'd visited had listened to his Izzy woes—that he wanted more time with her and to help with her animal phobias—and she'd suggested the animal shelter. She, too, volunteered there and if she got an adoption out of an unconventional date, she'd be pleased. A sound idea, since Petey, the hyperactive ruffian, really *did* need a brother and Izzy might benefit from a jaunt around some animals that couldn't get to her without someone unlocking their cages.

Curtis pushed off the wall and shook his tingling hands. His wolf had receded some and he'd come out of the danger zone. A smiling staffer came his way with a cup of water he gratefully accepted and an offer of coffee or soda he declined. He indulged her light conversation. The pleasant chatter helped reign in Clear-Skies and soon he felt fully human and the master of his faculties.

*

Izzy started to uncurl from the bench when a chuffing wuff from across the playroom rooted her to her seat. It was a Siberian standoff.

Nook sat again, his belly no longer kissing the tile. His frosty blue eyes assessed her, and when she met them, he didn't shy toward the wall. Was that a good thing? She couldn't remember if direct eye contact with an animal was good or bad, but Nook didn't turn aggressive. He looked away first, gave another wuff like a quiet belch, and did the hokey pokey with one paw, placing it forward, then drawing it back.

Nook wasn't loud. He didn't run around or jump up. Izzy liked that. She didn't like how fearful he seemed. That he'd been hurt without cause, crippled in his own way. He didn't deserve it.

Slowly, Izzy eased herself to the tile floor and positioned her legs in a wide vee. She rubbed the floor between her knees with her left hand and dusty grime accumulated on her fingertips. Nook's head bobbed and he stretched his muzzle in her direction and sniffed. Puckering her lips, she made kissy noises and patted the floor. Nook obeyed her summons and darted forward.

Startled at the sudden reaction, Izzy jumped back and Nook froze, looking from her to the wall as though unsure of his place. What did she expect when she sent such mixed messages? With her left hand, she reached out and Nook skittered back, whining a little. She kept still and left her arm outstretched.

"Noo-ook." Izzy sung his name in a two-note melody and rubbed her fingers together like she had a treat.

Air hissed through Nook's nostrils and he shook himself. Inching closer, he sniffed at Izzy's hand. She itched to give him a comforting pat and prove she wasn't a threat, but she didn't. Patience rewarded her.

Nook took the final step and nudged Izzy's hand, licking her fingers and getting a good whiff of her scent. She let him investigate for a while before petting him. At her movement he retreated, dancing away and then re-approaching. When he came near enough, she placed her hand between his flattening ears and scratched. Eventually, he relaxed and soaked up the attention.

Izzy ran her hand over Nook's head and back. A ring of thin hair and tough skin circled his neck. He squeaked when her fingers brushed that spot and she stiffened.

"I'm sorry," she said and dropped her arm.

Nook followed her hand and pushed his head under it. Soundly corrected, Izzy caressed him. His ears were so soft. They slipped through her hand when she stroked them. With a large yawn—she swallowed at his many sharp teeth—he stretched out between her legs and rested his head on her thigh. He was a pleasant warmth beside her, like Curtis had been sprawled next to her in bed.

"Wow." Curtis's voice drew Izzy's attention. He and the volunteer leaned on the half-partition, observing the cozy scene. "Looks like someone made a friend."

Izzy made a face. "You think?"

"Affirmative," Curtis said. "Sit tight you two."

Curtis entered the playroom and Nook went on high alert. His head lifted, his ears perked and when Curtis stepped next to Izzy, the dog's upper lip curled and the beginnings of a growl started in his throat.

"Easy boy," Curtis said and brushed the back of his hand over Izzy's cheek. Nook's growling ratcheted up, but as she leaned into Curtis's touch—his ease radiating through her—the dog quieted and lowered into her lap. He watched Curtis with guarded blue eyes.

Accompanying Izzy on the floor, Curtis put his arm around her. Every ten minutes or so, he tried petting Nook. After forty, the dog allowed it.

"His last owner must have been a big guy," Izzy said, wondering what it was about Curtis that Nook didn't like.

"He and I will have lots of time for get-to-know-you. Unless *you* want to adopt him, that is."

"Not quite ready for that. My complex is pet free anyhow."

"Then he'll have to settle for Keene property. Good thing huskies dig wide open spaces."

Nook answered with his cough-like wuff and thumped his tail on the floor when Curtis scratched behind his ears.

*

Meat sizzled in the pan Curtis manipulated on Izzy's tiny stove. Perched on the counter to his left, she steadied a mixing bowl filled with half-smashed potatoes, milk, and butter. She rotated her left wrist, her hand cramping with the mashing she'd accomplished.

"That's at least two meals for me," she said as Curtis spatulaed her steak onto a cooling plate. Red juices pooled in the black porcelain. "And we need some leafy greens to go with all these proteins, carbs, and fats."

"Green? Blarg." An exaggerated shudder shook Curtis's shoulders. "No leaves. No pods. More flesh."

"Then what are you having for a side dish?"

"Mmm . . . bacon?"

"Steak with a side of bacon?"

"Fantastic idea, Isabelle. Pass the pork."

"You're serious?" Izzy picked up her work again. Sloppy potato mixture wormed through triangular openings in the masher.

"Deadly." He pointed the spatula at her throat like a blade. "Tell me where you're holding the pork and no one gets hurt."

"Fridge, meat drawer, lower right."

Curtis snatched the utensil away and eyed her suspiciously as he rummaged in the fridge. Twenty minutes later, steak and a stack of bacon sat on his plate alongside a hillock of mashed potatoes covered in shredded cheddar. Izzy halved the meat he'd prepared for her, spooned some of her mash next to it and decided to forego toppings. They sat together at the circular table next to the large window dominating the east wall. Curtains and sheers open, the starry night sky over the neighboring luxury condos added an elegant touch to their homey meal.

"When I come down next weekend," Curtis said around a cheek full of steak, "you want to come back up to the lodge with me?"

Izzy's fork clanked against her plate. Her throat constricted and she had trouble swallowing the morsel of beef she chewed.

"Nook's comfortable with you," he went on, advocating his case for her visit. "The more he sees me with you, the more comfortable he'll get with me."

The relatively simple adoption process took about an hour, a few questions, a little paperwork, and a checkup for Nook who wasn't fixed. Curtis didn't want him breeding any strays. Scheduled for Tuesday, the operation would be quick with recovery slated for Friday, just in time for pick up and transport to DeConing.

"I'll think about it," Izzy said. "It depends how much progress my soloists make." She gave the safest answer. The invite threw her off guard and her immediate response was "Yes, yes, yes, yes, a billion times, yes!" That couldn't be healthy. Time without him would give her perspective and she could hash out this whole mess with Dr. Turner. "Did you take care of all your business in town today? You looked pissed in your car this morning." She didn't bother with subtlety in her conversational shift.

When Curtis answered he kept his eyes on his food. "Lodge management BS. My business was seeing you, a few local friends, and snagging a new bud for Petey. Mission accomplished." He flashed her that smile that begged for reciprocation.

"Problems at the lodge?" Izzy asked. Her mouth curled up to match his. No matter how hard she tried, she couldn't be a serious fuddy-duddy around him.

"Aren't there always. Spending a weekend away brings all that crap to the forefront." Curtis's gaze grew distant. He appeared almost desolate. "I wish I could spend more time away."

"You can't delegate?"

"I wish I could," he said.

Dinner was delicious if imbalanced. Curtis couldn't do eggs, but prepared dinner like a chef. Taking care of herself wasn't a problem for Izzy, but food wise she was limited to meals with less than four uncomplicated steps. She couldn't remember the last time she'd had a real dinner, side dishes and everything, in her apartment. If it wasn't salad with baked chicken breast on top, it was something she ate at a restaurant.

"The steak was great," Izzy said while she rinsed their plates. Hot water rushed over her hand and pink liquid dish soap scented the steamy air with flowers. "Did you enjoy your meat and meat?"

Curtis's hands appeared on the counter at Izzy's sides, his arms trapping her in place. She felt him at her back, his breath on her neck when he spoke.

"One of my physical appetites is wholly satisfied." He nipped at her neck and a tremor passed through her like a ripple over water.

"You have a lot of appetites," she said.

"At times I am a product of my hungers and I give them free reign." Curtis shut off the tap. Water pattered from the faucet into the sink's steel bowl, thunderously loud in the loaded silence. Curtis turned Izzy to him and her damp rag plopped on the floor. He placed a line of soft, questioning kisses along her jaw. She answered those questions when her mouth found his. How could she deny him when he did such wonderful things to her body? Would he stay the night again? What her heart needed from him was at utter odds with rational behavior.

Running her left hand through his hair, Izzy flecked her tongue at his lips before he slid his between hers. Arms wrapped around her and his palms traveled to her ass, which he squeezed. Then he lifted her onto the counter. With his hips, he knocked her legs wide and filled that space with his bulk, grinding against her, thrusting as though nothing, save skin, separated them.

Desperately, they tore at each other. One hand Curtis clamped over the back of Izzy's neck while the other slipped beneath her tank top and up to knead her breast. Her nipples stood out against the fabric of bra and shirt. She wanted to reach down and squeeze the cock riding against her sex, making her damp and ready, but she couldn't, not with his mouth and body bearing down on hers, pushing her back toward the sink. The faucet prodded her back. Reaching her strong arm over his shoulder and back, she anchored herself to him.

Breaking away, Curtis said, "Hold onto me," and hoisted her off the counter. Izzy gripped his hips with her legs and circled her arms around his neck as he carried her to the bedroom.

Tumbling Izzy onto the bed, Curtis did away with her shirt and jeans, tossing everything in a sloppy pile in the corner. He added his own shirt to the top of the heap and climbed onto the mattress, getting her out of her harness.

"I can do it," she said, fighting him.

"Yes, but I want you naked now." Curtis's adept fingers had her harness loose in a second and he whipped it off, setting her prosthetic on the nightstand. He discarded her bra and panties and, with his hand on her chest, pressed her flat on the bed.

Izzy arched her back in an elegant curve as he trailed a finger between her breasts and down to her shell-like stomach where he circled her navel. Her belly fluttered, contracting under his light touch.

"Where are your condoms?" Curtis asked, continuing his circling. His eyes lingered at the shadowed patch between her thighs.

Through quickening breaths, Izzy answered. "Nightstand. Bottom drawer."

His teasing ceased when he went for them and she relaxed only to jump up when she remembered what else lay in the bottom drawer of her nightstand.

"Wait!" she said.

But it was too late.

Chapter Seven

"Oh, my." Curtis stared into the open drawer. "Maybe you were alone for a couple of years, but you certainly weren't lonely."

Izzy shoved him, but he stubbornly kept his place. Right next to her remaining condoms sat her vibrator, fleshy, pink and unavoidable. When she pushed him again, he caught her, wrapping an arm around her back and canting her chin up with his free hand.

"When do you use it?" His dark eyes were serious and uncompromising.

"Curtis." Izzy struggled and his hold on her eased.

Wedging his head in the cradle of her neck and shoulder, he kissed her throat, coaxing her with ardor. "Don't be embarrassed. Tell me. I want to know when you like it."

On principle, Izzy resisted, then gave in to his nuzzling and sweetness. "In the evening during the week. On weekends, first thing in the morning. Sometimes in the late afternoon on Sunday when I'm bored."

"Mmmmm. Show me?"

The unexpected request was unexpectedly enticing. Moisture and warmth pulsed from Izzy's sex.

"You want to watch?" she asked.

Curtis took her earlobe with his teeth in a light grip. His bite sent a delicious shiver over Izzy's scalp, her flesh alive to every sensation no matter its subtlety. "I love it when you perform," he whispered.

Nudging from him, Izzy lowered her head. Finally, she reached for her toy, taking the weighty device in her palm and scooting until her back met the plush, cool give of pillows and her cushioned headboard. With her foot she pushed Curtis and he moved to the end of the bed, adjusting himself through his denim.

In private, Izzy preferred the security her comforter provided. When she pleasured herself she did so under the warmth and down of her bedclothes, eyes closed, bent knees tenting the sheets. With an audience she couldn't afford a drawn curtain. Getting comfortable, she let the pillows support her back and her head rest on the headboard. She bent her legs and, haltingly, spread them. Curtis's fixed attention on her exposed entrance bordered indecent. It seemed the light whispers of air over her wetted skin came from him, as though his intense gaze itself touched her. The twitch of his smile and the devilish cast to his expression drove her sight downward to the body she stroked for his, and her, amusement.

Watch me, Curtis.

Glistening curves and crevices of pinked flesh parted, widened for the blunt head of the cock with which she teased herself. She traced her opening and massaged her clit, uttering a high, surprised sound at the tickle of a hundred tiny feathers from within. Moving lower, she penetrated herself with the first inches of the toy, watching herself stretch and accept its width. Her lids fluttered and her eyes rolled back.

The mattress rocked. Curtis stood, his eyes trained between her legs as he shoved his jeans and boxers down his thighs. His prick sprang free from the lowered clothing. His hardness and length galvanized her and she pushed the toy deeper, until its secondary, curving appendage—a jutting protrusion like a finger attached to the topside of the surrogate cock—brushed her clit. She pushed the toy as deep as she wanted Curtis and, catching his attention, she told him so with her eyes, emboldened by his nudity and unabashed interest. He paused his stripping and his lips parted in surprise. She turned the toy's dial base and it came alive inside her.

Vibrations coursed throughout her inner walls and the little finger at her clit danced against her swelling bud. Izzy murmured words made incomprehensible by pleasure and her hips involuntarily worked against the device, rubbing herself harder against the massaging finger. Curtis seated himself once more at the end of the bed and gripped the base of his cock, moving his hand up the shaft, fingers pinching when he crested over his engorged head.

Izzy's hand shot out. She didn't want Curtis at a distance, both of them stroking themselves to solitary climax. The vibrator slipped when she beckoned for him. Its teasing protrusion moved from her clit. What she wouldn't give for her other hand back. A frustrated cry escaped her and she moved the toy back in place, glaring at Curtis and his sly, knowing smile.

"You want me there?" he asked, glancing at her stuffed passage and tugging on the head of his cock. Walking on his knees to her, Curtis bent and clasped her wrist, urging the device free. Izzy resisted. "Playing hard to get?" Leaning forward, he sucked her pert nipple into his mouth, flicking his tongue over the sensitive tip. Her sex throbbed around the vibrator and her teeth cut into her bottom lip.

"I do want you," she said. "But not there."

Curtis's nose brushed hers when he raised his head. Confusion glazed his eyes. Izzy captured his mouth with hers, coaxing his tongue between her lips, sucking on it as she drew back.

"I want you in my mouth."

A ragged breath rushed from Curtis at her suggestion. One eyebrow hooked up like a question mark and she answered with a stunted nod. Kissing Izzy a final time, a glancing caress compared to how they'd devoured each other in the kitchen, he righted himself, inching forward on his knees, his prick jutting and level with her face. Hands braced on the wall, he stared down at her and curled his hips until his cock grazed her lips, its skin soft and delicate like a bit of fine velvet.

Izzy opened her mouth, but she didn't take him inside. Instead, she maneuvered her head, letting the tip of his shaft trace her open lips. Salty fluid from the clear bead welling at his crown's slit moistened her skin. She swept her tongue over her wetted lips and swirled it over the divot dimpling his head.

"Izzy," Curtis mumbled and pressed his cock to her mouth. She still hadn't opened wide enough to accommodate him and he moved his hips impatiently. His tip bumped her lips and brushed across her cheek before moving back into position. "Izz—"

She sucked him in. Hot, ridged flesh stretched her mouth wide. Curtis groaned when she rocked into his reactionary surge, her hand momentarily abandoning the vibrator to grip his ass. His muscles tensed as she pushed him further, dictating his depth and rhythm until he took over. Fingers curled around her ponytail and pulled her carefully forward. Hair surrounding his groin tickled her nose and lips. She drove the toy deep into herself, mimicking his thrusts.

Each muffled cry Izzy gave around Curtis's thick shaft spurned him on. His cock nudged the back of her throat before sliding out and driving back in. She didn't know how or from where she pulled her courage, but she kept her eyes locked on his, communicating exactly how much of him she could take. A lustful sheen made his brown eyes glassy. Sweat glistened on his forehead and dampened his dark hair.

The vibrator hummed deep within Izzy and climatic chills rippled in her belly. The little finger wriggling at her clit stoked her pleasure higher. Her hand frenzied at the promise of release, bearing down on the mounting sensation. Tilting her head, she opened her throat for Curtis who pushed as deep as he could and she was filled utterly at either end. That fullness—his prick swelling in her mouth, the vibrator stretching her sex—broke her and she came, her throat contacting around his cock and initiating his release. He jetted inside her, hand vise-like in her hair while the other cupped her jaw, his thrusting erratic and forceful. She swallowed the searing liquid he spilled. It left a strange tang on her tongue and at the back of her throat. She did not move away from him, knowing how sensitive men were immediately after they came. Even slight pressure could be painful. Instead, she relaxed around his length and let him recover.

Sliding from her mouth, Curtis stroked Izzy's cheek as he gazed down at her from hooded eyes, lazy in the aftermath of his climax. "You ok?" he asked, chest pumping like a billows.

Izzy planted a kiss on his softening cock that shone with her enthusiastic attention. "Very." She switched off the vibrator and eased the toy from her slit.

Sitting back on his heels, Curtis slumped onto the bed, watching her while she cleaned the device and put it away.

"Come here," he said when she finished and held his arms open for her. Izzy crawled into them and let him position and pet her. She dozed against his chest, wondering what exactly she wanted with this man and what exactly he wanted from her.

Chapter Eight

Curtis didn't sleep. Couldn't. He held Izzy while she slept, his eyes burning and gritty with wakefulness. He buried his face in her soapy smelling hair. If they never left her bed they could hide from the world, from the pack, from Rapid. He squeezed her too tight and she wriggled and grumbled without waking.

Golden light pierced the blinds above the bed, striping Izzy's face and shoulders. Curtis inwardly cursed the morning, but he didn't stir. He knew when Izzy woke, sensed it somehow. They lay spooned together, each aware of the other's consciousness, comfortable with silence.

Breaking their stillness, Curtis pressed closer to Izzy, his erection cradled in the cleft of her buttocks. She shifted up and back and her downy lips, already damp, pushed at his crown. He took the wordless invitation, trailed his hand—the one not attached to the arm wedged under her—down her back and over the curve of her hip. Sliding his palm between her sandwiched thighs, he elevated her top leg. Her slit was now open to him and her breath hitched as he stroked her up and down with his cock, the motion similar to her demonstrated foreplay with the vibrator the night before.

Curtis learned fast. He hadn't requested her performance simply because it aroused him—blood thickened his cock at the memory—but also because he wanted to learn her wants, to know when and how she craved her fucking. Knowledge was power and he armed himself with it. The more he knew of Izzy, the closer they grew. Soon, she would hunger for what only he could give her and she would be his. Her slippery, heated little mouth conformed around him and he drew in a deep breath through his nose.

I need a condom, he thought while the hand of his arm tucked beneath Izzy, which had long ago found her breast, idly fiddled with a pearled nipple. He needed a condom or else he'd do what he wished: slide home naked inside her and fill her up with his come like he had her mouth. The idea tempted him, marking her body as his, sealing her with his scent. His protection. With him inside her, beside her, nothing could touch her that meant her harm. That choice, however, came with potentially life altering consequences for which they weren't ready. When he had kids, they wouldn't be the result of selfish impulse.

Sheets *shished* when Curtis sat up. He turned toward the nightstand, but before he reached the drawer, Izzy caught him by his prick, her firm fingers wrapping around his base. It ticked in her hand, syncopated with his ratcheting pulse. She tugged at him gently and her reddened lips pouted and her expression turned demanding.

Curtis laughed and twisted for the drawer. "One sec. I'm getting a condom."

"I'm on the pill." Abandoning his dick, Izzy pulled at his waist and her short nails raked over his torso. He shivered. "I'm all right without if you are. Unless there's anything I should know about your health."

Curtis angled back to face her. "I'm healthy," he said, stunned at how closely her thoughts mirrored his. Well, maybe not all of them. She'd already proved she stood on her own two feet, whether a burly man had her back or not, and who knew if she'd ever considered children. But she wanted him as close as he wanted to be. This was good.

"Then leave it?" she suggested.

His brain spluttered out. A few yanks to his cerebral starter cord got his *thoughts put-put-putting* along.

"All right." He swallowed and lay on his side and turned Izzy away from him, recreating the comfortable position from which they'd strayed.

He snaked his arm back under her and the nubs of her spine bumped him as he gathered her to his chest. Throwing his other arm over her, he brought his hand to her face and touched her lips. Humid breath whispered over his fingertips.

"Open up," he said into her ear.

Izzy obeyed. That she heeded his casual command without question heightened his arousal and he rotated his hips, arranging his length more comfortably at her backside. Maybe he wouldn't mind being her Alpha. He slipped two fingers into her mouth.

"Suck. Like you did last night."

This time she hesitated. He started to pull free and the pitted texture of her searing tongue gave his flesh a tantalizing stroke. She had to know he wouldn't force her, but Christ he wished she'd do it. Six words had pushed him from aroused to agonized and no amount of rearranging could quiet the dull pain of anticipation spreading through his dick. Suddenly, she sucked his retreating fingers hard, pulling them, massaging them with her lips and tongue as she would his cock. The hardness banked along her bottom she trapped in her thighs and rode, his length gliding through her wetted slit. Curtis grunted at the unexpected stimulation. His balls tightened, preparing to jettison his semen out over her stomach. Any more of her bucking and sucking and he'd lose it. She fought him when he attempted to draw his fingers from her mouth. Her teeth cut into his toughened skin.

"Punishing me?" he asked, finally extracting himself.

"Only a little."

"Well, you'll regret it a little later."

Izzy clamped her thighs around his cock in response, but went limp when Curtis's fingers, which she'd so helpfully moistened, went to her clit. The bundle of flesh budded at the pads of his fingertips and her whole body went fluid. With her distracted, he liberated his prick and, using the hand keeping her at his chest, found and caught her delicate wrist. He positioned her where his fingers played and set her hand over his.

"Show me. I want to do it right," he said.

Izzy stroked his knuckles and up over his wrist. Dark hairs there trailed against her touch and little shiver-bumps stippled his skin when a violent tremor wracked his body and raised his cock. She seemed very smug about his reaction.

Squeezing his fingers together, she moved his hand just above her clit so he barely touched her. Not what he expected. What he did with his tongue must not be what she needed with his fingers. Rapidly, she moved his hand back and forth while he rolled one of her nipples in his unoccupied hand. She corrected his pressure—this touch was so slight yet she panted under it—when he tried taking over. Once he understood her needs below, she left him and toyed with the breast he didn't. Her head tilted back into his chest. Her mouth opened in a silent cry and her belly clenched.

Curtis withdrew his hands and swore he heard a needle scratching off a spinning record. Izzy gritted her teeth and growled.

"Not so fast," he said and closed his mouth over her nape, kissing her there, then raising his head. "I know everything you need now. You're at my mercy."

"But—"

Lifting her leg, Curtis entered Izzy with one sure stroke. Her slick passage accepted him with no resistance.

"Ah." His jaw clenched. She was tight around him and so hot. Without the latex barrier, sensation drilled into his brain, permeating his every nerve. Clear-Skies, who'd nestled behind his heart, lashed out, wrapped around the beating organ, and sparked. Curtis groaned when he adjusted himself deep within her, his balls resting on her inner thigh. Just as his wolf spirit relaxed around his heart, Izzy undulated against him and he grabbed her shoulders, keeping her still.

"Wait." His heaving chest pushed her forward. "You're not making me come yet." He circled his arms around her, locking them together. True, he did need a moment to tamp down his excitement, but he also needed Clear-Skies to back down. The wolf couldn't be prominent now or he'd take her too rough. Calmed, the wolf spirit shrank and dimmed to a faint, blue candle flame wavering in his breast.

Movements slight, Curtis rocked with Izzy. Fitted inside her to his base, his rolling massaged a place deep within that had her limp and moaning. High, breathy cries punctuated his movements. Eager for mindless release, she reached for her sex, but Curtis restrained her.

"I told you you'd regret punishing me." He trapped her complete arm to her chest while his unencumbered hand hovered over her clit. Like this, her inflamed apex brushed his fingers whenever he rolled into her. Izzy threw her head back on his shoulder and scored his earlobe with her teeth. He drove faster, fingers moving freely over her mound, stimulating the tender bud housed within the flesh. It was too much for her this time—color flushed her breasts and crept up her neck and cheeks—and Curtis let her go.

Digging her nails into his confining arm, Izzy came, crying out obscenities. Her passage convulsed, constricted around and milked Curtis's cock. He didn't wait for her to cool. Releasing her, he pushed her leg higher, gave himself room, and pounded into her. The suck-release, suck-release of her body ignited him and his jerking orgasm chased the end of hers. His spasms threaded out the diminishing shivers of her climax.

It took a long time for their breathing to fall into the steady rhythm of relaxation. Curtis didn't draw out right away. He softened inside Izzy, enjoying the residual warmth and the gentle pulse of her body. Hand resting gently around her throat, his thumb stroked the tendon he'd never nibbled. She drooped, lazed along the cradle he made of his body. When he did move— difficult as his sapped energy made him feel like he waded through honey—he kept her comfortable and kissed the spot in the middle of her shoulder blades and flipped onto his back.

"Can I hop in your shower before I head out?" Clear-Skies rippled at the pull of longing in Curtis's gut. The wolf didn't want to leave either.

"Sure," Izzy said, a hint of a smile at her lips. "That is unless you planned to lick your balls and pee in the corner."

Curtis's lashes lowered and he laughed a private laugh before launching out of bed. "Your corners are safe from me." He ambled to the bathroom, his heavy cock swaying with his stride.

*

Izzy left the shower to Curtis, comfortable in pajama bottoms, a loose tank and the clinging scents of sex for the moment. She gathered the clothes he'd pitched in the corner, stale from two days of continuous wear, and yelled through the cracked bathroom door if he wanted his things washed. He consented, the shower spray muffling his words, and she puttered out front with a large bundle of clothes tucked under her left arm. Absent the warmth and steam of the shower against her face, the front rooms were chilly. Hiking up the thermostat, she ventured to the utility room and shook out their jeans next to the washing machine.

Curtis's cell phone flew from his pocket and clattered on the hardwood floor.

"Shit." Izzy swiped back her hair and bent for the device, anxious she'd busted it. Images of her crushed smart phone and its pricey replacement flashed in her mind. The cell landed in an upside down vee and stood up like a pup tent. She snatched it up as two texts came through, strings of characters populating the green screen before she could flip it closed.

You there?

She more important than us?

Squinching her eyes closed, Izzy snapped the phone shut and pursed her lips. The lighted text burned colors on the backs of her lids. She squeezed the cell and set it on the dryer. Single-handedly, her chores so practiced without her prosthetic that she was as fast with it on or off, she emptied thick, blue detergent into the already running wash and let the lid slam shut. She found Curtis's jacket and wallet on the coffee table and placed his phone next to them, glaring at it like a treacherous thing as she plunked down on the couch.

She hadn't snooped, had she? She hadn't meant to read it. It was an accident. Not like the text had to be about her anyway, and if it was it was Curtis's problem and he wasn't treating her like it was. Better to forget it. She hadn't done anything wrong and asking him about it would be nosy and clingy and a perfect example of everything she hated about herself.

"Pondering the secrets of the universe?"

Jerking her head from her hands, Izzy stared at the tan, towering man framed by the hall entrance to her bedroom. Covered only in a white towel wrapped around his waist, he stretched his arms overhead, his shadowed navel peeking above the terrycloth.

"I'm all wet," he said, slicked back his damp hair, and drummed his fingers on his taut stomach.

"You'll be dry when your clothes are. If you're going to sit, make sure you do it on the towel," Izzy said.

"Yes, ma'am." He saluted her and adjusted his thick sarong. The towel opened for a quick flash of his groin before he draped the cloth around his hips, rolling the top edge for security.

"You are standing in front of a window," Izzy said as he strolled to the couch and took a seat. He propped his feet on the coffee table, crossing them at the ankle.

"No one saw." Curtis picked up the remote and switched on the TV, somehow finding a basketball game in under three clicks.

Izzy leaned against the armrest and stared past his feet. "Your phone was making a lot of racket."

"Was it?" Curtis's brows came together and he leaned forward for his cell. Whipping it open, his eyes scanned the logged texts with an impassive expression. He closed the phone on his chest and let it rest there where it rose and fell with his breath. "Good times never last," he muttered and rubbed his eye.

"Lodge stuff?" The words escaped her lips before she pinched them shut.

"They can get by without me," Curtis said without humor.

"If you have to leave now, I can dump your stuff in the dryer."

"No," he said. "Leave it. They can wait."

Izzy reclined against the cushions. Maybe the messages really hadn't been about her, but if they had she was glad to be more important than whatever or whoever awaited Curtis at the lodge. Sinking into his side, she watched the game, her eyes taking in movement and color while her mind wandered to her duties for the coming week. She switched their clothes from machine to machine and when the dryer's alarm buzzed, her chest got a little heavy. Her weekend guest pulled on his clothes in the utility room and tossed the damp towel in the hamper. He scratched the back of his neck.

"Will you think about coming up next weekend?"

Izzy nodded while Curtis shrugged on his coat at her door.

"Give me a call sometime this week so I have an excuse to stop working, ok?" he asked.

"All right," Izzy said and Curtis took her by the cheeks and placed a noisy kiss on her forehead. He disappeared down the hall, the clomp of his boots on the stair and his booming voice when he greeted someone below lingered in his absence. When she shut the door, she was very aware of how empty her apartment was even with the noise of the surrounding residents on a Sunday afternoon.

Chapter Nine

Crisis at the Glazier Studio meant Izzy soon forgot the ominous texts from persons unknown. Mimi Sims, cast as Clara, fractured her ankle at softball practice and showed up to class Tuesday evening on crutches, her damaged foot stuck in a big, blue boot. She swore she'd be fine in time for the performance, but a call to her parents revealed doctor's orders were four weeks with the walking aids and an additional two weeks to a month of rest without. No sports or strenuous activity. There were tears and tears when Izzy informed Mimi's understudy Suzanne—Su-zahn, the girl stressed whenever anyone got it wrong—she'd take over the part. Izzy placated Mimi by making her the understudy coach. By the end of class, Mimi beamed with her power over her understudy and Suzanne was red faced over the girl's admittedly harsh corrections. Choreography needed changing. Suzanne didn't carry the same exuberance as Mimi. She'd need a lot of Izzy's attention in the coming month.

Tuesday evening also marked Arty's return. The bum shambled back and forth on the other side of the studio's picture windows. Izzy closed the blinds and called the cops. She must have checked the door locks six times while she shut the studio down. Arty was gone when she emerged but came back Wednesday morning when she opened. A Styrofoam cup of coffee gripped in his chapped and palsied hands shook, spilling dark brown liquid on his coat sleeves and the pavement. He knew enough not to get too close and mumbled near incoherent apologies for his botched mugging before holding his hand out for change. Izzy remained tight lipped and shut herself inside the studio, warming up for her ten a.m. class.

The Montessori school down the street booked her early Wednesday and Friday slots. There was no real structure needed for classes geared for three to four years olds, just freeform movement and dance games. Izzy thought they might like to play with the big parachute at the end of the hour and yanked the wadded fabric out of the storage closet at the back of the girls' changing room.

Class flew by with shrieking toddlers swaying in the studio like tiny trees and flitting beneath the ballooning parachute before it touched the floor. Anyone trapped underneath became a "parachute bug" and had the cloth billowed around them to their squealing delight.

Izzy nabbed an early lunch after the toddlers, led by over-caffeinated, highly animated teachers, paraded out of the studio. Two private sessions with girls prepping auditions for summer intensives followed that afternoon. She thought at least one of them had a good chance. The other needed another year of hard work and significant improvement. When her evening classes ended, she finally had a spare moment to go over calls she'd missed on the studio's answering machine and to note two missed calls on her cell. One came from her therapist, the other from Curtis.

Izzy called Dr. Turner back, confirming their nine p.m. appointment then stared at her phone for the next five minutes, her thumb hovering over the "call back" button next to Curtis's missed call. In lieu of conversation, she sent him a text.

Sorry, I can't call. Dr.'s appt.

His reply came quick.

This late?

Therapy, she answered. *Call you tomorrow?*

Sure. Night!

Texting brought a taste of Curtis's infectious good nature to mind and an emptiness behind Izzy's sternum yawned wide. She'd kept herself so busy she hadn't had time for thoughts of him or what a good time they'd had together. How he fit comfortably in her schedule, insinuating himself in her heart and life as though he'd always been there and merely returned after an extended absence. She scowled at her phone. Who was he to barge into her life and why did she let him? Since when did she need anybody? She'd gotten over Alan's death and her arm and her whole life unraveling all on her own. Nothing should have changed.

Izzy recalled the pride that warmed her last Sunday while she and Curtis had watched the game. When he'd chosen her over his problems at the lodge, she'd had the same sense of satisfaction that came after she'd mastered a difficult balance or turn. Healthy validation came from within. That it came from his estimation of her was an enormous red flag.

*

The suite of offices Dr. Janet Turner shared with her associates was almost a second home, but the comforting atmosphere never banished Izzy's trepidation at sharing her innermost secrets and blackest thoughts. Confession was hard no matter how much you did it, and she'd done therapy for years. She'd spent a significant bout of childhood and adolescence on a couch discussing her once debilitating anxiety and quicksand depressions, her fits of self-deprivation and obsessive rituals, ballet included. All those offices and doctors melded into one innocuous, slap-dash memory like a smeared oil painting, the therapists and their surroundings all calming and without personality. Even the waiting room of the Couppola building's psychotherapy suite was different.

Dim lighting prevailed, but there was no innocuous, soft music piped from overhead speakers or a stereo concealed behind potted ferns and rubber plants. Art covered the walls. And not the pay-no-attention-to-us watercolor prints or framed Klimt posters bearing the artist's name in dominant, serif capitals. Paintings stacked upon paintings and decorative masks and relief sculpture tiled the wall in a haphazard Tetris layout from floor to ceiling. A couch and two deep-seated armchairs upholstered in mahogany leather surrounded a block of marble, which served as a coffee table. Izzy sat on the couch. Its splitting leather rasped at her palm and the backs of her thighs and she sank into the well-worn cushions.

Up-to-date issues of *Vogue, Craft, Make, Wired,* and *The Economist* mingled on the marble slab with supermarket paperbacks and jacketless, hardcover rescues from the public library. An area rug under the marble was reminiscent of a forest floor in autumn, its plush weave shot through with hunter greens, russets, and flecks of faded gold. Kicking off her flats, Izzy curled her toes in the thick fibers while she waited on Dr. Turner. The smell of brewing tea preceded her therapist's arrival.

A pale, rosy cheeked, heart-shaped face capped with a sleek black bob poked through the waiting room door. Carmine lips spread in a wide smile.

"Ready for me, Isabelle?"

Izzy sprang from the couch. "Yes, Dr. Turner." She followed the taller, curvier likeness of Bettie Page, complete with artfully sculpted brows, down the long hall to her office. They stopped briefly at the kitchenette where Dr. Turner poured herself a mug of green citrus tea from a ceramic pot. Gold rings gleamed on all her fingers, matching the braided torc circling her white throat and the heavy scarabs stretching her ear lobes, stamped with twin cartouches on their backs.

Dr. Turner shook her head. "You're never going to call me Janet, are you? Tea?"

"No to both, thank you. 'Dr. Turner' is more conducive to my process." Izzy had to maintain some sense of structure to these meetings. Dr. Turner wasn't like any psychologist she'd ever met. She dressed like a yoga instructor crossed with an Oxford professor. Black, swishy pants flared around her gold, snakeskin pattered sandals, and a crisp, white button-down blouse drew in at her waist and fell over her wide hips. With a patient's consent, she chain-smoked cloves during sessions and glided effortlessly between a trio of personas: mother, best friend and incisive therapist. The combination made Izzy completely open while never doubting the formidable psychologist waited in the wings should trouble brew.

"How have you been coping since our last session with fear?" Dr. Turner asked as she sashayed into her office. "Have you given my suggestions any thought?"

Izzy tagged after her therapist into a room as full of character as the woman. Dr. Turner had a cat fetish and a streak of Egyptologist. Pharaohnic black cats adorned with lapis and gold necklaces and hoops through their ears coolly observed the eclectic space. Cousins to the regal felines, lucky cats of various sizes beamed from end tables and window ledges, the biggest and fattest positioned next to Dr. Turner's afghan covered sofa. Spangled with gold glitter, it smiled at each patient who sat—as Izzy did now—in the Laz-E-Boy opposite the therapist's couch and, when encouraged, waved its mechanized paw.

"I went back to Keene Lodge," Izzy said as she rocked back in the chair.

Dr. Turner reclined on her couch, legs up, a yellow legal pad balanced on her lap. She twirled a well-chewed ballpoint pen. "Feet first as always. Did you confront anything unexpected?"

"Curtis Keene."

Dr. Turner's brows went up and she made a "do tell" motion with her hand.

Describing their meeting and the weekend that followed ate up half the session. Dr. Turner didn't speak until more than three minutes of Izzy's silence elapsed.

"You've told me nothing but good, yet you're frowning. Why's that?"

"Why would anyone go through so much trouble over one person? Just to see them?"

Making a note on her pad, Dr. Turner straightened her posture and gave a thoughtful sigh. "Sharing a trauma with someone is a powerful thing. There might be a bond for him you don't yet understand."

"Or motives I don't."

Like slivers of glass, the texts, which Izzy had kept from her thoughts most of the week, had burrowed into her brain since she and Curtis's brief correspondence at the studio.

Is she more important than us?

Who was us? Lodge people? Did Curtis's co-workers or employees have such unrestrained access to his private life? And if they did, what threat did she pose? He didn't strike her as the type who shirked responsibility.

"Has he given you a reason for mistrust?" Dr. Turner asked.

Her foot dancing around over her knee, Izzy admitted her unintentional invasion of his privacy. Dr. Turner nodded.

"Accidents happen. Is the text what's bothering you or your violation of Curtis's boundaries?"

"Both."

"What is it about the contents of the texts that strikes you most?"

Thinking, Izzy folded her arms over her stomach. "The 'her over us' thing. I don't want to compete for someone's attention or affection."

"You've been in a situation like that before?" Dr. Turner's pen scratched against her pad.

"Competition's a big part of being a professional dancer. Standing out. Vying for roles. It's exhilarating career wise, but I don't want it bleeding into my personal life."

"Has it before?"

The therapist's room dimmed and an image wavered in Izzy's vision. A girl, belly curving outward in a pale pink leotard, legs sheathed in white tights, and feet in pink slippers wobbled in *plié* before rising into a strained *relevé*.

"Mom, look. Mommy, watch me!"

Watch me, Curtis.

But little Izzy's mom would not be distracted. She bent her dark head over Alan's blue duffel, making sure her son had everything for his Monday baseball practice.

"Mom, you're not watching!" Little Izzy rocked back on her heels, her loosened bun hanging off her head.

"In a second, sweetie."

Little Izzy didn't want seconds, she wanted now. Lower lip jutting, she dropped to the floor and glared at her brother's bag and his ugly, stinky baseball junk.

Blinking the memory back into the shuffle of fixed stills from her past, Izzy focused on Dr. Turner, whose lips puckered and relaxed as she observed her patient.

"If I didn't have everyone's attention when I was little, I wasn't happy. And I hated," her voice caught on the word, "Alan sometimes."

And when those angry feelings surfaced during a session or on her own time, Izzy's soul withered and crumpled like a dead leaf. How dare she feel anything but good for her brother? Alan had loved her. He'd sacrificed himself for her. Sure, he could be a great big jerk, but that was part of the brother thing. What she'd hated was the competition. Compared with his accomplishments, all her personal triumphs seemed negligible, then and now. A ballerina couldn't compete with a surgeon. She'd danced. He'd saved lives. Died saving hers.

"Sibling rivalry is normal," Dr. Turner said.

Izzy shrugged. "I guess, but there were still these awful twinges of it when we got older after I moved to New York. He stayed close to home. Mom, Dad and Alan were the Three Musketeers. They always felt like the real family."

"You were the interloper?"

"Feels that way."

"Feels?"

"Yes," Izzy said, confounded at Dr. Turner's fixation on the word. Two clicks later and she realized she'd used the present tense. Feeling like an outsider in her own family hadn't gone away with Alan's death, it had intensified. In her mind, she didn't deserve her life, selfish thing that she was. She should have died that day at Keene Lodge, not Alan. Nothing she did, no accolade she won could fill the vacancy he left. She was a grim monument of her family's tragedy, and so she avoided them so she would not burden them or herself with the memories. Vocalizing those thoughts should have been her next step, but Izzy didn't take it. She knew Dr. Turner didn't miss the loaded quality of the silence. While her therapist didn't press the issue, the sharp-minded woman wouldn't forget it either.

"What's your biggest fear about this budding relationship with Curtis?" Dr. Turner had set her pad and pen aside after completing her notes.

"That I'll need him as much as I needed them. Mom and Dad, I mean, and Alan. That nothing he gives me will be enough. That I'll want precedence above all things."

"And if he wants you at the top of his priorities?"

"No one wants that." Izzy plucked at a nonexistent bit of lint from her sweater.

Dr. Turner narrowed her eyes. "Are you going to the lodge this weekend or are you going to use these texts and your inadvertent breach of this man's privacy as a barrier?"

Izzy didn't respond right away. Seconds ticked by on the red cat clock above Dr. Turner's fastidiously neat desk. Its eyes and tail swished back and forth and its rhinestone studded bow tie sparkled in the lamp light.

"I think I'll go," she said.

*

"How fares Casanova?"

Curtis flipped his phone shut and glared at Gerome, who perched on the back of the main building's couch, an unwelcome cawing buzzard hovering at his shoulder. In fact, the text he'd just read had come from Izzy. His heart had jumped when he saw her name on the green-lighted screen. She would come, and she'd asked if she could call that evening to discuss their plans.

Of course, he'd typed out with his clumsy thumb. That she hadn't called during the week for small talk had dented his ego. Maybe she hadn't found him irresistible and charming. Impossible. Aggie, his dad's second wife and Curtis's honorary Ma, always said those were two of his most attractive qualities.

"Number three is compassion," she'd said and slapped him gently on the cheek.

Curtis rolled his eyes. Compassion got a wolf zip in a pack, no matter where it got him with the ladies.

"So, is she coming? Or do I get a crack at her?" Gerome made a kissy noise right in Curtis's ear. Clear-Skies flooded his veins and coiled through his bones like liquid ice. Fists clenched, he strove to ignore the taunt, but he didn't call back his wolf. If Gerome kept at it, let the beast come. They'd teach the pup a lesson he'd had coming for a long time.

Gerome *oofed* when Melinda shoved a construction itinerary into his gut. "You could make yourself useful instead of pissing off our Beta. You're monitoring cabins six through ten. All the Alpha ass-kissing you do won't be for shit if you split the pack, yeah?"

"Aw, Lin, I don't want nothing happening to the pack. I just want a turn with the bait meat before Rapid gets to her and there's nothing left but scraps."

Curtis saw red. He leapt to his feet, spun, and dropped a growing, warping hand atop Gerome's skull. Claws burgeoned from his fingertips and dug through skin and bone. Gerome shrieked when Curtis pitched him backward. The man's body sailed overhead and slammed onto the coffee table, his lightweight frame no more burden to Curtis's spirit-bolstered strength than a jumble of bound twigs. He leapt on Gerome and dug his claws into the man's cheeks.

"No. Wolf. Will. Touch. Her." Curtis's voice distorted to a growl. Gerome's bones creaked in his grip. Blood wept from the punctures in his pack mate's cheeks and the deep grooves torn from his scalp.

"Stop. Both of you." Thomas's command cut through the whining buzz in Curtis's ears. "Curtis, let go of Gerome and get hold of yourself."

With no choice but to obey, Curtis released his pack mate and drew Clear-Skies back. Straightening and shaking, Gerome looked murderous, his reddened face—its wounds already healing thanks to Leaf-On-A-Swift-Stream—twisting with contained rage. He likely would have retaliated if Thomas hadn't intervened.

"Gerome, Melinda, get to your cabins. Work crews are already unloading. I want a few minutes with Curtis."

The Alpha's eyes didn't leave his Beta's while the rest of the pack filed out. When they were alone Thomas said, "You're losing it."

"No." Curtis couldn't manage more than single word answers and stunted phrases with Clear-Skies so edgy.

"Have you heard from the lady in question?"

Bringing his chin down in affirmation, Curtis dug his now human nails into his palms. Pain brought his wolf further in check. Clear-Skies's essence no longer threatened his senses or reasoning.

"I have."

Thomas raised an eyebrow. "And?"

"She'll be here. Tomorrow if I have my way."

"Good work." Thomas took a seat on the couch. Curtis remained standing. "And your plan once she gets here? I'm doubting the wisdom of my choice with that little display. Dispassion is a wolf's greatest asset. A wolf who would be leader, anyhow. That's why I make the plans and you execute them. Give me a run down." He curled his hand in a "come here" gesture, rested his elbows on his thighs, and cradled his chin in his hands.

At attention, Curtis informed his Alpha what he planned for Izzy. When he finished, Thomas sucked in his cheeks.

"So, we're to tiptoe around her, then? A tall order for a bunch of rowdy dogs."

"We can do it, Thomas. Quietly. We're smart enough. We can scale the wall instead of smashing through it."

Thomas rose and clapped his Beta on the chest. "Whatever you say, son." Clear-Skies went spiny at the condescending endearment and freezing, spectral spikes lanced Curtis's heart. He sucked in a breath.

I am not *your son.*

"You get one shot at this. If I think you're slipping, I'm taking over," Thomas said.

"I'll handle it," Curtis eked out through gritted teeth.

Chapter Ten

Thursday evening, Izzy called Curtis and figured out her trip to DeConing. His tone as they planned carried a touch of resignation she didn't understand, but he sounded more pleased than anything. Whether she'd accepted Cutis's invitation or not, Izzy had planned to close the studio on Friday and Monday and, along with a verbal reminder to all her students, had posted paper notices on the doors, a banner on the website's front page, and an announcement on the answering machine.

Curtis would pick her up Friday afternoon, they'd fetch Nook, and head to the lodge. Izzy mentioned driving herself so he wouldn't have to drive back to the city on Sunday, but he insisted on humans and dog in the same vehicle. If Nook got anxious, he wanted her close.

At Izzy's apartment by eleven a.m., Curtis leaned over and shoved open the passenger side door. The interior smelled of wood and Curtis's deodorant, which came across strongest. The scent teleported her back to middle school, trudging through the halls between classes and brushing by a boy she'd liked. He'd smelled the same as this man, clean and natural. Music blasted from the stereo, a cacophony of shouting men and distorted guitars and thundering drums. Curtis dialed back the volume and Izzy's heart, which jittered with the pounding bass, thanked him for it.

"I like to blast it on long trips by myself. Pick something out if you want."

Retrieving the black canvas CD case at her feet, Izzy flipped through Curtis's collection. He didn't own a single album she'd ever listen to. *C'est la vie.* She selected a band she'd at least heard of and slid the disc into the player.

Nook was happy to see them. Well, he was happy to see Izzy. His tail wagged when the volunteer for the day led him out from the back of the kennel. He still shrank from Curtis, but gave his new owner's palm a curious lick when he offered his hand. Leash wrapped around her fingers, Izzy led the husky out of the shelter and corralled him into the backseat of the Jeep. Nook spent most of the ride to DeConing with his nose at the cracked rear window or pressed to Izzy's cheek. Sometimes he paced behind the driver's seat and gave his new master an inquisitive sniff, retreating if Curtis paid this any mind.

Keene Lodge's parking lot was deserted. Izzy frowned at the empty spaces as the car came to a halt and she unbuckled her seat belt.

"Light season?" she asked.

"No." Curtis grabbed his cell from the circular cup holder in the partition between their seats. "We're renovating all the guest cabins, so we closed until the end of January. November through February are spotty months anyhow. We pick up in March."

Taking stock of the nearby grounds, Izzy noted wire stemmed signs for Davenport Construction Co. planted in the frost-covered earth, black trails of tire tracked mud, and a lone forklift parked near mountainous stacks of fresh lumber. The forklift's yellow paint job struck the gray and black landscape like a patch of sun she wished would make an appearance through the low clouds blanketing the sky. Her shoulders drooped. This wasn't the sort of cover that broke up in the late afternoon. It could snow.

Curtis commandeered Nook's leash when they released him from the car. Izzy circled to the trunk for her duffel when Curtis called to her.

"We'll come back for your bag. I want to introduce Nook and Petey first. If it's too cold, you can head inside the main house. Should be a fire going and I won't be long."

"That's ok. I'll come, too."

Izzy followed Curtis up the hilly incline. Ice crunched with her steps. Taking her prosthetic in his free hand, he helped her up the slope as Nook strained against his lead, catching scent and sight of the other dog. Having her right hand held like her left made her uncomfortable, but there was no one to notice if her fingers didn't twine around his, and she didn't pull away.

In a tizzy inside his pen, Petey pushed his shining, black nose through the wood slats, wuffing at the approaching company. He pitched back and forth, barking and barking when they hesitated several feet away. Curtis handed over Nook's leash to Izzy.

"Would you hold him a minute? I want Petey calm before we get the two of them together."

Vaulting over the gate, Curtis pelted to the middle of the fenced in plot and Petey tore after him. Crouching, Curtis slapped his hands on his thighs and teased the dog. "Where's your ball? Where is it?"

A flash of white sped over the dead grass and disappeared into a raised doggy hutch. The Samoyed emerged with a red squeaky ball crushed in his teeth. The ball, its inner squeak deflated with use, wheezed in a steady beat as the dog trotted to his owner.

Part of playtime consisted of Curtis trying to wrestle the ball from Petey. Each time he reached for the toy, the dog jumped away or tossed its head. Walking away from the hound, Curtis enticed the animal to him with his apparent loss of interest. Somehow, he intuited when Petey encroached into his personal space, whipped around, and chased him across the lawn, finally scooping the dog into his arms and wrenching the ball from his jaws. The moment his paws touched the ground, Petey's head dipped low and his butt wagged in the air. A rousing game of catch ensued. Nook yipped and tugged against the leash whenever the ball arced over the play space.

"Go ahead and let him in," Curtis said, eyeing Nook's swishing tail.

Izzy unlatched the gate, coaxed the husky forward and un-tethered him, grateful for Curtis's tight grip on the back of Petey's neck. The Samoyed clearly wanted to properly greet all visitors in his territory with a facial tongue bath and tried slipping his master's ironclad hold. Providing distraction so she could slip outside the pen, Curtis released Petey and lobbed the ball to the back fence. Both dogs bounded after it. Being closer, Petey got there first.

There was a time out while the dogs circled and sniffed each other. Petey happily barked and jumped all around the new addition to Curtis's makeshift family. Nook wasn't half as hyper or gregarious, but took the attention in stride, giving the Samoyed's snoot a lick or two, which Petey tried to dodge and supplant with his own fierce grooming to the husky's ears. Occupied with each other, they forgot the fetch game and Curtis snuck up and plucked the discarded ball from the ground. He jogged to the gate where Izzy waited.

"Can you stand a few more throws?" The ball went up and down as Curtis tossed and caught it and Petey dashed to his master, abandoning his new sibling to squirm his way up to his purloined toy.

"Sure," Izzy said and smiled, hoping she concealed her discomfort. It really was a blustery afternoon. Maybe she would head inside after all. "He doesn't get cold out here all day?" She nodded at Petey who twisted under Curtis's arm and snorted when he couldn't close his jaws around the ball.

Pushing the dog's head down, Curtis said, "Samoyeds and huskies are cold weather breeds, but there's a doggy door in the porch." He waved at the glass-enclosed deck tacked to the back of the main building. "It's heated. When the weather gets rough he heads in there or his dog house." He threw the ball away and the brothers chased it down. A minor squabble broke out once during play when Nook beat Petey to the ball. Curtis settled that in a moment with a single, baritone shout. Another time he threw the ball too far and it went over the main building's roof.

"Ah, gimmie a sec," he called to Izzy and hopped up the porch steps, opening the windowed door and entering the covered deck.

Izzy leaned on the fence and watched the dogs cavort. Perhaps she'd join them once Curtis got back. Throw the ball herself. Looked like fun. They weren't vicious wolves, after all. They were Curtis's family.

Completely absorbed in her musings, Izzy didn't hear the nearing footsteps at her back and only realized she wasn't alone when someone—someone very strong—grabbed her arm and she couldn't stop herself from screaming.

Chapter Eleven

"Whoa, hey! Sorry about that!" The man—and woman—at Izzy's rear backed off. It was the man who'd grabbed her and there was something about him, besides his disregard of personal space, she didn't like. His blue, blood-shot eyes never stopped moving. They roved over her body head to toe and his appraisal made her feel greasy, like she stood on a stage offering him her backside for a crinkled dollar bill. The woman, wisps of red hair escaping her wool cap, watched him, lips compressed.

"You're Isabelle, aren't you?" His raspy voice raked over her like grimy fingernails and she shuddered. His flicking eyes lingered on hers when he spoke and she felt compelled to look away, which she refused to do. Instead, she stared right back at him and rolled back her shoulders.

Fuck you, she communicated wordlessly. This lanky whip of muscle and ropey extremities would not intimidate her. A feral cast to his eyes and stance reminded her of a desperate, mangy dog and swallowing became difficult with her suddenly dry throat.

The man's upper lip twitched and he moved forward. The woman grabbed his arm.

"Gerome," she said, warning. Behind them, Nook growled. He and Petey took in the confrontation, Nook with teeth bared and Petey for once motionless. The Samoyed's tail, ears, and eyes were all alert.

The front door blasted open. Curtis leapt down the main building's front steps, nearly tumbling when he hit the ground. "Hey, hey!" He sprinted to the trio, skidding next to Izzy.

"Curtis." Gerome dropped his head and backed in line with the redhead. "Just introducing ourselves to your new," he inhaled sharply through his nose, "friend. You've been the talk of the lodge, Isabelle. We're pleased to meet you." His toothy smile was as warm as the ice at their feet.

"Yeah." The redhead butted Gerome aside with her hip and extended her mittened hand. "I'm Melinda, Isabelle, and this is Gerome."

Izzy took Melinda's hand and shook it. The girl—for now that Izzy had a good look at her she saw the redhead slouched with the careless posture of youth, like nothing much mattered or affected her—was a lefty, thank goodness. While Melinda spoke, her gaze moved between Izzy and Curtis and often rested there, some silent communication passing between them. Despite the redhead's welcome, which struck Izzy as genuine, she was shut out of this group as surely as if she milled in another room, staring out at them from behind bulletproof glass. And she couldn't stop the thoughts. Wicked little things like winding, black vines snaking in her brain.

Had either of these two sent the texts? If so, was it Melinda? Lily studied the girl looking so intently at Curtis. Her gray eyes were striking set against her heart-shaped face flushed with cold. Her chin came to a delicate point and her sweet, pink lips made a perfect bow. A smattering of freckles patched her temples and the bridge of her nose.

"Knock it off, Lin," Curtis barked out of nowhere. What the girl had done to provoke Curtis, Izzy didn't know, but his features were severe as sharpened metal. She sidled closer to Curtis, touching his hand, and Melinda's eyes lowered.

Creaking from the lodge's direction momentarily diffused the strange tension. A man as large as Curtis, possibly thicker, with a head of silvery hair, ambled down the steps. The screen door banged shut behind him. He took his time coming to the foursome. Melinda and Gerome moved aside, clearing his path to the pair standing hand in hand. Curtis wrapped his arm around Izzy's waist.

"Welcome back, Curtis," the silver-haired man said.

"Thomas," Curtis replied, nodding.

Thomas had a deep voice, powerful, but very quiet. When he turned to Izzy she had to look away from him and her cheeks got hot. He made her feel like a little girl. A little girl up to no good and, for some reason, she could not bring herself to face him as she had Gerome. Curtis made the introductions. There was an odd formality to their interaction that was somewhat parental, like Curtis presented her as his date to the prom.

"Thomas, this is Isabelle."

"So I gather."

Thinking it bizarre to stare at the ground during the conversation like a misbehaving student, Izzy adjusted her sightline to Thomas's chin. She could raise her eyes no further. One side of his mouth curled up.

"Pleasure to meet you, Isabelle." Thomas raised his volume as though he addressed the entire group. He held out his right hand for Izzy's and she cringed. She couldn't be rude. She let him take her prosthetic and watched his mouth quirk. "And what are the two of you up to today?"

The question was aimed at Curtis but Izzy answered, slipping her stiff limb from Thomas's grasp.

"I think I'd like to hike one of the old trails I used to love when I came up here with my family. After Curtis shows me his place, that is."

The rebellious little snot in her inwardly piped up, *We'll be back before ten p.m., safe and sound and tucked in bed,* but she squashed that inner voice. She wasn't a child and she already had a father. This man had no control over her. None.

She locked eyes with Thomas, who seemed surprised. The flicker of that *something* she could never make out, shadowed at times in Curtis's stare, went unguarded in his eyes and she recoiled. Whatever that something was, it was alien and threatening and it peered through the older man and into her, cowing her usually feisty spirit. Thomas was a window, a slight, fleshy membrane separating her from a vast and horrifically dark gulf teeming with chaos. Far away, thunder rumbled. Curtis pinched her hip.

"Ow!" Izzy pushed at him, but Curtis held her in steady. When she turned back to Thomas, he looked toward the woods. She saw his eyes in profile. Imagination had got the best of her. There were no alien presences invading herself or Thomas. Dr. Turner no doubt would have attributed the delusion to Izzy's indignation at bowing to a perceived authority figure. Arrogance told her nothing natural could have affected her that way, so her mind had given her a supernatural reason. God, she could be so nutty and neurotic.

"Sounds like plan," Thomas said to Izzy and then to Curtis, "Come see me before you hit the trail."

"Not a problem," Curtis said.

*

They didn't leave Nook in the pen and he was a handful. All the strangers and Izzy's distress must have spooked him. He growled at Curtis and resisted her when she tried hooking him to the leash. After lots of cooing and kissy noises, he relented to the tether and they packed him in the car. Curtis shouted goodbyes to Melinda and Gerome as they backed from the parking lot and then they traveled a winding road to Curtis's cabin.

The house sat away from the road, partially surrounded by the woods that grew thicker at the cabin's rear. Weathered gray slats and posts comprised the front porch and siding. A shingled roof sloped over the porch and sagged into the supporting beams so the whole structure slouched forward. If it hadn't been for the copse of evergreens framing the dreary scene with a deep green luster, Izzy felt she would have stepped into an old black-and-white frontier film.

They parked under a covered carport attached to the cabin's right side. There wasn't a driveway. Curtis simply went off the road and drove over his lawn.

"I'll lay a slab of concrete one day," he said to her raised brows.

Izzy took charge of Nook, wrangling him from the Jeep to the cabin. Curtis threw her duffel over his shoulder and met her at the front door, hand shoved in his pocket for his keys.

"Do you own Keene Lodge?" Izzy asked as he unlocked the door.

"They don't call me Curtis *Keene* for nothing." Kicking the door wide, he waved her in.

Inside, the light was murky. Thin, blue curtains faded by time and sunshine covered the windows, filtering the already meager light fighting through dense cloud cover. Nook padded inside and snuffled around the floor and furniture.

"Then why do I get the feeling Thomas runs the show around here?"

Curtis brushed passed her. His boots thunked on the wood floor as he crossed the room and switched on a standing lamp Izzy hadn't perceived in the gloom. Yellow light exposed a cozy, very masculine, living area. A massive flat screen and hand-me-down black leather couch crowded the east side of the room. Over the back of the couch hung a thick, patterned blanket. Two standing lamps and a pair of surround sound speakers book-ended the couch. Curtis stood next to the lamp he'd switched on, flicking the bowl shaped sconce at its top when the light guttered. The flicking, which made a tinny *ping-ping* sound, stabilized the bulb.

"Thomas manages the business end of the lodge so, in a way, he's my boss." He glanced at Nook. "Let him wander around."

Izzy removed the leash and the husky explored, disappearing down the dark hallway in the center of the back wall. A knotted rag carpet runner stretched from the front door to the shadowed entrance and split the living area from the kitchen. Curtis shouldered her duffel on the flimsy card table serving as the centerpiece of his dining set.

"You don't want to run the business yourself?" Izzy rubbed her arms. Gray ash piled in the fireplace to her left, but the room held none of the warmth from the spent fire.

"Keenes have owned this land for generations. It was my grandfather that really made it what it is today. My dad inherited the business and the land, but he made Thomas his partner when he decided to expand. After Dad passed I became the official owner and kept Thomas involved because he's the better manager." He looked askance and folded his arms. "Or so he tells me."

"Sorry about your dad."

Curtis smiled. "Don't be. He was ready to go when he did."

"What about your mom?" Izzy hadn't realized how little she knew about Curtis's past until he'd mentioned his father.

"Never knew my biological mom. My dad's second wife, Aggie, went to live with her sister out in Carmel after Dad died. She has her own wine blog thing and I get about ten emails from her a day."

"She sounds nice."

"She is."

Izzy pressed her lips together and they made a soft, popping noise when they parted. "Melinda seems nice, too. I didn't mean to screw anything up with them out there if I did."

"Our stress levels are all set to eleven because of the construction. Don't worry about that group. Especially not Lin."

"What did she do that pissed you off?"

Drumming his fingers on the card table, Curtis said, "Who, Lin?" His eyes lowered. "Yeah, I guess I snapped at her, didn't I?"

The outburst had been completely out of character from what Izzy knew, or thought she knew, about Curtis. He was nothing if not patient and kind.

"It's hard to explain," he said. "I've known her since she was thirteen and we have that brother-sister way of getting under each other's skin with just a look, you know?" Curtis's eyes clouded for a moment when Izzy said she did know, then he said, "What trail did you want to hike?" and cut off further discussion about Melinda, Thomas, or who was top dog at Keene Lodge.

"The one to Rock Spout Falls."

Curtis's brow creased. "You sure?"

Hugging herself, Izzy nodded.

"All right, then we'll take the dogs for a stretch and when we come back I'll get a fire going and," he hooked his foot around the fridge door and popped it open. Bottles clinked. He peeked inside. "I suppose we'll feast on grilled cheese and beer."

Izzy laughed.

"A grocery run might be in the cards."

Chapter Twelve

Curtis met Thomas in the main building as he'd promised. Spinning like a miniature comet in his chest, Clear-Skies paced. Convincing Izzy that no tension strained the ties between his pack mates didn't make it so and the hard set of the Alpha's jaw as he stared out of the lodge's north facing window reinforced the feeling. At the window, Curtis watched what his Alpha watched: Izzy and Melinda. At the sight of the redhead, Curtis folded his arms and widened his stance.

Brother-sister silent communication, my ass, he thought. What Lin had done to him out there had nothing to do with any emotional connection they shared.

Intellectually, Curtis knew Clear-Skies was an entity of some intelligence and, if he wished, he could "speak" with the spirit. There was no need. Curtis could count on one hand the number of times his wolf communicated anything other than "danger" or "hungry" or "tired." Otherwise, he received impressions of feelings or instinctive responses and little else. Even when the spirit swallowed Curtis's entire being, this did not change. The beast had more control and containing him required dedicated resolve, but they were never one. Barriers existed between them that Curtis would not bring down for his own mental and spiritual well being. Melinda suffered no such compunctions.

Lin and her wolf, Nettled-Clover, swam in each other like spectral fish in an aetheric tide (her words). Where one ended and the other began, Curtis didn't know and that disturbed him. At times, she—his adopted little sis—scared the hell out of him.

"Try it," she'd said to them all on more than one occasion. "It's like this ultra deep meditation, and then I understand her and she shows me things. They remember all their hosts, you know. All those memories, all those feelings? It's freaking amazing."

Curtis never entertained the suggestion. Dipping too far into the spirit had one sure result: madness. When Lin spent too long inside herself, he saw it in her. It manifested as a strange gleam in her eye, her mood rapid firing from elation to snappish moodiness. Sometimes she'd stare at a fork or phone like she had no idea what they were or what purpose they served when she had her fangs and a wolf call deep in her throat. During those times, Curtis watched her, waited for her mood to level out, and planned for the worst. If she lost herself to the wolf . . . he rubbed his eyes. He couldn't think about it. As it was, her plumbing of Nettled-Clover produced curious side effects.

Lin not only conversed freely with her wolf, but could also communicate with others' wolves. Curtis had felt Nettle-Clover's spring green essence brush at his heart when the pack had confronted Izzy. He didn't know what Lin had searched for, but she'd crossed the line and he'd snapped. Seeing her chat up Izzy made him fidgety. Could she read a human soul as she did a wolf spirit? Would she dare?

"Have you scented him?" Thomas's question pulled Curtis back into himself.

"Not yet. That could change once we take to the trail. She wants to head to the falls. Might be too much for Rapid to resist."

"If history's any indication he'll be cautious. Her scent might not be enough to provoke him. Blood would be better."

Enemy, Clear-Skies's proverbial hackles raised and he became a sharp angled, blue line.

"No," Curtis said both to his Alpha and to his wolf. "He'll come when he catches her scent. He'll wait for night cover. We'll set up a wide perimeter around my cabin. When he comes, I'll smell it and I'll call the pack. We'll box him in and take him down." And there'd be no way to keep their secret if Izzy got in the way. He'd have to tire her out, make sure she slept deep tonight. Besides a hike, he had an idea or two that made his lips and his dick quirk. Sex, even solitary style, worked wonders when he suffered insomnia.

Thomas didn't argue with him. His dark eyes tracked Izzy's movements, the flinging gesture of her left hand when she spoke to Melinda. The women looked happy, but Curtis wanted Izzy out of Thomas's sight.

Enemy, Clear-Skies sent to him. The spirit hadn't compressed into his normal ball of blue flame. Maybe Curtis should practice communicating with his wolf as Lin suggested. He'd wing it for now.

Not our enemy, Curtis thought at Clear-Skies, *our Alpha.*

When the wolf didn't respond, Curtis shrugged and set off out the door. Just as his hand alighted on the knob, a feral voice whispered to him.

We should be Alpha.

The condemnation lodged in Curtis's brain like a bone shard stuck in his throat and he pounded his fist to his chest as though clearing it. No, they couldn't be Alpha. Thomas would never back down and he couldn't kill the man. Unless . . .

Curtis stared at Izzy. All the protective instincts he struggled to keep at relative bay reared up within him. The surge of wild emotion fed his wolf. Clear-Skies swelled larger and larger beneath his breastbone. Curtis massaged his sternum. The spirit felt like a wad of bread and peanut butter he had swallowed too fast. If Thomas threatened Izzy, there was no telling what Curtis would do.

*

Outside the main building, Izzy hung back on the screened front porch while Curtis spoke to Thomas inside. She wasn't eager to be back in the property manager's presence. Curtis assured her he wouldn't be long and promised to help corral Petey. From the Jeep's backseat window, Nook gave her sad eyes. When the front door clicked open behind her, she spun, her smile wilting when she found Melinda and not Curtis holding the retractable leash. The girl had removed her cap and an astounding mass of red curls surrounded her head in a fluffy nimbus.

"Hi." Melinda took a careful step forward, seeming to read Izzy's wariness. "Curtis mentioned you guys were taking the dogs out. Thought I'd give you a hand with the fuzzy Tasmanian devil in there. Petey's kinda overwhelming." She went to the screen door and held it open. "You coming?"

Hesitancy around Melinda was ridiculous. If she were the infamous texter, then hanging out a bit might smooth any ruffled fur. Izzy followed along as Melinda skipped down the steps. Dark wash jeans hugged the redhead's curvy hips and thighs and tucked into work boots that had seen better days.

"Listen," Melinda said, enticing Petey to the gate with a crumbly Milk-Bone she produced from her pocket, "I wanted to apologize for Gerome. He was a huge dick to you earlier."

"That's kind of you." Izzy couldn't keep the bile from her voice. She didn't think any amount of hanging out could change her feelings about Gerome.

"Not really. I just want to make sure that impression doesn't rub off on me." Melinda attached Petey's leash to his collar while he crunched his treat. Tan crumbs sprayed the packed dirt. Realizing his predicament, the Samoyed thrashed in Melinda's double-handed hold. "Ugh, this effing dog. Unless you're Curtis he's only calm for five minutes at a time and only when he's bribed." She shouted threats that did nothing to subdue the animal, so she forked over two more Milk-Bones. Petey went for the treats and settled down.

"You work here?" Izzy asked. Melinda seemed young for a full-time employee.

"Yeah," she said. "I work the main desk a lot. Look pretty," she gave her hair a dramatic fluff and batted her lashes, "answer phones. I do nature hikes and mounted trail passes, too. Sometimes I help Curtis with maintenance stuff when Thomas and Gerome are tied up."

They leaned on the gate and Petey's crunching tided over the fizzled conversation. Fixated on the dog, Melinda didn't seem to notice Izzy's eyes traveling in her direction every few seconds. She bit back all the questions bubbling behind her lips. Making her inquiries benign wouldn't disguise the third degree when the subject was another woman.

Moistening her lips, Izzy said, "Curtis says he's known you since you were thirteen."

Melinda dipped her head in an attempt to hide her knowing grin and patted the top of the gate. Petey jumped up and she kept him occupied with lots of pats and scratches. "S'right."

"How old are you?"

"Nineteen."

"Six years." Izzy sighed and quietly added, "You must be close."

"I could put together a slide show if you'd like. 'Curtis and Lin's Precious Moments.'" Melinda elbowed Izzy's side, giggled. "Would you prefer a PowerPoint presentation?"

Nerves tweaked Izzy's laughter. Time for a subject change.

"Working here doesn't interfere with college?"

Melinda shrugged. "Higher education isn't really for me. I might take courses at the community college next year, but Pops and I need the money I make here since he went on disability." She toed the scuffed top of her brown boot. "You like Curtis?"

Steeling herself for the reciprocal interrogation, Izzy said, "Of course."

"How much?" Melinda's chin jutted.

"Plenty for a little over a week of knowing each other. You want a pie chart?" Izzy smirked and Melinda blushed and rapid clicked the button on the retractable leash.

"Just asking since me and my Pops pretty much adopted him." The mischievous glint in Melinda's eye dulled and her smile flickered. "I'm the baby around here and he's the closest thing to a big brother I've ever had. If you make it through the weekend, you should come up more often. It's crap being the only girl here twenty-four-seven."

If you make it through the weekend struck Izzy as an odd way to couch the request, but Melinda already waved Curtis over to the pen before she had time to say anything about it and all she could do was nod absently.

Chapter Thirteen

Snow fell in short, gusty bursts as Izzy and Curtis picked their way over the frozen trail of rocky terrain broken with upgrown, gnarled roots thick as her arm. These weren't icy flakes that clung to hair and lashes, but rounded pellets that peppered their heads and shoulders and bounced off the ground. The dogs snapped at them when they popped up or tried to catch them in their jaws before they hit the ground. Curtis and Izzy didn't speak. She'd retreated into herself soon after the forest enveloped them and his chatter had quieted when her answers dwindled from single words to soft grunts.

Memories overwhelmed Izzy, the wintry scene before her superimposed by the shimmering mirage of the May afternoon that so drastically altered her life. Tragedy had no place on what, to her mind, had been an idyllic day. Washed in dreary grays and dirt speckled whites, this bleak setting better suited bloodshed and tears. Wind blew mournfully through the pine and tossed her hair about her face and sliced at her cheeks.

The trail had changed over the years, trees grown, brush cut back or left to intrude onto the well traveled ground. Now and then a certain bend in the path or interlacing of branches overhead triggered a time flash and, instead of Curtis in front of Izzy, Alan looked over his shoulder and laughed, egged her on while they raced to the falls.

Like Billy Pilgrim, Izzy came unstuck in time. Immediately A.A., she'd become almost used to the disorienting flights her mind took when she smelled something that smelled very Alan. A certain spicy soap, expensive hair product, the sweat and mildew tinged odor of stale athletic gear, all of them plunged her down through time malleable as warm lake water. Yesterday became today and today ten years past, and down that one turn on the

116

trail her brother waited and this Izzy—armed with foreknowledge if bereft a limb—would pass the ghost of her ignorant and too curious self and lead Alan away from his doom. That old Izzy was just a shade. Substandard. So what if she died?

"Izzy?" At Curtis's word, time fixed. Today was today. The fugue passed, but another and another came over her as they trudged on. An insistent word or two from Curtis jolted her to reality until they came to the last place Izzy had seen her brother.

She knew the place instinctively and her legs rooted to the ground like slender saplings. No amount of encouragement from Curtis or butting nudges from Nook moved her. Nylon padded the warm fingers that curled around her arm and touched her face.

"You still with me?" Curtis asked.

"Here. It happened right here, didn't it?"

Curtis sighed and squeezed her upper arms. "About. That's what I remember. I'm surprised you do."

"I do and I don't." Izzy let him bring her to his chest and she rested her forehead on his shoulder. Nook planted on his haunches at her side, but Petey, the kinetic fuzz-ball, circled the pair, winding his leash around them. "I remember us racing. I remember stopping because I thought I saw something out the corner of my eye. We were always one-upping each other spotting wildlife. The shadow I saw was big, and I thought if I saw a deer or fox I could throw it in his face if he beat me to the falls."

The forest and trails were bare of all but the heartiest foliage in winter. Summer, as it had been at Keene Lodge B.A., choked the woods with green and Izzy had to part a tangle of thicket and vine to unveil the creature she sought.

"I don't know what I thought I'd see," Izzy said. "Animals run from people thundering around their territory. Alan called for me. Maybe he'd noticed I'd fallen behind."

"Those eyes are so clear in my mind. They were bright yellow. Surrounded by tree shade and black fur, they were terrifying. Demonic."

"Izzy—"

"I had the strangest thought when I saw it. I thought: Are wolves really that big? This wolf's too big. And I couldn't move, so I called to Alan and said 'Alan, there's a wolf.' I said it like it was nothing. Like I told him the coffee was done.

"I backed out of the brush. I don't think I did it fast, but it leapt at me and the only thing I could think to do was put my arm up and close my eyes."

Petey whined.

"It crushed me. I thought everything inside me had broken or burst and I couldn't breathe." Izzy's throat and lungs constricted in sympathetic response to the memory and she struggled to continue, words coming between shallow, panicky breaths. "I couldn't get air to scream. It was so quiet before Alan came. The wolf didn't snarl or bark. Not until Alan tried to save me.

"Then I thought it was me screaming. Men don't scream like that, so high and shrill. That was my brother." Izzy said it like she didn't believe herself. She didn't want to. She lifted her head and looked at Curtis who seemed very far away. "I don't remember you at all."

Curtis stroked her hair. "Why do you do this to yourself, Izzy?"

"Catharsis. I'm supposed to feel a release. I don't feel anything."

"In my experience," Curtis said, untangling them from Petey's leash, "catharsis can't be forced. The mind knows when it's ready. When it's not—"

Head snapping westward, Curtis tensed under Izzy's hands. Squinting, he sniffed twice and pinched his nose.

"When it's not?" Izzy strained to see what startled Curtis. Nothing roamed the tree line she discerned. Guiding her with a finger against her chin, Curtis pulled her attention back to him. Whatever he'd heard or seen couldn't have been important.

"When it's not, the mind shuts parts of itself off to protect the whole." Hard, strange eyes met Izzy's. They possessed a strangeness similar to what she'd perceived in Thomas's expression. Or did they? When she blinked Curtis's face was his own, tanned and creased with laugh lines. His eyes were Curtis's eyes, rich as milk chocolate and touched with echoes of mirth. "We get this." He trailed a padded finger down Izzy's cheek. "Blank expression, glazed eyes, lackluster attitude." He glanced at the slate gray sky patterned black with the forest canopy's lace. "We should head in. Weather's gonna get bad. We need to drop Petey off at the main house before hitting the store."

"And Nook?"

"He'll come with us."

Curtis had relaxed somewhat, but the dogs hadn't. Both Nook and Petey's muzzles pointed west, their nostrils flaring, taking in scents Izzy's dull senses couldn't detect. Their sickle tails were erect and still, their ears up, and their postures rigid. Petey's lips curled back from his teeth. A few tugs on their leads brought them around and they all traipsed out of the woods, the dogs stopping every so often to sniff and perk their ears and Curtis pausing to type away on his phone when he wasn't scanning their surroundings. The sky didn't look so angry though the wind buffeted them, but if it had the dogs and Curtis on edge who was she to argue?

Izzy huddled in the back of the Jeep with Nook, heater on full blast. A toasty setting for Izzy, whose deadened fingers and toes pricked and tingled as they thawed. The temperature had Curtis shiny with sweat five minutes into their drive. He shed his gloves and coat and flung them onto the vacant passenger seat. Intermittent flurries thickened to true snowfall when they pulled up at the grocery, a small, corner store about two miles from Keene property. The hand painted sign atop the brick building read "Obander's." Through the car window, she spied a copper bell hanging inside the front door. An elderly man loitered behind the counter. He read a paperback he clutched in two hands, its front cover folded over and pressed to the book's backside. When the bell tinkled, he placed a finger where he stopped and waved at Curtis, who snagged two black plastic baskets from the stack next to the door.

Packing the trunk with a dozen brown bags, Curtis hopped in the driver's seat and navigated the worsening weather. He hunched over the wheel and squinted at the road obscured by waning light and swirling powder.

Izzy was a ghost at dinner. Nook curled at her feet. A fire crackled in the grate behind them. She and Curtis shared the tiny card table. Plates of food and Mason jar glasses brim-full of blush colored, cheap wine—it left her mouth tasting metallic—left no room for forearms or elbows. She picked at her food. The rough and watery texture of cooked meat oozing juices nauseated her. Deep in contemplation, she didn't notice Curtis's absence from the table until he returned to clear her setting.

"I'll do it," Izzy said with a half-hearted lurch from her seat.

"You," Curtis laid a hand on her shoulder, "need a long hot shower."

Izzy sniffed herself. "Do I stink?"

"No, but you haven't come back to Earth yet and I think it'll do you good." He deposited her plate and half drunk wine jar on the counter, stood her up, and marched her down the hallway and through a door on the right to his bedroom. She hadn't explored the cabin as Curtis had her apartment, hadn't had the energy since their aborted hike. The room was, like many things male, utilitarian. Not a lick of embellishment adorned the tables or walls. In fact, he had but one framed picture in his bedroom and it looked out of place, too small for the space where it hung.

A man—he had to be Curtis's father, they looked so alike—and woman smiled out from the frame. The man had his arm around the woman's shoulder, squeezing her in a half bear hug. The woman, her ash blond hair wispy in her eyes, had one hand flat on the man's chest. She wore a yellow rain slicker. Was she Curtis's real mother or was this Aggie? Whoever she was, she had a kind face. The questions went unasked. All Izzy could do for the moment was be led into the bathroom. Repellent, the idea that she needed coddling, that she needed her hand held like some shuffling invalid. The back rooms didn't have the benefit of a fireplace, so Curtis fired up a space heater wedged in the corner before pulling her into the connected bathroom.

A clear, green shower curtain patterned with daisies hung from metal rings and lined the inside of a well-used claw foot tub. Curtis got the water going while Izzy floated, phantom-like in the doorway. Everything around her seemed distant and trivial. She shook her head. What an awful guest she was.

"I'm sorry about this, Curtis."

He sat on the lip of the tub, one hand under the spray, testing the temperature. The mirror over the sink fogged. "Nothing you can do about it, Izzy." Pushing up from the tub, he went to her and worked at the belt threaded through her jeans. Her body swayed as he tugged the leather from her belt loops. She pulled her shirt over her head and her fingers slipped over her harness's buckles. Steam from the shower had collected on the plastic and the moisture made her left hand clammy. Curtis took over and loosened her prosthetic.

"After Dad died, Aggie used to space out a lot. For days sometimes. I'd leave one morning and she'd be sitting on the couch staring straight ahead. I'd come home and she'd still be there by herself in the dark. At first, I didn't know what to do, but if I got her up and moving, talked to her, she'd come out of it."

"I don't know why she left with you around."

"Because I reminded her of Dad. The family resemblance is strong. She'd call me Rob by mistake." He held onto Izzy's harness and prosthetic. "I'm going to put this in the bedroom. I'll be in the workshop across the hall. Come get me if you need anything. I'll have my headphones on." He tapped his ear and left Izzy to the shower, which did do her good.

Hot water brought Izzy out of the stratosphere and into her body. Curtis's eucalyptus scented shampoo tingled on her scalp. His cake of green soap smelled like him and steam made the fragrance a heady perfume. When she cut the spray and stepped from the shower, she shivered and wrapped herself in a towel. Patting herself dry, she went to the bedroom and, finding her duffel absent, padded to the front room, leaving Nook snoring at the foot of the bed.

Light from the dying fire illuminated the living area and shifting reds and oranges highlighted the rough shapes of the furniture. The floorboards, worn shiny from years of foot traffic, were smooth and cool under Izzy's bare feet. She found her duffel on the sofa where Curtis must have moved it so they could dine. Unzipping the bag, she rifled through its contents, searching for her pajamas.

Something thunked and skittered on the porch outside. Izzy never would have heard the noise in the city. The quiet of the woods out here was a tangible thing with its own weight. No disruption went unnoticed. She thought it might be a fox or chipmunk, but when she heard the scampering again, Nook's nails clicking over the hardwood floor came to mind. Curtis had groused earlier when they had dropped Petey off at the main house, complaining that the Samoyed often jumped his pen in bad weather and wandered to the cabin instead of holing up on the heated porch. If Petey had come to the cabin, she couldn't leave him out in the cold.

Towel cinched at her breast, Izzy crossed to the window next to the fireplace—heat from the embers warmed her legs—slid her stunted arm between the threadbare drapes, and parted them.

The storm had spent itself and the night was clear, save for a cloud or two scuttling across the starry sky. Fresh snow glittered in the moonlight like a blanket sprinkled with crushed diamonds. Petey wasn't out on the lawn and Izzy didn't see him on the left side of the porch.

Lambent, yellow eyes met Izzy's when she turned to the right. A gray wolf stared up at her so close to the window its snout was barely an inch away from the glass. She shrieked and shot back, stumbling right into the folding chairs and card table. She fell in a heap with the toppled furniture. Chairs clanged against the floor like struck gongs. One of them knocked her shin. The table conked her head and her towel crumpled around her waist. She couldn't get her breath and choked, breasts shaking with her sobs.

Curtis almost tripped over Nook when they both galloped into the living room. Cursing, he shoved the husky aside with his bare foot and knelt next to Izzy. Enormous headphones cupped his ears and their cord dangled down his chest. He yanked them off and tossed them into the hall.

"What happened? Are you hurt?" He lifted the chair off her leg and righted the table and felt her head. "I don't feel any lumps."

Izzy spoke between hitching sobs. "I'm not hurt."

"Then why are you crying?"

A keening howl answered for Izzy. Blood crawled through her veins like a hundred thousand tiny insects. Their thorny legs scritched under her skin. She froze and her muscles coiled for flight. Tears came silently, hot trails gliding down her cheeks. Curtis stroked her back and stood. He peered out the window.

"Is it out there? Do you see it?" Izzy whispered and sniffed. Her voice was nasal and her face felt puffy. She rubbed her bruised leg.

Curtis nodded and crossed to the front door. When he reached for the keys hanging from a hook near the doorframe Izzy shot up. Her legs tangled in her towel as she rushed to him. Leaping, he caught her before her chin hit the floor, taking all her weight as she regained her balance.

"Don't open the door, Curtis, please." She clutched his shirt with her whole hand while he steadied her and kicked away the towel.

"Wolves don't come near people, Izzy."

"Like they don't attack people, either?" She awaited his retort with wide, watery eyes. When he didn't speak, she said, "Please, don't go out there. I don't want to lose you, too." She bawled into his shoulder. Flannel rasped her bare chest and coarse denim brushed her thighs. The cold button above his fly stamped her belly.

"All right, all right." Curtis's breath heated her damp head and he put his arms around her.

"Fuck." Her voice shook. "This is so stupid."

"What is?"

"Crying." Acknowledging her tears and his tender response to them somehow exacerbated her fit.

"It's fine," Curtis said when she quieted some and petted her arms. "But if you snot on my shirt we're finished."

Izzy choked. Crying and laughing didn't mix. "Stop it."

"I mean it. I'll toss you and that fussbudget dog in the car and haul the both of you back to Tavella. Some lines aren't meant to be crossed." He kissed her forehead and his hands skated lower to massage the small of her back. "And not that I don't prefer you naked and in my arms, but aren't you chilly?"

"Impossible next to you." Snaking her hands under his shirt, Izzy's fingers skimmed over his fevered skin. His stomach trembled. On tip toe, she craned her neck and placed a kiss on his neck and at the corner of his mouth.

"Feeling better?" Reaching lower, he cupped and pinched her ass, patted her bottom. "Not afraid anymore?"

"It's out there and can't get in, right?" She guided his face to hers and grazed his bottom lip with her teeth.

"Mmm. Mmm hmmm." Moving his head back and forth, Curtis brushed his nose against Izzy's. He took her chin between his thumb and index finger. "You're all wound up. If I laid you on the floor and did what I want to do, would we count that as taking advantage of your fragile emotional state? 'Cause I don't want to do that."

"I do."

Fierce need for him zinged through her like she'd mainlined three double espressos. Joints and extremities fizzed with it and she flung her arms around his neck, taking his mouth with hers. Fear compelled her haste, the wolf at the window a horrific reminder of pleasure's brevity.

Hurry. Take what you want. Take it now before it's gone.

Anything could happen to the man she kissed. What sense was there in cowering on the floor when he made her body sing with bliss? His fingers dug into her cheek as she pushed and bustled him to the wall.

"No, you don't," Curtis said. He spun Izzy around and forced her back to the wood paneling between the door and fireplace. Grooves between the panels scraped her back. He had her by the shoulders, pressure from his hands forcing her slightly down. Red light from the last of the fire shone in his eyes like glare from a camera's flash. Closing on her, his tongue darted out and curled over her parted lips. Wet flesh stabbed into her mouth and she opened wider, pushing her tongue into him. His jaw worked against her and his hips thrust forward, the ridge of his erection prominent against her leg.

With a shake of her head, Izzy wrested herself from Curtis's lips. Uncanny light still flickered in his eyes and she shied from it. It made him wild, feral, frightening. His white teeth gleamed when he smiled. Bowing his head, he scraped those teeth against her throat. To her over sensitized skin they seemed sharper. A hand gathered and wound around her damp hair. Water trickled down her arched spine as Curtis squeezed and pulled, drawing her head back, exposing more of her throat to him.

Buttons slipped between Izzy's fingers. She couldn't see with her head yanked back, but Curtis's shirt flapped open and her palm moved over his naked chest. The outside world and the beasts stalking it weren't reality. Existence ended at the hard wall at her back, at the radiating body crushing her to it. Beyond their twining limbs was void, infinite and empty until they said it wasn't so. And right now it was not so.

Curtis mouthed her neck, washed the delicate skin there with a flat tongue. Lower, he teased her nipple, pinched it in his lips and gently with his teeth. Both breasts responded to his play. Their tips tingled and hardened. Lower still, his fingers pressed between her legs, quashing the buzzing arousal hooded behind her aching lips. He ran his fingers over her slit, coaxing a slide of fluids from her heated entrance.

Weak legged, Izzy fought to keep herself upright. She grasped at Curtis's jeans button, unfastening the closure and splitting his zipper. She shoved her hand through the metal teeth and rough denim and wrapped her fingers around his hard cock, threading it through his boxers and opened trousers. Curtis grunted against her breast. He sucked and tugged at her nipple as he drew back, releasing the budded flesh with a wet smack. The blunt head of his erection nudged her belly. Aiming him downward, she spread her legs and raised her hips, moving to take him inside. Before she could, he crouched and lifted her, his cock sliding free of her curled hand. He slung her over his shoulder. Free of his grasp, her wet hair dangled forward and swished. Water droplets patted the wood floor as he carted her to the couch. Situated on the sofa's back ledge, Izzy wobbled when Curtis let go.

"I'm gonna fall."

"I've got you," Curtis said and circled an arm around her back. He urged her legs wide with his knee and positioned himself at her opening. Delicious pressure had her gasping and stilted his breath as well.

Torturously slow, he plunged into her and she stretched wider and wider. Her mouth opened, but she didn't make a sound. His hips kissed her inner thighs and he pulled back. Air hissed through his clenched teeth. Wetted from her tight channel, his cock glistened between them. Needing that fullness, Izzy gripped his ass and tugged him closer. One deft maneuver later and he untangled himself, slipped from her entirely—the shock of it made her whimper—and pinched the swollen tip of his cock as she reached for him, teetering on the couch. He steadied her with his free hand on her thigh.

"I'm too excited," Curtis said. Clear fluid welled at his tip and traveled down the under-curve of his shaft. Releasing himself, he caught her other thigh and dropped to his knees between her legs.

Breath whispered against Izzy's thighs and her wide-open sex. Placing his thumbs in the crease of thigh and groin, Curtis spread her moistened lips further and lapped at her, wriggling his tongue into her passage. Izzy laced her fingers in his hair and tugged at his scalp and writhed under his attention. Tongue circling her clit, he inserted two fingers into her and worked them back and forth as he sucked her throbbing bud into his mouth.

"Curtis. Curtis!" She was so close. He grunted his acknowledgement and rose, sliding his cock up her cleft and massaging her clit with his head. She clung to his neck and coaxed his mouth with hers as he slipped down and penetrated her with a shallow stroke, which was all she needed to send her soaring.

Izzy came moaning into Curtis's mouth while he drove himself in to the base. Her spasming sex clamped around his shaft and she thrust up her hips to meet his. Their bodies clapped together hollowly.

Veins corded in Curtis's neck as he pumped into her. His breaths came quicker and quicker until he jerked inside her, hot fluid spilling from him. In his arms, she felt his muscles bunch and flex with his release. He held her like she was the one thing keeping him on Earth. His head fell to her shoulder, which he kissed, his lips moving up her neck and to her mouth. Easing from her with a shudder, he raked his fingers through her hair and tilted her head back so he could kiss her more deeply. Sweat dampened his skin and her palm was sticky with it.

Izzy slid from the couch, leather pulling from her thighs and bottom like clinging film. She swayed on her feet, but Curtis had her. Cheek against his chest, she held onto him, delighting in the great thump of his heart, the tide-like rush of his breath. He was so present and large and definite. She had the sense nothing could compromise him. Never mind the wolves at the door. In his arms nothing could touch her. What could ever go wrong when he held her like this?

*

The day hadn't gone as planned—they'd ended it well, anyhow—but the results satisfied Curtis. Izzy slept soundly under his arm. The light sound of her breathing mingled with the soft hum of the space heater.

Too hot.

He worked himself over the covers, careful not to disturb his bedmate. After her scare, he figured she'd be wide awake for hours. Fucking Gerome. Loose perimeter didn't mean stake out his goddamned porch. Clear-Skies had been so keyed up, Curtis was surprised he didn't sprout a tail when he took Izzy on the couch. Their romp and the adrenaline crash from her fright must have sapped her energy. He yawned and his heavy lids drooped. Where the hell had his stamina gone? Ah, but this was normal. On his own turf in the aftermath of mind-blowing sex? He was lucky he hadn't passed out already.

Another yawn stretched his mouth so wide the chapped skin on his lower lip split and stung. The tip of his tongue darted out and he tasted salt and copper. Stretching out, he curled his toes. Sleep wasn't for him tonight. All his systems had to stay on high alert; nose filtering the air for Rapid's proximity, body and wolf ready for action.

Night's-Rapid-Water's acrid musk had tinged the crisp smell of the coming storm on the trail that afternoon. From what Curtis could tell, his pack mate had been miles off. He hadn't smelled the wolf since.

Come on, Rapid, Curtis thought. *Don't you dare screw me.*

If the wolf didn't come tonight and they didn't catch him, Thomas would consider Izzy's blood forfeit. There would be no concealing the pack's true natures then. If she knew what they were, that a significant part of Curtis melded with the beast she feared and hated, what would she do? What would Thomas do?

He'd use it as an excuse, of course, to get rid of her if Rapid didn't. *Humans mixing with wolves never ends well,* the Alpha had quipped on more than one occasion. *Mundanes who know our secret end up targets. Keep your lips zipped unless you want that on your conscience.*

Curtis wriggled to a new, somewhat cooler, position above the bedclothes. He'd deflect any proverbial (or literal) bullets aimed at Izzy. Just because he was a wolf didn't mean they couldn't be together. Aggie hadn't been pack and his dad had made it work—Thomas's naysaying had done nothing to prevent it. If Izzy loved Curtis, she'd accept Clear-Skies, too. He brushed his own spirit against his wolf's icy essence, which contracted, pulsed, and spun. Clear-Skies gave him the wolf spirit version of the cold shoulder.

Izzy would accept them. She'd be fine with it. Maybe.

Well, couples kept secrets from each other all the time, didn't they? She might never have to know. Curtis's head sank into his pillow, which sighed out a rush of trapped air. No way he could keep a secret like that forever. The space heater clicked, punctuating the importance of that conclusion. Roasting air acted as a replacement comforter and settled over him like heavy wool.

Damn heat.

It made his brain fuzzy and sluggish and with Izzy next to him and the mattress so comfy it was almost too much to keep his eyes open. But he had to. For Izzy. For Izzy he had to . . . stay . . . awake . . .

Chapter Fourteen

Pounding at the door.

Izzy's eyes fluttered open. Body heavy with sleep, she couldn't be certain she dreamed the pounding or not. Whoever knocked knocked again—an insistent cop-knock—and she had her answer. The comforter fell into her lap when she sat up. She draped it back over her chest awkwardly with her right arm as though the third, intruding presence might spy her somehow through the cabin walls. With her left hand, she shook Curtis who snoozed beside her on top of the covers. His snoring stuttered and he turned on his side at her disturbance yet he remained unconscious.

"Curtis," Izzy said and shook him again.

Grumbling, he sniffed and his lips twitched and he tried to draw her to him. Evading capture, Izzy scrambled out of bed and he latched onto her pillow instead. Snoring resumed. The knocker knocked.

"Shit." Izzy found her pajama bottoms and Curtis's flannel shirt in the orange glow coming from the space heater. She'd hiked up the flimsy pants and fastened one button on the shirt before the rapping started up again, this time going on and on like a two ton woodpecker. How could Curtis not hear that racket? She recalled he'd mentioned that he could sleep through nuclear warfare, but she hadn't taken him seriously. Her mistake. Though she would have preferred he answer his own door, whoever stood out in the cold sounded impatient and who came knocking in the middle of the night if not for an emergency?

Nook stood alert in the bedroom doorway. When Izzy passed he whined and bumped his snoot on her ankle. She looked at him and he coughed out a low wuff and paced, looking back and forth from the front room to the bedroom. She was nervous, too.

Confronting a stranger at night in half-buttoned PJs wasn't exactly safe. She cast off her reticence with a shake of her shoulders. She'd check the peephole in the front door, let whoever it was know Curtis was coming, and jump up and down on the man's chest if that's what it took to rouse him.

Floorboards creaked under Izzy's careful steps. The knocking had ceased but picked up again when she came a few paces from the cabin's entrance. The front door trembled under another volley of knocks and its hinges rattled. She almost turned back, then went on her toes and put her eye to the spy hole's chipped gold rim. The cold metal ring brushed her cheek and eyelashes. The convex image of a man in a wide brimmed hat stood on the porch, flashlight in hand. His gold badge gleamed in the moon's soft light. A ranger.

Something must have happened on the property, Izzy thought. *Something terrible.*

The wolf!

In a tumult of panic and guilt, all Izzy could do was stand there, caught in the furor of her raging thoughts. They should have told someone about the wolf when they saw it. Reported the animal to the authorities. Wolves didn't leave the safety of their forests unless they were starving or mad or both. When a wolf treaded human territory it meant they were desperate and, in her mind's eye, Izzy pictured someone else—Amanda first, then Dr. Turner, Claire, Travis, Melinda—in bloody tatters because she'd indulged herself with Curtis, wandered off the trail when she should have exercised self-restraint and responsibility.

Snatching the keys from their hook, Izzy fitted the right one in the scratched and dinged fixture and the lock clicked back. She threw open the door. Frigid air swirled around her. Icy tendrils curled beneath her clothing, caressing her calves and the under-curves of her breasts.

"What happened?" Izzy asked. "Is anyone hurt? Is everything all right?"

The ranger took a deep breath and shifted his weight. His hat shadowed his eyes, leaving his thin lips and grizzled chin exposed.

"Ma'am." The ranger's words came slow and slurred like one side of his mouth was dead, like he couldn't form the right sounds. "I need Curtis Keene."

Izzy put her left hand to her head. Of course, he'd want the property owner if something was wrong. He wouldn't tell her. "Wait right there," she said. "I'll get him." She whirled, so many frenzied thoughts zipping through her mind she forgot to ask him in or shut the door.

Izzy didn't make it three steps. Weight barreled into her from behind and she pitched forward, belly flopping onto the hard wood floor. When her forehead struck the planks it sounded like someone dropped a brick from the ceiling. A film of wavering, bilious green glazed her sight as her head swam. She retched, tasted acid that burned her chest and the back of her throat. Choked gurgling escaped her, but there was no air for screaming. The ranger's body crushed it out of her. From the darkened hall she heard Nook's frantic yips.

The ranger's weight eased up and Izzy gasped. Fabric tore above her as she scrambled for the bedroom, the walls and hall tilting like she rode a nauseating ride. She stumbled. Shreds of the ranger's khaki shirt fell over her head and neck and a massive, black furred paw crashed down in front of her, barring her escape. She screamed and flattened herself to the floor. Hot labored breath steamed against her back and a rumbling growl shook her insides. Sickle-like claws carved deep grooves in the wood as the ranger's— the creature's—paw convulsed and elongated, bones snapping and popping into new and horrific shapes. A tortured howl deafened her, the cry somewhere between demon and beast. Something in that much pain couldn't be an immediate threat.

Dodging the tree trunk appendage in front of her, Izzy crawled to the hall. She didn't look back. Her head pounded like a second heart. The organ itself lurched and fluttered in her chest like a wounded sparrow. She had to get to Curtis and Nook. They had to get out. When her fingers skirted the shadowed edge of the open hall, a second blast of humid breath blew back her hair. Like spectral flames in the dark, two amber eyes shone from the gloom. Arms and legs rebelled though Izzy urged them backward, somewhere, anywhere away. She couldn't move as the thing emerged from the hall.

The beast was silver and gray. Its ears flattened against its head and its lips curled back from a glistening set of enormous fangs. Its target was the creature howling at Izzy's back, but when it passed, it took her in, shining nose inhaling her scent and lambent eyes narrowing. Curling into a tight ball, she mumbled jumbled snippets of what prayers she remembered from childhood, tacking pieces of the Lord's Prayer, Hail Mary, and the Apostles's Creed together in an incoherent, Catholic pastiche. Prayers likely had nothing to do with it, but the beast passed her over. Its belly and tail grazed her head and back and then she did not feel its presence. Still, she did not move.

A thunderous crash drew Izzy from her defense and she scampered into the shadows before daring a peek behind her. The silvery beast had thrown the black ranger into the ashen fireplace. Khaki tatters littered the floor and clung to the ranger-monster's dark fur. He'd tripled in size, dwarfing the silver wolf—for they were wolves, she realized, wolves of unnatural size—that had thrown him. Crouching, the silver wolf seized and trembled and Izzy watched its shape distort.

It grew faster than its opponent. Legs bulged and lengthened, bones twisted and cracked, and the creature that went on all fours stood upright, its sleek head half a foot from the ceiling. Leaping, it sank its teeth into the ruff of the black wolf struggling in the grate, throwing a spume of ash into the air. Like a crocodile with a captive gazelle, the silver wolf thrashed Izzy's attacker back and forth. The ranger finally swiped one of its clawed paws at the beast's muzzle, smacking it to the ground, and twisted free. Large as its white-gray cousin, the black wolf rose, a thick pelt of glossy fur covering its massive body. Aggression arced between them—silver wolf sprawled next to the fireplace and black wolf looming over it—a resonance that vibrated Izzy's body like a struck tuning fork. Muscles cording, the black wolf prepared to strike his opponent, but when his nostrils flared—white clouds huffing from his nose and mouth—his head snapped toward the hall where she cowered.

Izzy scooted back as the black wolf stalked toward her, her hand and bare feet squeaking over the wood planks. Its footfalls sent tremors through the floor and made the furniture jump. She could get to the bedroom, but what then? Out the window? What about Curtis and Nook? Had the silver wolf killed them? Blood hadn't stained its muzzle—she'd had a clear view of that—but she couldn't see Curtis rent in a dozen gory pieces and keep her sanity. Thinking, in this case, was a mistake. She should have followed her instincts and fled, but she'd hesitated one second too long. When the black beast hunkered down she knew she couldn't escape and sanity became the least of her concerns.

The dark wolf sprang and Izzy screamed and flailed back. If the animal's weight didn't crush the life out of her, its teeth would snap her in two. Mid-leap, the silver wolf cannon-balled into its side and the animals careened into the couch, sending the furniture crashing into the flat screen and tumbling the standing lamps and speakers. The silver wolf regained its footing first, reared back, and bayed. Windows rattled with its bellow. Distant howls answered the call and the night filled with a haunting refrain.

The ranger-wolf scented the air and its eyes searched Izzy's hiding place. It made one useless dash for her, but its lighter cousin cut him off, snarling and snapping its jaws.

Dropping to all fours, the dark beast loped from the living room, out the open door, and into the night. The silver wolf gave chase. Its claws plowed deep furrows in the floor, corkscrew curls of wood shedding from its paws. Over the white blanketed lawn, Izzy saw the flitting shadow of her attacker pursued by a mercurial shift of liquid moonlight. The silvery wolf's coat blended almost perfectly with the snow. Izzy couldn't visually track its pursuit, so she listened, waiting until it was safe to leave her cover. Yips and barks grew quiet as the chorus that had answered the silver wolf's ululation. If she wanted out, now was the time. She didn't have to think it over.

Izzy sprinted to the bedroom.

"Curtis? Curtis!"

He wasn't there. No body, no blood, no nothing. The comforter crumpled in a heap on the floor by his side of the bed. She checked the bathroom, threw back the shower curtain. No one.

"Nook?" Her voice bounced off the walls and tiled floor.

Quiet whines came from the bedroom. Izzy's shins bumped the space heater when she rushed into the adjoining chamber. Burning coils seared her skin. She yelped and ripped the cord from the wall, cursing when she kicked the thing and stubbed her toe.

"Nook?"

The husky whimpered beneath the bed. She got on her knees and peeked under the box spring. Nook huddled against the back wall.

"C'mere, boy." Izzy patted the floor. The dog didn't move. "Nook. Nook!" She tried infusing Curtis's commanding tone into her own. The sobs strangling her words ruined the effect. "Nook, please." Tears streamed down her cheeks and she put her hurting forehead to the floor. She couldn't wait for the dog. She had to go.

"God, please stay under the bed, Nook," Izzy said as she snatched her prosthetic and hurried to the living room.

Picking through the debris from the smashed sofa and overturned TV, Izzy extracted her duffel. She stowed her harness inside and pulled her boots on over her pajama bottoms. The keys still dangled from the door, chiming while they swung. Ripping them from the lock, she held the ring in her teeth, the tarnished metal bitter on her tongue.

Izzy's coat lay like a shadow by the splintered card table. There was no time to put it on. She threaded it through her bag's straps and headed to the door. Maybe Curtis had escaped to the main house? She could check, but would he have left her behind? She snatched the pointed fire poker she spotted from the ash strewn grate just in case. Couldn't be too careful.

Clomping down the front steps, Izzy scanned the lawn and the trees blackening the edges of the property. She didn't see or hear anything. Cold numbed her face and arms. Her breath plumed white and her tear tracks froze on her face. Her boots squeaked when they sank ankle deep in the snow. Fresh tracks from the rampaging beasts cut blue shaded troughs in the sparkling and pristine white. Wading in the opposite direction from the wolf tracks, she made her way to the carport.

A large shadow swallowed Izzy's as she trekked to the Jeep. Spinning, she swung the fire poker at whatever came up behind her. Thomas caught the weapon in one hand and yanked it from her feeble grip, bruising her cold-burned fingers. He caught her under the arm with his other hand and scowled.

"You're not going anywhere." He ripped the keys from her teeth and hauled her back to the cabin. Izzy squalled and thrashed the entire way.

Chapter Fifteen

Inside, Thomas stood up one of the collapsed folding chairs and sat Izzy in it, pushing her down hard by her shoulders. Then he set up one of the lamps, switched it on and shut the front door. Without a word, he leaned against the windowsill by the fireplace, opened the shabby drapes with the pointed end of the fire poker, and waited. Did he know what was going on? Izzy couldn't keep quiet. Not with Curtis in danger.

"Something's happened to—"

"Shut your mouth and keep still."

Izzy's voice cut out and her jaw snapped shut. Blood burned in her cheeks and she surely took a layer of enamel off her back teeth when she ground them, but she didn't speak. She couldn't. Her mouth wouldn't open. When she tried shouting, air came up in her throat and stuck there like a burp she couldn't expel.

The wooden window frame creaked when Thomas clenched it and his jaw muscles ticked as he stared out the glass. Time passed in silence until heaving grunts and heavy plodding from the porch broke it. Claws raked the front door. The small, stifled voice within Izzy screamed, and her raw throat tightened and clicked when she swallowed. She didn't want any of those creatures getting back in.

Thomas cracked his knuckles, neck, and opened the door, ignoring Izzy's frantically shaking head. The silver beast stalked inside followed by a smaller, dark gray wolf on all fours. Instinct dictated she make herself as small as she could on the chair, but her body wouldn't react. She couldn't take her eyes off them. Trapped there, she couldn't help but drink in the sight of them.

The wolves were frightening yet utterly beautiful. The gray wolf simply appeared an overlarge version of the actual animal. The silver one was something out of a dark fairy tale. His—she saw now the silvery wolf was a he and wondered how she'd missed his, ah, masculinity before—coat shimmered like the snow carpeting the lawn. Beneath his luxurious pelt was a powerful and enormous body. Izzy's eyes bugged out in disbelief.

Humanoid in his upright stature, the silver wolf's legs were in a permanent semi-crouch, knees bent to support his upper body. His bipedal stride had appeared awkward when he'd entered the cabin. Izzy doubted he covered long distances on two legs. The white tips of his retracted claws poked from his hand and foot-paws and the points of his fangs jutted from under his black upper lip. Shoulders and chest went up and down as he inhaled and exhaled and the floor dipped a little where he towered before Thomas, the old wood straining under his prodigious weight.

"Well?" Thomas held out his hands. The property manager seemed not at all intimidated by the beasts. In fact, his manner suggested he ought to be obeyed. And the wolf beasts did obey.

The smaller gray plopped on his hindquarters and gazed up at his monstrous partner who let loose a coughing series of wuffs, growls, and grunts. His gestures as he communicated were very human and, if Izzy hadn't feared for her life, she would have found the scene comical.

"Change," Thomas said. "I can't get the details with you like that." He waved his hand at the looming silver. The humongous wolf dropped his head.

The seated gray immediately convulsed and Izzy winced at the painful sounding process. Hesitant, the silver wolf paced back, looked in her direction and back at Thomas. Why the hell did they obey him?

"A little late for cold feet, Curtis. Change."

Curtis?

Izzy's heart gave a sickening lurch. Snorting, the silver wolf tensed. His skin rippled, fur standing up with the passing tremor, and its shape changed, dwindled, while its companion's stretched and grew. Fur and claws retracted, muzzles shortened, and where two wolves once hulked stood a very human, very naked Gerome and Curtis.

*

Changing always left Curtis hurting for a good five minutes afterwards, like he'd scrubbed himself with fine grit sandpaper. His skin was raw and hypersensitive, and the currents of air coursing over his body were near unbearable for the first few seconds. Disorientation accompanied his discomfort. Sound, texture, and color screamed at his senses and his Alpha's voice, though quiet and threatening, reverberated in his ears.

"Did you kill Night's-Rapid-Water?" Thomas asked. He leaned on the fire poker he held like a cane.

Curtis heard his Alpha but he barely comprehended. Izzy distracted him. He opened his mouth to respond, but no words came. When he'd entered the cabin with Gerome, her face had held the same burned-out quality it'd had when they'd come off the trail to Rock Spout Falls. The faraway look in her eyes had quickly twisted to shock, then anger when he'd shifted to human form. She regarded them all with unconcealed fury, dark eyes flashing. Charm and explanations probably wouldn't get him out of this one.

"Curtis." Thomas snapped his fingers in front of his Beta's face and Izzy swam out of focus.

"We couldn't catch him," Curtis said, folding his arms.

Gerome suppressed a laugh that came out like a snort.

Curtis went on, "He was always the fastest of us and he'll always know the terrain better. The woods are his first home not his second."

"That's why we brought her up here." Thomas jerked his head at Izzy and heat bloomed in Curtis's chest and crept up his neck. "I didn't think Rapid could smell her and leave her alone even if it meant crossing our territory."

My territory. Mine. Rocking on the balls of his feet, Curtis rolled his head around and shoved his hands in his armpits before he balled them into fists.

"He might be a pure wolf, closer to animal than man, but he knows us," Thomas continued, either unaware or uncaring of his Beta's mounting agitation. "Our lure won't be effective a second time without some additional . . . encouragement." He ambled over to Izzy's chair and braced the fire poker he held against her seat. Behind her, he clasped the metal chair back and leaned over her.

The dominant and possessive display stoked Clear-Skies from a candle flame flicker to a torch of blazing incandescence. Spirit fire shot from Curtis's chest to his core, the freezing burn chewing through his belly and sparking out his pores. The wolf wanted out and Curtis's vision tunneled. He shrank inside himself and the internal discordant howl of his enraged inner beast rang in his ears.

Not now, Curtis strained against the transformation. *We can't change now. We'll hurt Izzy.* He concentrated on his Alpha's face, keeping his expression carefully neutral. If Thomas and his wolf, Mountain's-Might, sensed the Beta's defiance, nothing would stop them from tearing each other, and everyone else, apart.

Thomas smirked. "So, tell me, what exactly went wrong besides 'we didn't catch him?'"

Gerome gave Curtis the I'm-not-taking-the-fall-for-this face and Curtis's upper lip pulled back. Debrief, though he resented playing twenty questions, helped him regain control. Articulating his thoughts kept Clear-Skies from tearing loose, the wolf's reactionary instinct brought in line by reason.

"It's my fault," Curtis said. "I fell asleep. I didn't smell Rapid until he was in the cabin and already changed. He'd masked his scent with his human form and with the ranger's clothes." No doubt a missing person alert would go out in the next few days. Unless the authorities found the unfortunate man's body, that is. Curtis didn't think they would. If Rapid didn't consume his kills, he hid them well. "I didn't signal the pack soon enough because I was distracted."

"You don't say?" Thomas drew Izzy's hair over her shoulder, tangled it in his fingers, pulled her head back, and took a deep whiff of her neck. Though her face was tilted up, Curtis saw her eyes widen with terror. Her throat convulsed when she swallowed and his acute sight narrowed on the erratic flutter of a pulsing vein. That delicate spot he'd kissed lay exposed and vulnerable and he had to protect what was his. He felt his blank expression contort and he edged forward. Thomas baited him. He knew it. This was a test.

Is she more important than us?

Of course she was. And because she was, Curtis couldn't rise to his Alpha's taunt. He couldn't give Thomas an excuse to get rid of her. Cheeks working around his gritted teeth, he stepped back in line with Gerome and the heat he knew colored his neck set his ears aflame when Thomas stroked Izzy's head.

"Maybe if you weren't so distracted." Thomas fisted his hand in Izzy's hair and yanked, making the skin on her forehead taut. "Maybe if you weren't fucking the bait," he jerked her head back hard and her eyes squinted, watered, "we wouldn't have to do things my way." Two drops leaked from her eyes and slid down her already tear-tracked face.

"Thomas." Curtis strode toward them, gunning for Izzy. He'd had enough.

"Curtis, shut the fuck up and get back in line."

A violent force worked on Curtis. The Alpha's power hit him as if Thomas had thrown up an invisible wall. Circumnavigating the barrier was impossible. The wall pushed at him, then twisted on itself, creating a thrumming filament that speared his core and pulled him backward like a strung puppet. The string hummed with Thomas's intent and ripped through his Beta's body in a shock wave, making his eyes jitter and his muscles spasm. Clear-Skies leapt away from the tendril of power skewering his host, and when Curtis tried to resist the command, he felt his insides tear.

Once he obeyed and returned to Gerome's side, the pain ceased. The power spent itself and diffused. Curtis's arms hung like dead weight. Fighting the order had hollowed him out and Clear-Skies had become a pinprick of white-blue light hidden deep within his chest, his dominance quashed by the Alpha's will. Thomas rounded on him, dropping Izzy like an uninteresting bit of prey.

"You assured me. You said you'd take care of it. I trusted you to handle Rapid." Thomas came a hair's breath from Curtis's face, so close a fleck of spittle struck his chin. "You fucked up and I don't even know why you're smiling, Gerome." The Alpha glared at the subordinate wolf in Curtis's periphery. "All that means is more bitch work for you.

"Curtis, your priorities are clear. You stay here and baby-sit. Gerome, wait for me outside. We'll be tracking, so change quick."

When the door swung shut behind Gerome, Thomas laid his hands on Curtis's bare shoulders.

"Your head's in the wrong place. It always has been with her. You're my second. *My* Beta." Thomas squinted at him. "Did you really think I'd let you life-mate a cripple? I didn't order you to get her up here for you to fuck her. Don't look away. Look at me."

Curtis did and he understood it was not merely a pup's disobedience that clamored inside him. He hated this man. Had tolerated him so long out of deference to his father's respect for his business partner and friend. But Robert Keene was long gone and Thomas had somehow—no, Curtis knew he'd allowed the man to do it—sidled into his father's place, wore his father's role like a misshapen mask. The mask's distorted mouth gaped as it lectured him.

"The only reason that woman hasn't run screaming from you is my influence. She's weak and she's not your mate. Quit acting like she is. After tomorrow, that girl is a face on a milk carton. She's the next shitstorm on CNN. Get used to it." Thomas pushed off Curtis and slammed the front door when he exited.

*

A weight Izzy hadn't realized settled on her lifted with Thomas's departure and the rest of her truncated warning came tumbling out, "—to Curtis."

At the mention of his name Curtis moved to Izzy, arms outstretched. Another man's hands on her was the last thing she wanted right now. Her skin and hair still smelled of the property manager, his overpowering cologne. The fragrance made her think of men who wore fat, gold rings and met in smoky back rooms. Where he'd stroked her hair and neck she imagined glistening trails like a snail's silvery tracks.

Body and voice free, she leapt out of the chair, snatched up the fire poker, and brandished it at Curtis. Unhindered by the weight that had kept her paralyzed and silent, her body felt very light, like she'd trained herself to run with ten-pound weights attached to her arms and ankles and had just loosened the excess ballast. The right sleeve of her flannel shirt flopped over her incomplete arm.

"What the hell are you and what the fuck is going on?"

Curtis stopped where he was and held up his hands as a man would at gunpoint. The dull tip of the iron poker dimpled his chest. "Calm down, Izzy."

"*Fuck* you. I'm bait? Weak?" Shock from the attack and at seeing two wolves morph into men had overwhelmed her indignation at Thomas's scathing remarks. It had taken a moment for the full effect of his words to hit her. And this man—if he was a man— had stood by and accepted it. It made her gut twist. Inside, she hurt all over, her organs suddenly too large and crowding each other in the flimsy casing of her body. "Do you have any idea what it takes to be a principle dancer in a major company?" She prodded him in the gut with the poker.

Curtis *oofed* and shook his head, rubbed his tummy.

"I used to be the fucking best," her voice caught and she blinked back stinging tears. "Now I'm a face on a milk carton?"

"I didn't say any of that."

"But *he* did, and it seems like everyone agrees with whatever he says and does whatever he wants."

Curtis looked bewildered. "Thomas is our Alpha. A direct order is almost impossible to disobey."

A direct order?

Shut your mouth and keep still.

So, that's why she hadn't been able to move or speak, and when Curtis had stepped out of line he'd had to retreat when Thomas told him to. Curtis had to obey no matter what he felt, which—

Oh, God.

"He ordered you to bring me up here?" Izzy asked.

Curtis's Adam's apple bobbed up and down. "Yes."

The fire poker wilted in Izzy's hand. "That's why you came to the studio. It didn't have anything to do with my glove." The center of her forehead tickled like a hair-line fissure opened there in her skull.

"It wasn't just orders. I wanted to see you anyway." Curtis tripped over his words and took a half step to her before Izzy righted her weapon and drove him back.

"I hear you fine where you are. Why does your 'Alpha' want me here and what was that, that *thing* that broke in?"

"That *thing* was a Werewolf. I," he touched his chest, "am a Werewolf. We're not things. We're people . . . mostly. The wolf that attacked you tonight used to be part of our pack before he went sick. Thomas wants you here because we haven't been able to track him. When you came to the lodge last week, we scented him for the first time in years."

"But why would he come for me?"

Curtis played with his fingers. "Izzy, you're the only prey that's ever escaped Rapid." He couldn't look at her. "He's the one that took your arm. He's the one that killed your brother."

Chapter Sixteen

The back of Izzy's head got very heavy. She felt she couldn't hold it up. The tiny fracture she'd felt split the smooth bone beneath her forehead webbed out in a network of zigzagged lines. Her scalp prickled and her whole body went numb. Distantly, she thought, "This is what they mean by 'cracking up." Her ears rang. Curtis's lips moved as he approached, but the shrill warning tone—an emergency broadcast—in her ears obliterated his words. She swung the fire poker at him in a limp and poorly aimed swoop, unable to focus. Everything blurred. He caught the weapon as Thomas had and held onto the rod with two hands while she shoved it against his chest, the noises coming from her somewhere between sobs and shrieks. He wouldn't back off.

"Get away from me!"

"Izzy." Curtis's voice cut through the squealing whine. He pulled on the fire poker and braced her to himself before he extricated it from her feeble grasp and tossed it aside.

"Fucking Werewolf." She slapped his chest and shoulders. "Let go." She twisted and shoved away from him.

Curtis's coffee-colored eyes pulsed amber. "Don't jerk like that, Izzy." He blinked and the wild incandescence faded. "I told you: Sudden movements provoke the hunter's instinct."

Those strange eyes—eyes that had haunted every nightmare—framed in his familiar face pitched the room at an odd angle. She'd trusted him. *Trusted him.* Izzy's legs buckled and she stumbled back, catching herself on the wall as Curtis rushed to catch her. Flinging her arm at him, she staggered into the hall.

"Izzy, you're going to fall." Curtis went for her again. "Don't—"

Izzy shot down the corridor on rubbery legs and Curtis snarled behind her. His arms ensnared her and he slammed her, face forward, against the wall, his body hard on hers. Lips brushed her throat.

"Don't run." His voice rasped with a rattling growl and his muscles twitched and jumped. Shuddering, he combated the change threatening his body. Izzy felt the creature inside him ripple and stir beneath his skin as it fought for freedom. When he thrashed with it and growled again she kicked back and brought her heel between his legs, connecting with a bare and very sensitive spot. Howling, he dropped her and doubled over. She streaked into his bedroom, slamming the door just as he righted himself and gave chase.

Pounding shook the wall and Izzy retreated from the door. Her boot splashed in a puddle. She glanced over her shoulder and grimaced. Nook had peed. She shook the piss off her boot and skirted the mess. Emptying Curtis's dresser of clothes, she shoved the furniture against the door.

"Izzy," Curtis shouted through the barrier. "Will you listen to me?"

Izzy knew if he wanted in, her fortifications wouldn't stop him, but she had to make some effort to appease herself and he respected the extra walls she'd erected. She hugged herself and stared at the dresser-bolted door, absently fretting at the end of her stunted arm.

"Why aren't I a Werewolf?" she asked.

"What?" Curtis spoke around labored breaths.

Izzy swallowed. "If a Werewolf bit me, how come I haven't turned into one?"

"Doesn't work that way."

"Enlighten me." She had to keep him talking, distracted, while she figured something out.

Curtis sighed. "Being a wolf isn't viral. Or genetic. A spirit makes us change."

"You're possessed?"

"I suppose. Some wolf spirits pick humans or wolves at random. Some stay with a family. Like mine. Sees-Through-Clear-Skies was my dad's wolf before he passed to me."

While he spoke, Izzy checked the windows. She could get them open, but Curtis, wolf or not, would hear it. She sucked on her upper lip and spun around. The noxious puddle in the middle of the room made her gag.

"Werewolves make a habit of eating people?" she asked once her stomach settled. That puddle had to come up.

"When they go sick they do."

"So, you get the flu and I'm dog food. Fantastic." Izzy's mind rebelled at this talk of spirits and wolves and shape-shifting men. Reason had taken a sound beating and languished, bruised and bloodied, in the far corner of her brain. The cracked shell housing her psyche teetered on the verge of total collapse, but rationalizing the improbable away wouldn't keep things together. She'd witnessed three men change from human to beast or vice versa. She wasn't on drugs and was mentally sound besides the odd fit of anxiety or depression. Still, she couldn't discuss wolf spirits with a naked man shouting outside her door without a surge of hysterical giggles tickling up from belly to throat. She suppressed those giggles.

The mind knows when it's ready.

Well, hers wasn't and if she didn't get some normalcy soon she didn't think her sanity would stand up to Werewolves, sick or healthy. Curtis had been lecturing all the while she mentally grounded herself and she'd missed the first part of his speech.

"—so we don't get sick like that. When a wolf snaps it's because the change got to him. Happens to pure wolves mostly."

"And they are?" Izzy crossed to the bathroom and snagged a damp towel hanging from the metal rack next to the toilet. A small, frosted window a few feet above the tank caught her eye. She judged the fit. She could get through it.

"Wolves that turn human. As opposed to a human turned wolf," Curtis said.

Izzy stopped short on her way to the puddle. "Oh my fucking God, you're not a reverse Werewolf are you?"

"No, I'm not pure. Would it have mattered if I was?"

"Would it matter to you if I'd been born a man?" Izzy asked as she knelt. With the towel, she sopped up Nook's mess. The husky poked his nose and paws out from under the bed.

"Fair enough. Can I come in?" Curtis asked.

"No."

"Izzy, I'm fine now. I got stirred up from chasing Rapid and Thomas's posturing crap and when you ran from me I couldn't help it. It won't happen again."

"At the moment I'm fresh out of trust."

"My balls are already busted. How many times are you going to kick?"

"I don't know. How many times have you lied to me?"

Curtis's punch shook the dresser at the door and his solitary framed picture jumped from its hook on the wall. The photo of Curtis's parents clattered on the floor and a crack split the glass. "Fucking, fuck! Fuck, Izzy!" Nook's nose and paws vanished under the bed skirt. "It wasn't supposed to happen this way." More pounding and crashing and a stream of curses that escalated in virulence and complexity punctuated his tirade as Curtis moved back to the living room. Sounded like he'd need new chairs. And plates. Didn't sound like his anger would fizzle for a while. That suited Izzy's plan fine.

Carting the yellowed towel into the bathroom, Izzy sat it on the toilet seat while she climbed onto the tank. Stuck with ice, the little window took some jostling before it cracked open. She wedged her fingers into the space and shoved the pane the rest of the way up. Grabbing the fouled terrycloth, she pitched it into the snow, banked high at the back of the cabin. Lucky for her, the window was low enough for her to wriggle through. If she'd had to lift herself she would have been screwed.

Left hand braced on the rough exterior timbers, Izzy shoved herself through the narrow opening head first. Front half hanging out of the cabin, she grunted at the window ledge biting into her stomach. She edged down the back wall. When her feet left the toilet tank, her unsupported rear weight pitched her off balance and she tumbled face first into a snow bank. She didn't fall far and was cold and uncomfortable more than anything else. Her legs and forearms were scraped from their brush with the wall and window. Bruises and abrasions. Nothing a Band-Aid couldn't fix. First, she had to get to a phone.

With Thomas and Gerome tracking and Curtis raging in his living room, she should be able to get to the main building and call the cops. Her cell had probably been crushed. No telling what Curtis had done to her duffel. She circled around the cabin and took off across the lawn, hugging the shadowed tree line so Curtis wouldn't spot her from his front window. Snow came up to her calves in some areas and she had to high step through the drifts. Her legs cramped up and slush clogged her boots and soaked her pajama bottoms. After she lost feeling in her frostbitten toes she couldn't decide if she should be grateful or really, really worried.

The wolf that clipped Izzy's side was all but invisible until it hit her. It shot from the trees and threw its weight into her, knocking her down. It tossed back its head and howled. Izzy flipped over and kicked it in the chest. Her powerful dancer's legs choked off what was undoubtedly a warning signal and toppled the beast. She scrambled up and made for the road, but the wolf flanked her before she got far. Hip-checked again, she face planted in the snow. Icy powder stuffed her nostrils and filled her mouth. With its front paws on her back, the wolf's weight kept her flat as it howled once more.

*

The remnants of the card table flew across the room and crashed into the toppled flat screen. Fuck tables and TVs. Who needed them? Not Curtis. Wolves needed nothing but the ground under their paws, the wind through their fur, a dry hole in rough weather, and meat in their bellies when they growled. An unbroken coffee mug rolled and knocked his foot. He kicked it and the ceramic shattered. Great, now all his tableware matched. He surveyed the wreckage of his living room and felt triumphant. The contents of his cupboards covered the kitchen floor in a broken jumble. Dents studded the drywall from his bedroom to the end of the hall. He'd made those. With his fists. And he'd make more if he felt like it.

Flexing his fingers, Curtis studied his bloodied knuckles. Tiny licks of blue flame curled from the shallow gashes and remade the flesh. Clear-Skies surged through his veins and his ears filled with the ringing rush of crashing waves. He felt shrink- wrapped in his skin and swelling pressure pushed against his skull and the backs of his eyeballs like his body was one big, puffy wound. When he opened his mouth he didn't bellow, he roared. Clear-Skies bucked under his skin. Why not let the wolf take control? He'd lost her. Even if he shielded Izzy from the worst of Thomas's cruelty, she'd rejected him. Them.

So what if he'd lied? He'd done it to protect her. She should be grateful. He'd given her food, shelter, protection. He'd had her body. She was his. His. What was truth anyway but a human construction and what was a human construction to someone more than human? There was no truth, only honesty and all he'd shown her of himself was honest. A wolf had no need for truth and lies. A wolf obeyed only instinct.

Curtis's insides twisted like a wrung cloth and he fell to all fours. Shifting perspective disoriented him a passing moment and he shook out the itching fur that sprouted from his skin. Snorting, he pawed at the floor and swung his head in the bedroom's direction. She couldn't shut him out that way. One kick of his hind leg and he'd splinter the bedroom door. When he was over her, she'd be his again and she'd want him. He panted and his balls drew up between his hindquarters. She wouldn't care what he was when he buried himself in her.

No! Curtis shouted inside himself, but he was so small in the cage of his body. Clear-Skies howled all around him and another wolf's song joined his internal baying.

Escaped, the she-wolf sang. *Escaped and captured.*

Curtis snarled and hurtled toward the front door, tongue lolling from his jaws, tasting wolf and woman and the citrus tinge of fear on the air. Using his head as a battering ram, he flattened his ears and bashed open the door, hearing metal snap and wood splinter. Skidding onto the porch, he spotted the black silhouette of Nettled-Clover perched atop his flown charge. He bared his fangs and flung himself over the front steps and into the snow.

Curtis would get Izzy back. He had to.

*

Sharp barks made Izzy's guard back off and she sat up, spitting out snow and wiping it from her eyes. The silver wolf—Curtis—sat in front of her and growled. In this form, he appeared as Gerome had: an unnaturally massive, but standard wolf on four legs. The huge, two-legged version she'd seen in the cabin must have been a special occasion thing, reserved for when they gobbled up helpless victims. He huffed at the second wolf, the one that had ruined everything, behind her. Smaller than the others and sleeker, its russet coat stood out from the silver and black speckled grays of its pack mates. At Curtis's chuffing command, she supposed, the red wolf lowered its head, stalked back into the trees, and vanished.

Circling Izzy, Curtis butted her back with his head. He wanted her in the cabin, but fuck if she'd go trooping back to her prison. If he wanted her he'd have to drag her.

He had no problems with that.

Bounding in front of her, Curtis latched onto the flannel and pulled, his head low to the ground and butt high in the air. He towed her about a foot before the flannel gave out between her flailing and his teeth. Fabric ripped and she fell back in the cushion of snow, chest bared when the shirt flapped open. She cinched the garment closed and sat up, brushing her hair out of her face with a toss of her head. Curtis shook himself and went for her again. Abandoning the flannel, she shoved at his muzzle. He ducked her hand, danced back, and his mouth closed around her left arm. She froze.

Wolves didn't have hands. Curtis had grabbed her the single way he could, but Izzy didn't care. She panicked and yanked her arm from his mouth. Though he hadn't bit her, the sudden jerk raked his teeth over her flesh and he drew blood. She pulled her arm into her chest and hunched over it, glaring at him.

"If everything went the way you planned I wouldn't know about any of this, would I? Would you ever have told me? I guess it doesn't matter since I'll be dead by Sunday. Convenient for you."

Curtis's hackles rose and he barked several times before hunkering down and changing. The shift took a minute. Izzy didn't bother with escape. She couldn't see the red wolf, but she knew it watched from wherever it hid. Splayed on his back in the snow, Curtis cracked his stiff joints, stretched, and sat up. Hunching into a ball, his nose wrinkled and he gave a human growl of discomfort.

"You're not going to die," he said through his teeth. "Rapid is. The pack will protect you."

"And what about when your sick wolf is dead?" Izzy's teeth chattered and she shivered. Her clothes were soaked and the material glittered with a thin sheen of frost. "Keeping me alive might be your plan, but what about Thomas's? Do you think he'll kill me or will he make you do it?"

Curtis flinched like she'd hit him and he grabbed her. "You're not going to die. I've gone against Thomas before. If it comes to that, I'll do it again." He didn't sound sure.

"You couldn't fight him in the cabin." Izzy didn't want him close right now, but he was so warm and she was so cold.

"I was pissed off. The Alpha's power affects behavior. He can command me to stop treating you like my mate. He can't make me stop loving you."

He said it so casually Izzy wondered if he realized he'd said it. She sagged into his arms and let him lift her. Together, they returned to the cabin.

Chapter Seventeen

The living room was a disaster. Not a huge change since Rapid's attack, but now glass shards crunched underfoot and the folding chairs twisted in a modern art heap. On its side, the standing lamp cast its light across the floor and the undersides of the ruined furniture. Izzy had stepped into an old-fashioned horror show. Any moment the monster would lurch from the shadows and wrap its claws around her throat. Except the monster walked behind her and he'd been one of the best things to come along in her life in a good long while. She kept ahead of Curtis as he trailed her into his bedroom.

She mused that he might have some trouble with the door, or at least pretend to, but he twisted the knob this way and that and the lock clicked back.

"Was never very secure," Curtis said and pushed the door open. The dresser gave him negligible resistance, groaning over the wood when he shoved it out of the way. Izzy jumped when it tipped over and crashed to the floor.

Hurrying to the opposite side of the room, Izzy pressed herself into a corner and eyeballed Curtis, who picked through the mountain of jeans, socks, and T-shirts she'd emptied from the dresser. He found a pair of boxers and tugged them on before stepping into some jeans. Seeing him perform these mundane tasks after observing the change unnerved her. Something so abnormal had no right disguising itself in Fruit of the Loom and Wranglers. His nose wrinkled and he sniffed, made a face.

"Ah, Nook." Curtis frowned at the spot where the puddle had been. Scratching the back of his neck, he glanced at Izzy and his expression communicated that he had a great deal to say, but didn't. Wise of him. Anything that came out of his mouth would be lost on her. Door locks and dressers he easily bypassed. Emotional barriers didn't cave to brute strength and Izzy's were three feet of iron and steel smelted over decades of fierce competition in SAB classes, the NYCB *corps* and years of trauma recovery. Her shields were impenetrable and she'd been an idiot to drop them for him.

Curtis left the bedroom to her, but Izzy didn't move from the corner. Walls at her back felt safe. She listened to his movement through the cabin; scrapes of metal on wood, the chink of swept glass. Satisfied she'd be on her own for at least the rest of the night, she inched from her safe spot, begrudgingly threw on some of Curtis's dry clothes, and headed for the bathroom.

A stack of soap, extra TP, and cleaning chemicals crowded the cabinet under the sink. Izzy grabbed a white spray bottle of all-purpose cleaner and found a ratty pile of rags next to the snaking pipes. She might have sopped up Nook's pee, but the floor was still nasty. No way in hell she could sleep with pee residue haunting her, if sleep were an option at all.

Spritzing generously, she scrubbed the floor, tossing each rag into the small trash bin she'd toted from the bathroom once they reached saturation. Even a round in the wash wouldn't get anyone to touch those again. She'd dump them out the window like she had the towel. Cleaning settled her frazzled nerves. By the time she finished, her hands weren't shaking. Werewolves might hunger for her flesh, but there were some obstacles yet surmountable on her lonesome. The bedroom smelled chemical fresh and Nook belly-crawled from his hidey hole, scenting the lemony air.

"You have anything you want to own up to?" Izzy asked the hound.

Nook quietly wuffed at her and sneezed.

After Izzy dumped the stinking rags out the window, she yanked the chain on the overhead light and crawled under the comforter. Nook curled beside her. She was achy-tired, but sound sleep eluded her and a fuzzy not-quite-dream state prevailed. One blink ago it was night, the next blink, morning. Yellow light, not the blue-gray of dawn, knifing through the drapes painted a blinding stripe across her face. Someone tapped on the door.

"Isabelle?" Melinda called.

Rubbing her gritty eyes, Izzy swung her legs over the side of the bed. Nook grumbled and his ears flattened as he stared at the door. Melinda spoke again when Izzy didn't answer.

"I've got some of your clothes. And food."

A millisecond later Izzy stood at an opened door. In a blur of fur and paws, Nook squeezed by the pair of them and shot out the door, tail tucked between his legs.

"Glad we're in this together," Izzy called after the dog and accepted the bundle of clothes wadded around her prosthetic from the redhead. She threw them on the bed and then returned for the proffered breakfast, hugging the greasy, brown fast food sack to her chest and savoring the smell of cooked bacon, cheese, and sausage.

"Mind if I join you?" Melinda held up a matching sack and smiled a shy smile.

"Are you co-habitating with a wolf spirit?"

Melinda's head bobbed eagerly. "Nettled-Clover. You totally nailed me in the chest last night, remember?"

Izzy kicked the door shut.

"Come on." The door muffled Melinda's voice. "Don't be like that."

Don't be like that, Izzy mouthed as she rolled her eyes and slid to the floor and opened the sack warming the hollow of her crossed legs.

"I had to tackle you. Didn't mean nothing by it. Hasn't Curtis explained anything?"

"I know all about obeying the Alpha and killing some crazy-ass ex-pack mate. And what's the deal with Thomas, anyway? What is he, the Wolf King?" The image pleased Izzy in a morbid way. She pictured the Alpha decked in a cavalier's garb and golden crown. He armed himself with the fire poker and lead an army of little wolves while she cowered in her nightclothes awaiting her white knight, err, nutcracker. Wolfcracker? "Forgive me if I'm not so quick to accept you holding me hostage and sacrificing me as a means to those ends." Izzy yanked a breakfast biscuit from the bag and bit into it. Steaming hot, the meat and cheese scalded her tongue. She blew out air to cool the contents of her mouth.

"It's not like we *want* to sacrifice you. At least, not me and most definitely not Curtis. Thomas always goes into kill mode whenever he hears about a non-wolf in on wolf biz and especially with this whole Rapid thing. Gerome is Thomas's bitch-boy, so he doesn't care if you die, but he's a retard, so who gives?"

"I give," Izzy managed around a mouthful of buttery bread and meat. "I don't want to die. Can't you let me out of here and track him yourself?"

"Hunting down a pure wolf is impossible without leverage. He knows how to cover his tracks and scent. He used to be all animal, so his instincts are bad ass. Plus he's got years of human experience and intelligence, and there's his wolf's collective memory if he can get to it. We can't let him run around. He's too dangerous. But you know that."

Ghost pain ached in Izzy's incomplete arm. "Yeah."

Eating occupied the women for a time, then Melinda said, "Your brother's not the only one he killed, you know."

The bite of biscuit Izzy swallowed lodged in her throat.

"There's been at least three others we know about. More than that most like. Missing hikers and all. It's why Thomas is so gung-ho, do-whatever-it-takes to get him. Wolves are supposed to protect their territory and the people in it. We've been sucking big time. I know it doesn't mean crap to you—wouldn't to me if I was in your position—but if risking your life saves who knows how many others? I don't like it," Melinda hurriedly added, "but there are other people in the world you have to think about."

Other people aren't me and they're not my family.

What was she supposed to do? Unselfishly offer herself for the greater good? Fuck that. She crumpled the bag and wrappers and stood. Choice was the difference. Giving up her life for a larger purpose should be her choice and it wasn't. Because some crappy Werewolf pack couldn't do their job, she had to cover their ass with hers? No thanks.

Stripping, Izzy shouldered on her harness without hearing another peep from Melinda. If she were the redhead, she'd want to imagine herself noble for all this, too. Izzy wasn't ready to change into her clothes yet and put on one of Curtis's huge T-shirts and a pair of boxers.

The front door slammed and Izzy heard the deep rumble of masculine voices and thumping footfalls. Melinda's back and heels knocked the door.

"Get out front." Thomas's voice was unmistakable. Melinda's light steps skipped up the hall. Izzy expected the Alpha to kick the door in. He didn't. He opened it and leaned against the frame. Crooking his finger, he beckoned her.

An itch prickled Izzy's belly as though all the slight hairs there wriggled in their pores. The sensation compelled her forward. She resisted the compulsion, uncomfortable as that was.

Thomas sucked his cheek and unhitched from the doorframe. "Come here." He pointed at his feet.

Now all her hairs tired ripping themselves from her skin. Burning spread through her muscles and a force pulled—actually pulled—at her bones. Her foot kicked out against her will. She ended up in front of the Alpha, bile rising into her chest like acidic Kool-Aid. Thomas clamped his hand around the back of her neck and marched her into the front room. Gerome, who'd observed her humiliation from his place against the far wall, followed close behind.

Melinda was nowhere to be seen. Nook wasn't out front either, but since Curtis had brought her back to the cabin she'd noticed the front door didn't quite close anymore. The husky likely got out while the getting was good. The little troop marched to the kitchen.

Clicking his tongue, Thomas shoved Izzy into Gerome's arms. "Hold her down on the counter. We need to get this over with before Curtis gets back."

Chapter Eighteen

While Thomas had a firm grasp of her neck, Gerome's fingers bored painfully into her arms and she struggled, grunted her protest. The man wasn't a wall of muscle like his Alpha, but he anticipated her weaves and bobs and held fast, making sure she'd have a nice set of bruises on each arm shaped like his fingerprints. They'd go nicely with the red and purple splotches on her legs. He steered her into the kitchen side of the living area. Her bare feet squeaked as they skidded over the floor. When dragging them didn't slow him down she made herself dead weight, hoping he'd drop her. No such luck. Her sudden slump stooped him over, but he gathered her weight, hauled her up, and slammed her into the counter. Its sharp edge banged her hipbones. Sparks exploded in her vision and she lost her breath. Harsh fingers twisted in her hair and smashed her face to the cool Formica. Gerome ground himself against her backside. She couldn't breathe. She swung out her arm, tried clawing at him with her left hand. Snagging her wrist, he forced her arm behind her back and laughed.

"I never got Curtis's attraction, but most women look good bent over." Gerome moved his hips in a hard, slow circle over her rear. Izzy kicked one of her legs back, but couldn't land a hit.

"Enough," Thomas said. "I told you to hold her down, not sexually assault her."

Gerome eased off, released Izzy's wrist, and moved away. Air rushed into her squished lungs. She gasped as Thomas, who'd taken Gerome's place behind her, yanked out her left arm and grabbed an intimidating kitchen knife from its wooden holster by the sink. He lowered it to her arm and she squirmed, attempted to buck him.

"Keep still," Thomas said.

Izzy's thoughts were mutinous but her body submitted and she went as stiff as a lake in winter. That her thudding heart didn't rattle the appliances set on the counter astonished her. One swift slash of the blade split the long sleeve of Curtis's T-shirt. Thomas collected the fabric and cut it free of the garment. He ripped the cloth in long strips then poised the blade at her shoulder. Its tip tickled then stung when he pressed down. Blood welled at the knife's point like a crimson pearl. She whimpered.

The front door banged open. Curtis appeared next to Thomas and latched onto his hand. Grappling, he got the knife up. They must have struggled because Thomas had trouble getting his words out.

"If I have to order you to let go, she will regret it."

Curtis immediately released the Alpha. Thomas rotated his wrist, which cracked. He set the knife down and scrubbed his hand over his face.

"Do you want to do this?" He gestured at Izzy's arm.

"We don't have to," Curtis started. "Patience—"

"You want to wait for Night's-Rapid-Water to skip out of the woods and into what he knows is an ambush? The only card we have left is his bloodlust and we're playing it. You have one choice: who makes the cut."

Curtis looked from Thomas to a point behind them where, Izzy supposed, Gerome stood and laid his hand on the knife. His fingers engulfed the black handle. Izzy caught his eyes and pleaded with him silently.

Please, don't do this. Please, don't cut me. Please, don't let them do it.

Faster than Izzy followed, Curtis swept the knife off the counter and rushed Thomas. Apparently prepared for a brawl, the Alpha brought up his guard and the men locked together in a shove off. Curtis's initial blow threw Thomas, but the Alpha caught himself on the counter and quickly regained lost ground, hurling himself into his Beta, the slap of their bodies' impact like cinder blocks knocking together.

"Back down," Thomas grunted. Their strength seemed matched.

Red-faced, Curtis roared against the command. Sweat streamed down his face and he plowed forward, trying to free his arms from Thomas's without giving the other man an advantage.

"Back down!"

The instant of hesitation the order induced gave Thomas the upper hand. He cocked back his fist and decked Curtis in the face. The force of his blow dazed Curtis and the Alpha followed with two more for good measure, sending his insubordinate Beta to one knee. Blood trickled from Curtis's left nostril like a red tear.

"Dumb shit," Thomas said, panting. "Stay down." Curtis had started to rise and the instruction made him a statue. "You want to challenge me? Good luck." He slid another knife from the holster and set to work on Izzy's arm, taking his time. She shrieked when he dragged the blade over her skin, but, under the unyielding weight of his natural strength and unnatural power, she couldn't fight. Thomas's body blocked her view of Curtis and if he reacted, she didn't see it.

Besides pain, Izzy felt the awful sensation of her skin opening under the knife. Sliced from shoulder to elbow, she tried very hard not to think of freshly cut steak. Hot blood seeped from the wound and wept over her arm. The room spun and nausea weighted her belly and made her mouth water. If she'd been on her feet she would have collapsed.

Tossing the red-stained knife into the sink, Thomas gathered the cotton strips Curtis had scattered when he knocked away the first blade. He pressed each strip to Izzy's wound and soaked up her blood.

"Idiot pup," Thomas muttered. "You think you could handle the lodge, this pack, on your own? We wouldn't be doing any of this shit now if you'd done the right thing back then."

The T-shirt strips sagged in a soggy clump next to Izzy's face. Their warmth glanced her cheek and she smelled her blood. Why couldn't she shut her eyes?

"If you had let Rapid take her that day on the trail, we could have had him. It would have been two bodies instead of two dozen, but you had to charge in like a fucking half-cocked hero—" Thomas growled and Izzy felt the beast writhe inside him. He squeezed her arm so hard her bones creaked and she cried out. Slowly, his grip loosened. "She was half gone already. You should have let Rapid have her." Thomas bent over her and his lips brushed her ear. "He didn't fight near as hard for your brother." He slopped the bloodied strips into his big hands and left the counter.

Curtis hadn't moved. On his knees, he stared straight ahead, his eyes burning amber. Other than the twitch of his lips he was still.

"Both of you get up and come over here," Thomas said.

Bereft of the Alpha's attention, Izzy slid from the counter and sank to her knees. Her throbbing arm was hot and swollen and her guts seized. She tried standing but her legs wouldn't cooperate and she collapsed onto the floor, cheek against the wood. Her brain wouldn't work right. Thoughts stuttered then leapt into bizarre trains of unrelated images, memories. One memory stuck, played over and over like a skipping record. Little Izzy sat, lips pouted, in front of her white whicker vanity, her father behind her with a soft bristled brush in hand. He passed the brush in the barest whisper over her hair, afraid he'd hurt her if he pulled too hard. It made no sense, but that's what she thought.

Alan's dead. It doesn't make any sense.

What role had Curtis played in her brother's fate?

Izzy followed the movement of feet along the floor. Before her were three sets of legs. The set facing her belonged to Thomas. The two facing away were Gerome's and Curtis's. She studied the heels of Curtis's work boots while Thomas doled out orders to his troops.

"Split these up between the three of you and spread them as far as you can."

Gerome whooped. "Chummin'. We're fuckin' chummin'."

Thomas ignored the interruption. "When you catch Rapid's scent, close ranks and flush him out. Isabelle and I will be waiting for him."

Chapter Nineteen

The pack, minus their Alpha, assembled at the mouth of the trail to Rock Spout Falls.

"You should have seen it. He *attacked* him. No way Thomas keeps him Beta after we're through." Gerome puffed out his chest and dumped some of the saturated cloth into Melinda's outstretched hands. She kept glancing over at Curtis, but she couldn't hide how the blood entranced her. Fresh blood for someone as enmeshed with her wolf as Melinda was a powerful stimulant. Her tongue swept her lips, which reddened and plumped when she flushed. The reaction was highly carnal. Curtis observed her inner struggle from his dispassionate state and a remote part of him heartened when woman conquered animal.

"You attacked Thomas?" she asked him, her voice small and careful.

Curtis almost couldn't answer. Too many conflicting emotions and concerns rushed just below his lofty detachment. Anticipation of the hunt had Clear-Skies dancing in his chest, his wolf snapping for release since his fight with Thomas. Mingled with animal excitement were a hundred worries for Izzy, rage that she'd been hurt on Thomas's watch—

Our watch, Clear-Skies snarled.

—that she knew he hadn't intervened while Rapid killed her brother. He'd had no choice. She had to know that after being subjected to the Alpha's power. Breaking free of it for her sake that awful afternoon almost hadn't happened, and he didn't think he'd ever felt pain as acute as that since. All his appendages were left intact, but his connection to the pack—a tangible, spiritual bond generated and tempered by the Alpha—had been damaged. He'd literally ripped himself from them when he went against Thomas and since then he could not tap their collective spiritual strength to bolster his own. He could have used a dose of that strength now. Functioning with all that doubt, guilt, and festering self-hatred that tossed the lower range of his thoughts in turmoil wouldn't fly. If he couldn't get it together, he placed his pack mates in danger. An absent Alpha meant the Beta took charge and here he was letting Gerome strut around like he had a chance at clawing over Curtis in rank.

"What he's doing is wrong," Curtis said, trembling with the effort it took to speak and control his wolf at the same time. "An Alpha is not just the leader of the pack. They're the heart of it. Thomas has lost sight of that. Maybe he never saw it."

Approaching his Beta with a portion of the cloth lures, Gerome snorted, said, "You're just pissed Thomas snatched your little chew toy. You'd better hope all he does is let Rapid rip her apart."

The lures exploded out of Gerome's hands when Curtis rammed into him like a linebacker. Making up in quickness what he lacked in strength, Gerome slipped Curtis's tackle and tried scrambling up. Trust the little shit to provide the focus Curtis badly needed. He leapt and caught the subordinate wolf and smashed Gerome face down in the grit-soiled snow. Using his pack mate's body for support, Curtis clambered up and straddled Gerome's legs. Fisting his hand in the man's hair, he pushed down. Smothering him briefly tempted Curtis, but they needed the other wolf for the hunt. Frantic moans and grunts accompanied Gerome's floundering. Curtis didn't let up. He slammed one knee into Gerome's nuts and his pack mate went floppy. Yanking up Gerome's head, Curtis came cheek to cheek with him.

"Here's what you'd better hope: you'd better hope when I ask Izzy what you did to her, it doesn't piss me off. I don't like where I'm picking up her scent on you. You'd better hope this plan works because if you hurt her for nothing, you'll be dealing with me on top of Thomas. And you'd better hope come tomorrow Thomas is still Alpha because if he's not, you'd better run. Got me?"

Gerome spluttered and choked on whatever slush he'd undoubtedly inhaled, but didn't convey anything like an answer. Curtis drove his knee upward and the man wailed.

"I didn't catch that," Curtis said.

"I've got you. I've fucking got you, so get the fuck off. You're going to pop my goddamned balls."

"Impossible when you've yet to grow a pair," Melinda quipped. She stood very still on the sidelines. Battle lust sparkled in her steely eyes. All their Wolves slavered for freedom. They needed direction.

Curtis cast Gerome aside and jumped up. Assessing their surroundings, he laid down the law.

"Pick all this shit up, Gerome." One his hands and knees, Gerome scowled over his shoulder at Curtis, but didn't argue. "Hang it from the trees, bushes, wherever, and keep east." Curtis faced Melinda. "You know what to do."

Lin dipped her head in acknowledgement of the non-question and shot off to the west. Keeping his eyes on Gerome while the subordinate wolf scuttled off, Curtis finally gave himself over to Clear-Skies and they ascended to their largest form. One thing he knew for certain: the old pack was no more. What he didn't know? If he could forge new bonds and lead whoever didn't end up dead.

Chapter Twenty

Anger burned through Izzy's fear like sun through early morning fog. Anger brought clarity, stability, and determination. She sat in the center of the cabin's front room and seethed. The cuts Thomas made—he'd sliced her other arm after Gerome and Curtis had left to mark the porch with her smell—were painful, but shallow. Terror had aggrandized her perception while face down on the kitchen counter. What had felt like a flaying slash was, in reality, a relatively neat incision. Considerate of the Alpha. She sneered at the man stationed beyond the open front door.

Outside, Thomas braced his hands on the wood beams framing the porch steps. Every so often his head snapped in one direction before he relaxed and continued his surveillance. Werewolf senses seemed preternaturally keen in or out of wolf form. Once, when the Alpha had left the porch to make a perimeter of the cabin, Izzy had shifted, uncrossing and re-crossing her pins-and-needles plagued legs, and Thomas had appeared in the doorway, scowling at her. She didn't think he'd been anywhere near the cabin's front and the floorboards hadn't complained with the repositioning of her weight, but he'd heard. Since he was there, she'd requested use of the bathroom, which he'd granted. He did not, however, grant her use of a sweater or pants. Blue with cold, her fingers and toes numbed, smarting when she tweaked or flexed them. Her extremities mottled with a tracery of red webbing, alligator skin, her mother called it.

If Rapid doesn't come soon I'll die of exposure. Izzy listened to the click-clickety-click of her chattering teeth. She curled into a tight ball. Nothing she did stopped her shivering. Without a fire or space heater and the front door wide open, the cabin had turned into an icebox. Her core froze and everywhere that wasn't cut or battered (or completely numbed) ached bone deep. What she wouldn't give for Nook's warm fur.

Or Curtis's.

Izzy giggled, the laughter as uncontrollable as her shaking. Thomas hissed for her silence and, while her hysterics quieted, her throat and gut spasmed with painful mirth that eventually subsided. All her feelings for Curtis hadn't diminished with her rage, they had complicated. Everything was a mess. The soft pink glow of her compassion and care and desire for him tangled in a mass of strangling, black briars. How could she still care about him? He'd lied to her, set her up. He'd let Alan die.

Orders, Izzy. He was under orders.

Yet somehow, Curtis had surmounted the smothering weight that now bore down on her vocal chords. She could not best Thomas's will, and trying hurt. Force, like creeper vines, constricted about her throat when she attempted speech. She leveled a fierce gaze at the pack leader. Because of him, her brother was dead. Curtis wouldn't have used an innocent man's life as a strategic chip in battle. If Curtis had been Alpha B.A., he wouldn't have ordered Alan's death.

Would a competent pack leader rely so heavily on the spiritual leashes binding his pack to himself? Didn't a good leader encourage loyalty and autonomy? Thomas didn't deserve the power he wielded and if Izzy got the chance, she'd take it from him. Exactly how she'd accomplish that feat she didn't know, but plotting her revenge kept her mind off the cold and the bloodthirsty wolf bent on swallowing her whole.

The sky was pink and orange before the first, faint howl carried on the still air.

On alert, Thomas craned his neck and stared westward. Rosy light skimmed his profile. The rest of his body, like the porch, was shadow. A second howl joined the first, then a third. Izzy's heart knocked her sternum on its way to her throat. They were coming.

Howling broke into barks and snarls. They were close, very close, if Izzy could hear that. Porch-side, Thomas peeled off the first of his clothes when a high-pitched yelp cut off the vocal posturing.

"Shit." He jumped out of his pants, kicked off his shoes, and changed. Izzy hoped it hurt like hell. Hoped he never got used to the pain. He stalked inside the cabin on all fours in his largest form, his coat the same black banded gray as Gerome's. White breath plumed from his black nose and his hackles rose. Pausing as he passed Izzy, he sniffed at her scabbed over left arm now chapped with cold, and terribly itchy. A swipe of his paw knocked her down and opened fresh slashes in her skin, drew blood.

A ragged scream ripped from Izzy's lips. The Alpha's control over her voice had lifted with the alteration of his form. She made a mental note of that and nursed her battered arm, heedless of the pain her jointed fingers caused. Her prosthetic hand came away red and tacky.

"Fucker," she said and bared her teeth at the massive wolf, who paid her no mind. He occupied himself licking her blood from his fur and claws. Pacing to the back hall, he went up on his hind legs and hid himself in the shadows. From the forest's direction, the crackle and snap of branches and a pattering gallop over the icy dunes signaled Rapid's approach.

Darkness, not a wolf, shot over the blue shadowed snow. At top speed, Rapid was a black blur of teeth and fur. He was so swift Izzy didn't have time to shriek when he bolted through the cabin door and shot straight for her. Not until Curtis crashed down on top of him, landing the mad wolf inches from her reddened and prickling toes, did she claim the wherewithal to cry out. Rapid snapped at her feet, confounded by the silver wolf sprawled astride his back. Stringy ropes of saliva looped and flew from the black wolf's jaws.

Izzy crab-scuttled away from the brawling pair and her flight fed Rapid's frenzy. He rolled beneath Curtis, bucking the silver wolf from his seat. A sharp kick of his hind legs caught Curtis's jaw and chest and tossed him back. The silver wolf crash landed near the open door and did not get up.

"Curtis!" Izzy screamed.

Regaining his footing, Rapid made a speedy appraisal of the living area and found his prey. He leapt at Izzy and—while her brain screamed *no, no, no!*—her body reacted. Shooting up, her right arm blocked what little it could of her face and upper body. Rapid knocked her flat. Back and skull cracked against the hardwood floor and flashes of green and pink exploded across her vision. She bit her tongue, tasted copper. The black wolf bit into her fake arm and yanked at it. Straps from her harness twisted and pulled, pinching her breasts, lifting her off the floor. Jaws crushed her prosthetic. Plastic shards pelted her cheeks and shoulders. Again she stared, transfixed by those same yellow eyes from her past. A curious calm descended upon her with the understanding that this moment might be her last. She observed the scene of her death with a clinical detachment.

Above Izzy, Rapid mangled her prosthetic, teeth grinding the steel skeleton housed in silicone-sheathed plastic. The metal armature squealed when it bent out of shape. She dropped her head back. Thomas towered behind her from the cover of the hallway, features serene as he oversaw the inevitable carnage, majestic as a king.

Had he watched Alan's death as he watched hers? She railed at his indifference. She wouldn't die. He couldn't order her to give up. She would get out of this and when she did, somehow, Thomas would pay. Thoughts of vengeance rolled through her brain like storm clouds when Night's-Rapid-Water started dragging her.

Ruined prosthetic clenched in his jaws, Rapid spun Izzy around on her back—her feet now pointing toward the bedroom hall—as he retreated to the front door. Her T-shirt, the collar strangling her, rucked up and the floorboards chafed her back. Her boxers caught on an old nail and tore. She had to slow him down, but there was nothing to grab. She had to get out of her harness.

Izzy had mastered the art of one-handed life, and she snaked her left hand under her shirt and found the fasteners first at her shoulder, then at her chest. Her deadened fingers worked the plastic buckles with practiced efficiency. At once, she came free and, unprepared for the abrupt loss of resistance, Rapid stumbled. Like a stretched rubber band, the harness snapped back and blinded him, its black back pad and straps smacking his face.

As Izzy scooted to the kitchen counter, Curtis, struck dumb by Rapid's kick, came to and flew up from his crumpled position. He careened into his ex-pack mate's side and knocked him over. Finally taking action, Thomas charged from the hall and joined his Beta in combat.

Back against the cabinets, Izzy intended to clamber up and swipe a knife from the counter, but a freezing line of metal butted her backside and distracted her. She discovered the fire poker sandwiched in a gap between counter and floor. Rolling out the poker, she clutched it, eyes darting to the writhing pile of muscle and dark fur in front of the wrecked sofa and to the two wolves stalking the felled beast they used to call friend. The floor bowed under their collective weight as the pair converged on their prey.

For all his speed, Rapid couldn't match the strength of Alpha and Beta. The Clydesdale-sized wolf seemed to intuit this and bolted. Rapid barreled through his former pack mates, yipping when Curtis's claws raked over his backside. The Beta's stunted lunge couldn't prevent the mad wolf's escape, but Curtis wouldn't give up. He loped after Rapid. The sprinting pair tossed up bits of the TV and disemboweled sofa stuffing as they fled the cabin. Izzy had survived her third encounter with Rapid. In the middle of her exhalation, a feral grunt reminded her she wasn't alone. The Alpha now had her all to himself.

Chapter Twenty-one

Thomas didn't come for Izzy right away. He waited, one ear cocked toward the door. She watched him, numb fingers squeezing the fire poker that rested heavy against her thighs. This wasn't over. Rapid was supposed to gobble her up. Maybe Thomas thought his old pack mate would make her death quick, devour her on the spot with the scent of her blood driving him like a drug. The Alpha hadn't considered whatever higher logic Rapid had cultivated during his human years would surpass the ravening predator's instinct. The wolf, though mad, had understood his vulnerable position in the cabin and had tried dragging her away. Perhaps he'd wanted to get her to a safe spot, a dark hole where his feast wouldn't be interrupted. Curtis had put a stop to that and had thwarted Thomas's efforts to keep his claws relatively clean. She knew the Alpha wouldn't let her go, so she wasn't surprised when he started across the devastated front room.

Using the poker as a cane, Izzy pushed herself standing and brandished the iron rod at the Werewolf in a shaking hand. Unlike Rapid, Thomas was in no hurry, but she knew he would catch her if she ran. No point in running. No point in fighting really, other than pride and no wolf could tear that from her, so she stood her ground. A silent prayer flitted through her mind for her parents and a slimy, slithery thing like a gob of congealed blood hawked up her throat when she said, "Fuck you." That gelatinous thing invisibly leapt from her mouth with her curse. A power all her own struck Thomas center mass and the wolf halted, tilting his head and sniffing. Formidable wills weren't regulated to the spirit possessed, it seemed, and he didn't come any closer. A foot away from her, he reached out a massive, splayed paw and she swung her weapon with all the strength she had.

The poker clipped Thomas's paw and banged his flank. Reverberations from the blow traveled up Izzy's arm and her aching fingers throbbed. It was all she could do to hold onto the rod. She'd likely hurt herself more than she'd hurt him. Growling his agitation, the Alpha knocked the poker from her and his left paw engulfed her throat.

*

The fight ended in a blink at the edge of the forest, finished with a snap of bones and a spray of blood. Flopped at Curtis's paws, Rapid's body shrank to its normal size, head kinked at an awful angle, tongue hanging slack from his parted jaws.

Enemy. Stop enemy. Must return. Must.

Curtis's jaws latched onto Rapid's neck. Steaming blood ran over his tongue and down his throat. He thrashed the body back and forth, creating a pit in the snow. Their enemy was dead. Still, Clear-Skies slavered for combat. From within his unleashed wolf, Curtis's view of the world came from the wrong end of a telescope, everything faraway and convexly distorted. The wolf acted upon the world and he was the guiding conscience, a brilliant mote of white light buried under two hundred and seventy pounds of muscle and fur. It was warm in his wolf body. It was safe.

Briefly, Curtis considered Rapid. The wolf, despite what became of him, deserved a better resting place than a shallow space swept in the snow. Going soft upstairs hadn't been his fault. But Curtis didn't have time for respect. One threat was gone. Another remained. He and the Alpha had unfinished business.

Kicking snow over the corpse, Curtis howled a warning to Melinda to stay away, to tend to Gerome. Rapid had all but gutted the weasel and he'd need all his strength if he wanted to outrun Curtis. When he finished his battles, no evil—and he considered Thomas and Gerome evil—would walk his land ever again. He'd be sure of it.

With a yipping bark, Curtis tossed up a spray of powder as he galloped from the forest, the yellow light from his cabin's front door a marker, a beacon drawing him to the final stand.

*

Thomas's clawed fingers constricted. Izzy scratched at the Alpha's arm and kicked as he squeezed. Her body needed air her gaping mouth couldn't suck down. Delicate bones in her throat and her windpipe would soon snap and collapse and her head would hang like a lead weight pinched off in a tube sock. Something acidic flushed her nasal cavity. Cold air stung her dry, bulging eyes. Dark spots blotched her sight of the Alpha. A high whine whistling in her ears almost obliterated a distant howl lilting like a dirge.

A violent jerk jostled Thomas to the left and he dropped Izzy. She fell to her knees. Gulping air, she soothed her parched lungs and lurch-crawled to the kitchen counter, barely dodging the bulk of Alpha and Beta as they warred overhead. Curtis had sunk his fangs into Thomas's shoulder. He drove his leader toward the ruins of sofa and flat-screen, raking the Alpha's back and sides with his claws before Thomas retaliated.

Izzy wasn't safe where she was and scrambled for the far corner of the cabin closest the fireplace, retrieving the fire poker just as the Alpha reached overhead and caught Curtis by the shoulders. Doubling over, he flipped his Beta forward, roaring when the hunk of fur matted flesh his Beta had latched onto tore from his shoulder. Slamming into the wall, Curtis crashed down head first. He rolled over, spat out the piece of Thomas he'd brought with him, and advanced on the gray wolf, evaluating his injuries. The Alpha wouldn't be taken by surprise. Snapping to attention, he threw himself at Curtis as the Beta sprang and they slammed together like two wrecking balls, hard muscled flesh smacking flesh. Locked in a grappling shove off, their hind paws slid over the floor as each strove for the upper hand.

Thomas lost ground.

Weakened from their fight with Rapid and caught off guard by Curtis's initial attack, he faltered against his Beta's strength. Rallying, he tossed his head back and bayed, releasing a blast of power. The silver wolf's muscles jumped and his fur bristled. His forward drive stalled and his amber eyes flared. The howling went on and Izzy saw it pained Curtis. She also saw him resist the Alpha's will, muscles cording, fangs gleaming, and foaming spittle collecting at the corners of his jaws. They were at a standstill.

Izzy, motionless in the corner, recognized her chance. If she meant to escape, she had to go now. She dashed for the unguarded front door, keeping an eye on the combating wolves. Neither was distracted by her flight and she passed through the threshold unmolested. Snow-covered lawn stretched before her to the black ribbon of paved road beyond and she was next to naked. Her lips pouted in determination. Frostbite was better than being eaten. When her bare foot hit the first porch step, a squeaking yelp from the cabin zinged up her spine. Reflexively, she turned.

*

A human shaped shadow flitted in Curtis's peripheral vision. Had to be Izzy. If nothing else came of this battle, she, at least, could flee. With Clear-Skies's strength and speed, he had thought to take Thomas down in one blow, but he'd held his wolf back when saw Izzy thrashing in the Alpha's grip. That recalculation had cost him. He'd wasted the element of surprise and gave Thomas time to regroup, to strategize, just what the old wolf did best. Of course, the Alpha had played his trump card and had blasted Curtis with the full force of his will.

Thomas's power over Curtis wasn't what it used to be, but it was enough. The howled command to back down wore at his resolve like the tide smoothed a stone. His wolf body trembled under the pressure and he had no pack of his own to call on for backup.

Howling for Lin and Nettled-Clover would only aid Thomas. The Alpha could control many individuals at once. Curtis was ignorant as to how and if he couldn't call up more strength, he'd never know. He was losing.

Cannot lose. Cannot. We are stronger. We are better!

Clear-Skies shook all around Curtis. His wolf arms buckled and his legs gave out. Confident of his Beta's defeat, Thomas had guarded against losing his balance and swept Curtis around, flinging him on his back. The Alpha did not hesitate. His jaws fastened onto Curtis's neck and his razor clawed forepaws ripped down his exposed belly.

Curtis yelped at the blinding pain.

*

Izzy couldn't run. Thomas had Curtis pinned and squirming on his back. The Alpha's broad backside obscured most of the silver wolf, but black blood pooled on the floor. Was it Alpha's or Beta's? She couldn't tell, but she knew Thomas didn't intend to mete out punishment. Curtis had crossed him three times for her sake and, judging from the squeaking growls Curtis uttered, she didn't think Thomas meant him to survive. At the claws of the Wolf King, Curtis would die.

No!

Starting back inside, Izzy hesitated. What could she possibly do? She couldn't fight a wolf and win. One flick of Thomas's wrist and her neck would snap. She had to think fast. While the Wolf King was strong, she was clever. Her sightline fell to the shoes at her feet, human trappings the Alpha had discarded when he'd changed. She didn't have to beat Thomas. All she had to do was distract him. Curtis could handle the rest.

Tucking the fire poker under her right arm, Izzy hefted one of Thomas's boots in her left hand and chucked it at him. She missed, barely grazing his leg. She hooked her fingers in the second boot's mouth, aimed, and pitched it at the Alpha's head. It clobbered him.

He snarled and whipped around, his muzzle glistening black. She balked and the hasty retreat triggered the wolf's lust for the chase. For the barest instant, she spied Curtis pitifully sprawled on the floor. His chest wasn't moving.

Not again. This can't happen again.

First Alan, now Curtis. Then Rapid, now Thomas. This was the part where Izzy fell to the wolf, but there was no one else to save her. She'd have to save herself.

Abandoning his lifeless Beta on the floor, Thomas loped toward Izzy, who drew her poker like a rapier and leapt back, heels skidding on the icy first step. She lost her footing and her stomach dropped with the downward pull of gravity. Arms pin-wheeling, she fell as Thomas rocketed into the air. Snow cushioned her fall, swallowing her like a frigid cloud. She still had the wind knocked from her and the drift slowed her down. She couldn't get up. The Alpha landed on top of her, his muscled arms bracketing her face, his hindquarters boxing her legs. His stinking breath steamed her face when his jaws opened.

Poised for the killing strike, the Alpha seized and choked gurgling rattled from his throat. He spluttered. Blood spattered Izzy's face and stippled the white snow. Wet warmth coated her hands like heated syrup and soaked her T-shirt and boxers. She looked down.

The fire poker stuck up like a lightning rod in her hand and Thomas had landed on it. It skewered his belly and he bled out, steaming ichors dissolving the snow. She couldn't take her eyes from what she'd done. She hadn't meant to. She'd only wanted to give Curtis time, space to end fight. She'd only wanted to defend herself.

Though badly wounded, the Alpha wasn't down yet. He lunged for Izzy's neck and she shrieked, shrinking further into the freezing carpet, eyes squinching shut. A sound like cracking ice made them snap open. She wished she'd kept them closed.

Curtis's hands were clamped around Thomas's head, which he'd twisted further than it was meant. With one last jerk, he pitched the Alpha off Izzy. The fire poker was pulled from her weak grasp, firmly tangled in the gray wolf's guts.

Prone in the snow, Izzy stared up at the silver wolf. Claw marks raked his chest and belly. His muzzle and fur was stained and matted with gore. He heaved out a smoky breath that blew back her bangs and lowered his head.

The Alpha was dead.

Chapter Twenty-two

Curtis changed.

In human form, his torn flesh already knitted together. If Izzy unfocused her eyes, she thought she saw tongues of blue light darting from his wounds, alchemizing the healing process, but that couldn't be. All that remained of the slashes across his face and torso were dark, raised scars. She wasn't so fortunate. She ached everywhere she'd been cut or bruised. Swallowing hurt. Her throat felt puffed up like she had the worst case of strep throat. She sat up and found herself at the center of an enormous Rorschach blot. All around her, the Alpha's blood had spread and stained the snow. Dazed, she turned her head in the direction of the body. There was a bare, human foot.

A firm hand captured Izzy's chin. Curtis made her face him, his fiery amber eyes still bright with feral luminescence.

"Don't look." Long and pointed, his canines dropped from the straight line of white teeth and his voice came out as a half-growl. Unable to maintain eye contact, Izzy stared at his bare chest, then lower. Below his waist, his stiff cock curved up to his belly.

Izzy's tongue passed over her top lip. "We killed him."

"We had to and we have to get inside."

"I don't think I can stand."

"That's all right."

Curtis got to his feet first and offered his hand. Izzy wobbled up without his help. She'd done something to her ankle. It wasn't broken, but walking pained her and the skin there stretched tight with fluid. Hobbling the few feet to the porch steps drained her and she gripped the railing. She had to recharge for the less than monumental climb. Whether concerned or impatient she didn't know, but Curtis came behind her and scooped her into his arms, careful to block her view of the lawn. Chivalry was welcome even though she could have made it inside without help.

Exposed to the elements all day, the cabin's inside was as cold as the outdoors. Icicles could have hung from the ceiling. Little piles of snow gathered in the corners of the cabin's entrance. Shutting the door with his foot—he kicked it three times before it stayed closed—Curtis paid the shambles of his front room no attention. He carried Izzy to the bathroom and set her down, leaving her for a short time. As she pulled off her blood-stiffened clothes, she heard the bedroom door click shut. By the time Curtis returned she was naked and picking the caked gore from her fingers like old, cracked scabs. Blood flaked onto the white tile and speckled her bare feet, which were little more than mottled slabs of frozen meat. Looking at them made her ill, so she looked at Curtis instead.

Curtis stared at her, amber eyes ablaze. Under his alien scrutiny, she felt hunted and vulnerable. She held still when he advanced. He stopped himself. At the sight of her, his cock twitched and he clenched his fists.

"I want you now," he growled out.

*

When Curtis had snapped Thomas's neck, he'd felt nothing. Not horror at what he'd done or any sort of power rush save the fight's adrenaline pumping through him. He'd had no idea if the Alpha's mantle had passed to him until this instant.

Clear-Skies wouldn't stay quiet and tucked away in his regular flame form near Curtis's heart. The wolf stretched under his skin like a translucent membrane, giddy with triumph and eager to exercise their increased dominance.

Mate. Izzy. Mate.

The wolf's instincts tangled with Curtis's desire, already running hot from the hunt and his victories in battle, and it was too much;

Izzy standing there bare and hurt and bloody and the smell of Thomas and Gerome and Rapid on her and her brown eyes wide and fearful. He wanted her so bad he hurt and her fear heightened his lust. Was that Clear-Skies's instinct or a shadowy sliver of himself swimming up from the depths of his soul? Was there a difference? There had to be, but he couldn't compartmentalize his wolf and Izzy transfixed them both.

"I want you now," he said, then it happened.

A flash of force like a small, ghostly hand pushing off his spine and zipping out from his gut had chased the last of his half-snarled words. He'd felt this new appendage strike Izzy and he hadn't drawn it back in, couldn't. Until she'd obeyed him, he'd had no clue what the sensation was. When she bent over the sink and displayed her back side at his demand, her upturned and split sex shiny with need, he knew he'd inherited the Alpha's power.

A metric ton of responsibility shackled itself to Curtis's neck and he bowed his head.

*

Near the sink, Izzy grasped the porcelain edge and bent over. She canted up her rear, offering herself to Curtis. She didn't think about doing this, she simply did it, her body responding to his whim. Body heat warmed her bottom and thighs when he came close. Callused hands stroked her back and his cock nudged between her legs, sliding up the cleft of her ass. Her heart pounded. His fingers dug into her hips when he resisted her invitation.

"Tell me if you want this." The harsh edge of Curtis's voice softened.

Izzy ached for him, but she was afraid. Why had she reacted this way? How could she be wet for him after they'd done what they'd done? Anger, fear, satisfaction at Thomas's death, and revulsion that his death pleased her, became confused with this need for Curtis that had suddenly flared inside her when she'd watched him transform. She thought she might throw up. Thomas and Rapid, her brother's killers, were dead. She and Curtis were alive. Knowing wasn't enough. The solidity of his body would assure her. She needed it, needed the nova of pleasure exploding between them, making them definite, re-affirming their frayed bond. Pleasure would banish these awful feelings, this sickness rolling in her stomach and tossing her head like a little buoy, wouldn't it?

"I don't know," she whispered into the drain.

Curtis snaked an arm around her chest and lifted her. He braced her against him and she felt his face in her hair.

"Later then," he said and moved away.

Curtis got the shower going. Since he'd come to her rescue last night, they'd been at odds. Secrets, his feral nature and kin, had eclipsed what she supposed she knew of him. He'd become a stranger again. Deception had been a sucker punch when, with him, she'd felt so at home. But what he was hadn't changed who he was, had it? Hadn't he proved that? Back muscles bunched while he worked at the tub and she padded behind him, placed her one hand between his shoulder blades.

The touch startled Curtis and he spun around. "No. Over there." The order came close to a series of barks, near unintelligible. He pointed at the toilet and she went without question or hesitation, plopping on top of the lowered seat.

What had happened to the will that gave the former Alpha pause? Curtis commanded and she obeyed, just as she had with Thomas. But the Alpha was dead, his power gone. Unless it passed to someone else.

Izzy forced herself to her feet, testing the theory formulating in her brain. Familiar compulsion traveled up her legs in a prickling wave that made her teeth itch. This was the Alpha's power and she didn't have the energy for rebellion. She sat down.

Curtis observed her reaction. A frown pinched his features. Twisting his back to her, he tested the jetting spray then held out his dry left hand.

"Will you come?" he asked, voice gentle.

Izzy awaited the inevitable urge to capitulate and catapult to his side. She didn't feel it. Her body stayed hers. He'd asked her to come, not told or suggested. Watching him warily, she rose and stepped into his waiting arm and he ushered her into the shower.

Tepid water shocked Izzy's frozen body. She hollered when the spray hit her, jolting numbed aches and pains to life. Biting her lip, she let the water wash over her and curled her pain-gnawed fingers and toes. Filthy water circled the burbling drain. Textured cloth brushed her back like a tongue and Curtis's spicy soap scented the steadily warming room. She leaned into the hand at the small of her back and winced when the soapy rag touched her slashed arm. The warm water already stung, but the soap lit her wounds like a trough of gasoline. She stifled the cry struggling to escape her lips. Bowing out of the spray, she took the rag from Curtis as they switched places and gingerly sponged around all her hurts.

Water sheeted over Curtis's back and buttocks and his tanned skin gleamed. All his wounds had healed. He slicked back his soaked hair, rubbed the green cake of soap over his scalp and chest. He lathered every inch of his body, palmed his groin, and rinsed himself. Izzy joined him under the showerhead, cradling his backside with her body. When she circled her arms around him, her breasts squashed against his back.

Passing over the bump and ridge of muscle, Izzy's fingers traveled down Curtis's abdomen, found, then stroked his rigid cock. A satisfied growl rumbled in his chest and his head fell back. Releasing him, her hand ventured lower. She cupped and hefted the heavy weight of his balls and gently squeezed as she pressed her open mouth to his back.

Disentangling himself, Curtis whipped around and ensnared Izzy's waist. His mouth came down hard on hers and his pointed canines gazed her lips. The low rumbling in his chest vibrated against her body, which was flush with his.

Had she made a mistake inciting his passion? She wanted Curtis, not the strange creature riding his body. Was there a difference? As his teeth scraped her jaw and his tongue flicked at the scalloped edge of her ear, she couldn't bring herself to care. She needed him—this—now. What he was, what they'd done, didn't matter. Not now.

Izzy guided Curtis back to her lips when he strayed too far to her bruised neck. He wrangled out of her handhold and backed her up with his bulk. Indelicate hands kneaded her ass and locked her hips against his ready erection. One hand moved and squeezed her right arm and she hissed around his kiss. Pain ripped though her shoulder and she pushed at him, drove them apart. She nursed her burning arm. Half under the lukewarm spray, water dripped from her hair into her face, blurring Cutis's form. The feral light in his eyes dimmed. Turning, he shut off the water.

*

A new power Curtis knew nothing about and couldn't control was the last thing he needed. He didn't need a reminder of how tenuous his control could become. When Izzy had locked herself in his room, barring his entrance, he'd almost lost it. The pack's turmoil, his helplessness, and the threat to the woman he protected had fed his wolf's frenzy. The need to dominate had threatened to consume him. If he would have forced himself on Izzy . . . he shook his head. That would never happen. The moment his inner animal had reduced him to that point, he'd fought back, asserted his humanity. Thomas was gone. So was Rapid. He'd soon deal with Gerome. With all threats eliminated, his inner beast couldn't snap through its restraints. If Clear-Skies tried, Curtis would master the spirit as he had when he first inherited his wolf. He could do anything for Izzy.

Tilting back his head, he let water from the dripping showerhead pat his crown. Clear-Skies simmered and bubbled just beneath the surface. The wolf hadn't retreated, but Curtis had stopped fighting him. He let the spirit hover like a secondary skin, explored where he ended and the wolf began, where they'd grown inseparable. Two beings, one body. Beyond their mingled vapors, buried in the depths of Curtis's belly lay the Alpha's power, a reddened coal, a glowing and un-tempered blade.

Declarations quickened the power. Curtis had felt it again when he'd told Izzy to get away from him—his restraint had depended on a generous swath of personal space—but the mechanics of the power had mystified him.

In the shower, with the rush of water in his ears, he began to comprehend. The Alpha's power had linked him somehow to Izzy. It forced an inarguable bond. He'd reached out with this new sense and had felt it pulling from his back like a glistening sinew. Reaching further, he'd felt Izzy's essence, her soul white and brilliant as his own, but clouded, surrounded by a thatch of curled and thorny blackness. The vision had cut out when Izzy had touched him, but he'd welcomed it, had let his hungers rise up and take him. Desire had trampled his better judgment.

Curtis balled his fists. Balance, he knew, was possible. He'd search it out. With practice, he'd find away around triggering the power or make it less of a slug with a baseball bat and more the fine cut of a scalpel.

Argh.

Thinking about scalpels conjured an image of Izzy helpless while Thomas cut her and Curtis on his knees, powerless at the former Alpha's side, a prisoner of his own long-standing cowardice.

There. He'd admitted it. But never out loud.

When Curtis's dad had passed, his inheritance had terrified him. Not the land or the lodge, but the wolf and the pack. Allowing Thomas to assume part of that burden had relieved him. He had sidestepped the perks and responsibility the role of Alpha bestowed. Boy, had that come back to bite his ass.

Curtis faced Izzy. Until he understood this power, he'd stick with questions, not demands. Reaching out, he pushed her plastered bangs from her eyes, then stretched and yanked a towel from the rack near the toilet. Arms raised, she let him wrap the terrycloth around her and drip dried while he stepped from the tub and patted himself off. When he crouched in front of the sink—he knew a first-aid kit hid somewhere under there—she took his place on the soggy bath mat and carefully buffed herself. Like an egret, she went on one leg, giving her swelling ankle some rest.

Curtis went to her, gauze and tape, cotton balls and disinfectant in hand. He concentrated on her face, but her hard and rosy nipples distracted him, the sensitive areolas surrounding them puckered with cold and arousal. The scent of her desire permeated the room like the soapy perfume carried on the lingering steam. His cock stirred and he swallowed. Clear-Skies tightened over his muscle and bone, infusing them, bringing Curtis's beast forth. The animal *now-now-now* of the wolf's mating drive made him grit his teeth.

Control. Balance. You are not the wolf. The wolf is part of you.

The inner mantra helped, but he still needed distance.

"Bandages first," he said to himself. "Bandages first." He stole into the bedroom where he dumped all his aid supplies onto the mattress and paused a few seconds to shake off Clear-Skies's bid for dominance. Noticing the toppled space heater, he restored the device and flipped it on. When he returned to the bathroom, he lifted Izzy and brought her to the bed, too.

Cotton balls exploded out of the package when Curtis ripped it open. One of them bonked off his nose. He rushed with the disinfectant and almost spilled it. Libido raced with logic. Logic only had to hold up while Curtis finished his work. There was no way he'd keep a level head after that. His sex drive wouldn't lose and when it took him over and he took Izzy, he knew he'd be closer to animal than man.

*

Everything Curtis did with his chemicals and cotton hurt like hell. As a ballerina, Izzy was no stranger to pain. She'd danced through excruciating conditions with a smile on her face and a springing bounce in her step, crying her eyes out once the curtain fell. Right now, stoicism didn't concern her. She had no audience but Curtis. Shouting proved cathartic when pain spiked beyond her threshold. Her swelling ankle rested on the bed and she mentally computed probable rest times. She worried. A ballet teacher MIA was a ballet teacher that didn't get paid. As soon as all her slashes were cleaned and padded, Curtis shoved all the first-aid equipment from the mattress and crawled over her.

Izzy sank to her back. The top of Curtis's head bobbed between her breasts. He licked a cool, wet path over her sternum and sucked at the plump bottom curve of her breast. Moving down her body, he came to the single aching opening that couldn't be quelled with medicines or balms.

Thighs in hand, Curtis lifted Izzy's bent legs and covered her throbbing sex with his mouth. She threaded her fingers in his hair. He feasted, tongue parting her slit, probing her dampened passage, and fluttering at her swollen bud. Various hurts became irrelevant at the galvanizing pleasure he invoked. It sparked in her fingers and feet, nipples and clit, traveled in a shivering wave from the top of her head to her soles.

Curtis raised his head and his damp, cool hair slipped over Izzy's fingers. His lips and chin glistened with her arousal and his haunting eyes didn't leave her face when he bit her inner thigh, holding the tender flesh in his jaws. He kissed her trembling stomach and came over her, pushing her knees to her shoulders. His cock traveled through her slit, making her gasp.

No, not this way. She'd had it with submitting to physically stronger forces.

Wriggling up, she brought her legs down and met him face to face.

Lips to Izzy's, Curtis tried to get her back down, but she fought him, put her fingers to his chest. Cupping his side, she pushed. She wanted him on his back. A snort and a shake of his shoulders communicated his displeasure. He nuzzled her cheek and fastened his fangs at the junction of her neck and shoulder. At her sex, his fingers tested her entrance and when she made a little high noise he surged upward, stroking and setting her core alight. He tried repositioning her again and she almost relinquished her ground if only he'd keep fingering her.

Releasing a frustrated growl, Izzy caught Curtis's wrist and slid him free of her sex. She sucked in breath at the sudden absence of pressure and her teeth cut into her bottom lip. With his waist trapped between her knees, she twisted herself, hoping he'd roll over. He didn't. Instead, he snapped at her, teeth a millimeter from her face. Pursing her lips, she steeled herself. Behind those wild eyes and bared fangs was Curtis. The wolf was a part of him and he wouldn't hurt her. Curtis had taught her a thing or two about canine language. Kow-towing some to his proverbial chest thumping would get her what she wanted, but how? Ah, she had it. She tipped back her head and exposed her throat.

That's about as submissive as you get without going belly up.

Dipping low, Curtis rested his teeth on her neck, holding her there as he'd held her thigh. Grumbling his acceptance of her gesture, he drew away and reluctantly turned on his back.

No sooner had Izzy straddled him, he was up and guiding her hips where he wanted them. She steadied herself on his shoulder and her mouth went to his. She gave him tender kisses, trying to recapture the reins of their lovemaking.

Slow, slow.

Amorous direction proved useless.

One powerful thrust of Curtis's hips housed him inside her. Moaning, Izzy ground herself against him, giving herself over to his urgency. Her entrance accepted and gripped his length. Breath escaped the fused seam of their mouths in hisses, their kisses deep and near violent. His fingers grasped the round curves of her ass and encouraged her frantic rocking. Fangs forced her mouth wide and once or twice, she came close to piercing herself on their pointed tips. She never thought she possessed a taste for pain or danger, but riding Curtis while he warred with his inner beast pitched her excitement sky high.

When Izzy climaxed, she arched back and screamed, clawing at Curtis's back. He buried his face in her chest, teeth dragging over her skin as he grunted and snarled out his own release. Within her constricting sex, his cock pulsed. Collapsing against him, she allowed his possession and command of her body. Arms secure around her, he rolled them over where they lay—Izzy's face to Curtis's chest—in a warm, sore tangle.

Chapter Twenty-three

"I tried to save him."

Izzy's eyes fluttered open. She drowsed, but hadn't lost consciousness. The space heater cast an ambient, orange glow in the otherwise dark room. Curtis's quiet voice held none of the feral gruffness it had minutes ago. Her lashes swept his chest when she raised her lids and he squirmed.

"I couldn't break out of Thomas's command. I tried, Izzy, I swear, but by the time I broke free, your brother was gone. You—"

Izzy hushed Curtis, putting her fingers to his lips. He moved her hand away.

"Do you believe me?" he asked.

Smashing her forehead to his chest, she wished she could disappear somehow, meld with him perhaps, stop being Izzy. "I do, but, please, I can't hear this now."

"But after tonight, you won't come back here, will you?"

As soon as he said it, she knew it was true. She'd initiated this tryst because she'd wanted to drown herself in sensation. Reaffirming their ties to each other, she'd told herself, that's what she intended. That was a lie. She didn't want to think about death and wolves or Werewolves and what she felt for Curtis, so she used sex—like she used work and dance and everything else—to shut it all away. But those thoughts and feelings wouldn't stay locked up and she couldn't have sex forever, though she wouldn't mind trying with Curtis. She ran a palm over his torso.

A bond shimmered between them still. Izzy fancied she saw it just on the edges of her vision, fine and glinting like a strand of spider silk, that delicate. Despite all she felt for the man beside her, this place, his kind, had taken too much of her blood and spirit. The thread connecting them also kept her bound to the past. It anchored her to the weight of insurmountable events that made each present moment so painful. In her mind, she wanted Keene Lodge buried and forgotten, but this grave was Curtis's home. Forgetting one without the other wasn't possible. Leaving Curtis made her insides ache. She could deal with the pain. She couldn't stay.

Someone tapped at the bedroom door.

Curtis rolled off the bed. His movements were relaxed, but Izzy tensed anyway, ready for another attack. Not bothering with clothes, he padded to the door and opened it. Though his body blocked the exterior view, she recognized Melinda's voice.

"They're gathering," Melinda said.

"And Gerome?"

"Gone already. Wouldn't even stay for Constance to check him out."

Curtis grunted. "I thought I smelled Constance. Would you tell her to come back here? I want her to take a look at Izzy."

"Yeah, sure boss."

Recoiling at the title, Curtis's backside hunched, the motion delineating each muscle. Izzy couldn't believe the pair carried on a conversation with him stark naked. Wolves ran around bare assed all the time, but human form was different. At least, it seemed it should be. Neither of them sounded at all perturbed.

"You're gonna have to say something to them, you know," Melinda said.

"I do. I want you in here while I'm not. No one gets past this—"

Scrabbling interrupted Curtis and a whining bundle of fur scooched by him and into the bedroom. Nook trotted to the disheveled mattress and leapt up. Izzy squeaked when he nuzzled behind her, his fur damp with snow and ice and very cold.

Curtis sighed. "No one but Nook gets past this door, ok?"

"Got it."

While Izzy shoved the soggy dog off the bed, Curtis came back.

"What's going on?" she asked.

Bed springs creaked when Curtis sat. "The local wolves are gathering."

"Here?"

He nodded. "They sensed the shift in power. They're coming to acknowledge the new Alpha."

It took Izzy a second to process that Curtis meant himself. His word hadn't affected her that way for nothing. Thomas's death meant he'd inherited the seat of command. Any order he gave demanded compliance. Her mouth went tight and her words came out strained when she said, "Did I want you just now because you ordered me to?"

"No." Curtis grabbed her by the shoulders, massaged them. "No. The Alpha's power affects behavior, remember? I could tell you to hop on one foot or spin in a circle, but I can't control your feelings or thoughts." The pads of his thumbs traced circles on the bare curves of her shoulders. "I can't make you want me. If you don't believe anything else, believe that." He searched her face for an answer she wouldn't give him and slowly withdrew his hands. Staring at his lap, he scratched the back of his neck.

"She's not pack, but one of the locals—Constance is a nurse and I'd like if you'd let her look you over, please." Izzy noted Curtis's careful wording. He made sure he phrased his suggestion as a question, made certain he gave her a choice. "Don't think you need stitches, but I'm no doctor."

Izzy agreed to a check-up and Curtis brought her one of his oversized shirts. He helped her get it over her head, then chewed the inside of his cheek.

"I'm Alpha now. No one can do anything to you without going through me. You wouldn't be in any danger if you decided you wanted to . . . you know, stay."

Izzy's eyes were unfocused when she said, "I see."

Abruptly, Curtis stood. "Either way, I'm making you pack ward."

When she didn't say anything to that, he explained.

"It means a threat to you is a threat to the pack. To all of us."

He made a face. "As of now that's me and Lin."

"You think someone will try to hurt me?"

"No, I just—" Curtis sucked in a deep breath. "I want you to know you're safe. Here." He brushed her bangs out of her eyes. "Anywhere." His face became pinched. "And Izzy, I need to know . . . that is, would you tell me what Gerome did to you when you were alone with him and Thomas? It's important."

"What he did to me? He held me down," the backs of her eyes stung and memories threatened to overwhelm her, "so Thomas could cut me."

"That's all?"

"Yeah." Izzy searched his face, trying to interpret what it was he wanted to hear.

"You're sure? It's just that before, I could smell him . . . " His eyes dropped to her lap and she understood.

"He got too close for comfort at first, but Thomas put a stop to that."

Obviously relieved, Curtis let out the breath he held.

"You might want to get out there." A tall, burly woman with streaks of gray in her blond hair leaned in the doorframe. "Natives are getting restless."

"Right," Curtis said and left Izzy with this unfamiliar, yet kind looking woman who didn't bat an eye at the naked man sidling passed her. She came and sat by Izzy.

"Constance," she said by way of introduction and not much after that. She inspected Izzy's arms—Izzy ooched and ouched when the bandages peeled up—and *tched* at the patient's throat, probed the painfully tender flesh with firm, careful fingers. "That'll be sore a while. Curtis did all right by you. You'll have scars, but everything should heal up nice and clean. You notice any inflammation and you get to a doctor, y'hear?"

Izzy bobbed her head in acknowledgment. The woman didn't have the power of an Alpha, but she struck Izzy as the no-nonsense type.

"Nothing broken in that ankle far as I can tell. Might want an X-ray for certain. Two weeks off it should do you fine to my eye. You need anything from me?"

Excusing the nurse, Izzy shook her head and Constance went about her business. When the woman strode out the door, Izzy saw Melinda crouched in the hall. The redhead offered a tired smile and shut the door, paying respects to her privacy.

From the bedroom, Curtis's voice came to her muted. He talked a while, interrupted by the occasional howl or bark. Izzy pulled the covers tight around her. She assumed Melinda guarded the door, but that didn't ease her mind. Sounded like a lot of wolves out there. How many could there be in Colorado? The world? A chorus of wailing cries marked the end of Curtis's speech. He didn't return to the bedroom immediately, but when he did he had her duffel in tow. He set it next to her.

"Lin can take you home tonight if you want. I shouldn't leave the property for the next couple of weeks. You could stay if—"

"No. I think home would be better for me right now." She looked at his feet when she spoke.

Curtis made a soft noise and touched her hair. He scrubbed a hand over his face and rubbed his eyes, turned away.

Inside her bag, Izzy found clothes and her phone. Curtis hadn't bothered with her destroyed prosthetic. They dressed together in silence.

Melinda had the Jeep started and warmed up by the time Curtis escorted Izzy outside. People she didn't recognize loitered away from the cabin. Red points from their lit cigarettes moved up and down like fireflies in the dark. A black patch in the snow marked where Thomas fell. The body was gone. She couldn't take her eyes from that patch as she situated herself in the passenger seat and shut the door. When Curtis knocked on the window, she rolled it down. He gripped the sill, but he didn't lean inside.

"Be safe, you two, all right?" His voice broke on the "all right."

"No worries, boss," Melinda chirped.

"Izzy, you have my number, yeah?"

"Yeah," she said, barely hearing herself.

"You need anything, you call . . . if you want to," he hastily tacked on to the order.

A slight jerk of her head served as Izzy's reply. Stepping away from the car, Curtis gave the hood a send off pat and trudged to the cabin, expression shuttered and distant. Izzy rolled up the window and let her mind go blank. Spacing out turned down the volume on sensation and muted sound. Still, she felt the minute twang in her heart when the thread running between herself and Keene Lodge—Curtis—snapped. Unmoored from the weight of the past, she expected to soar, but she grew heavier. Forsaking her slender lifeline, she fell.

And fell and fell and fell.

Chapter Twenty-four

Two weeks proved an accurate estimate for Izzy's recovery. That Monday, she called Claire, her instructing assistant, and had her take over studio classes and private sessions for the duration. Luckily for Izzy, Claire was a saint with a flexible schedule.

The first days Izzy slept, leaving her bed only for water and toilet. By day three, she craved a shower and exercise. She indulged in each, the shower longer than the exercise. Her ankle was just a little swollen now and she didn't want to push it. The awful bruises around her neck were deep purple and her voice, when she spoke, rasped. She spent a lot of time on the couch wrapped in an ice pack muffler. Thank God for winter and her ready supply of turtlenecks and scarves. Come the second week's end, she had her new prosthetic and sat in on classes, offering her discerning eye with Claire's instruction and correcting where need be, which wasn't often. The bulk of Izzy's studio work came in returning phone calls, wrapping up paperwork, and updating the website. A month and a half remained until the studio performance of *The Nutcracker,* which left about six million things to do. Six million to-dos blessedly distracting her from everything and everyone she'd encountered at Keene Lodge.

Dr. Turner saw Izzy right on schedule. The therapist's red lips twitched at the sight of her patient. The ghost of a frown wrinkled her pin-up girl features, but she quickly recovered her pleasant mask that concealed any worry she might have divulged.

Sessions up to the production were an utter waste. Dr. Turner tried engaging Izzy about her weekend with Curtis and Izzy dodged all the conversational lures. She discussed the upcoming show, her stress over her injury, and pressures coming from her professional track students and their parents. Personal life was a minefield she skirted. Besides wading through the emotional wreckage of that weekend, how could she spill her guts about murder and Werewolves? What would Dr. Turner do if she suspected Izzy had a psychotic, homicidal break? These were topics best shut away in airtight compartments with rummage-proof lids. There'd be plenty of time to unpack all that. Later.

Some evenings, Izzy scrolled through her contacts and stared at the name "Curtis Keene" and held her thumb over the entry. Always, she'd smash the home button on her cell, return to the main screen, and toss away the phone. Curtis never called or texted either and, gradually, a painful knot grew beside her heart. Izzy had danced through physical hurts and had lived with an unyielding welter of emotional pain. What was waking up with one more ache to her? As Rutger Hauer once said, "tears in the rain."

That knot wouldn't become a problem until after the production.

*

Glazier Studio's performances of *The Nutcracker* went off without a hitch. Parents cooed over the younger students in their snowflake costumes and loved it when the little flakes went off choreography for a wave at Mom and Dad or a blown kiss. Camera flashes went off like fireworks and blinded Izzy, who peeped at the crowd from the wings. The older pupils showcased their skills to standing ovations. Amanda and Travis, her Sugar Plum Fairy and Cavalier, were a hit. The Glazier Studio raked in a healthy profit that Izzy had decided to split with the local animal shelter. Reps and volunteers from the organization attended each of the four shows, manned adoption and volunteer information desks, and accepted donations. The partnership required a frenzy of last-minute coordinating, but was worth it. When Izzy dropped off the organization's check, she prepped herself for the cacophony of barking and sent up her mental armor. She discovered she didn't need it. Instead of terror, a persistent longing stretched in her breast. The dogs yapping at their kennel doors and the acrid scent of animal made her wistful.

She wondered how Nook fared and rolled her eyes when she thought of Petey.

When had that happened?

*

"Well, howdy stranger." Melinda spun in her desk chair and faced Curtis when he entered the lodge's main building. "Haven't seen you in a quadrillion years."

"Lies. I saw you three days ago," Curtis said, giving his feet an extra swipe on the welcome mat before letting the front door swing shut behind him. The construction schedule weighed fifty pounds. He'd come to kick back and prune the list of "dones," sick of flipping through page after wrinkled, crinkling page of annotated and crossed off projects. So far, they hadn't deviated from the original timetable. The February grand opening was right on track. Just in time for Valentine's Day. Curtis *harrumphed* and flung himself backside first on the couch.

Clear-Skies zipped back and forth in his chest like a comet, pacing. The wolf spirit had been at it since the day after his ascension to Alpha. They were both restless. Curtis pretended he didn't know why.

"You passed by my desk three days ago, but I don't think we've said one word to each other since Izzy bailed."

Curtis cringed and his teeth squeaked when they ground together. "Don't—"

"Use the *I* word? Why not? That's why you're all grouchy and not talking to anyone."

"That's not the only reason why." He rapped the burgeoning clipboard with the back of his hand. "I'm responsible for all this now. With Thomas and Gerome gone, I have to supervise everything and get a handle on the property manager stuff.

Thomas used to handle all that."

"What a load of crap. You know what he did. You just weren't doing it."

Lin was right, but Curtis wasn't telling her that. When it came down to it, taking over management of the lodge wouldn't be hard. Cold-blooded killer he may have been, but Thomas had kept thorough and meticulous records. Anything Curtis didn't understand about the property manager's duties came clear going over archived files. When the full staff came trickling back in January, he'd be more than ready. Surprisingly, it excited him.

Mine. Everything's mine. Except . . .

"If you want her back so bad you oughta call her instead of camping out at Pat's Pub and holing up at the bottom of a pint every night."

"I go for the pool, too." But Curtis's toes curled at the thought of a thick, dark Guinness. Dinner schminner. Who needed dinner with a dozen pints warming your belly? Images of delicious, tempting lager jostled out of Curtis's brain, replaced with the dark fringe of Izzy's lashes against a pale cheek, the way she stood so very still, so straight and silent. The way her face looked when he made her come, almost pained at first, then surprised, eyes closed and her shining, pink lips in the sweetest "O."

"And I can't call her anyhow." It was useless avoiding Izzy-talk with Lin. The girl never let him fucking slide and she never sugar-coated anything. She'd make some man miserable some day.

"You're just a big 'fraidy wolf." Melinda sniffed and her chair creaked.

Ah, finally she was wrong and Curtis jumped on it. Straightening on the couch, he leaned one shoulder over its back like a truck driver and pointed the pen he'd slipped from his front pocket at her.

"No, see, I'm not afraid. I'd love nothing more than chasing that woman down and changing her mind." He scratched his chin with the pen and grinned. "Lots of times. I'd love to call her up and say, 'Izzy, I miss you. Throw me a bone.' But I can't 'cause you know what she'd say after I was done making her feel . . . whatever it is women think. *Complete*, right?"

Rolling her eyes, Lin said, "Ignoring your sexism, what would the Izzy-in-question say?"

Curtis altered his tone in a nasal, falsetto parody of Izzy's. "But what if my feelings aren't my feelings? You called me and asked me to come over. What if it's your Alpha-ness making me love you." He cut the impression. "And then she runs off and we're at square one again, and I don't get two hundred bucks each time I pass it."

Lin stared at him, one rusty eyebrow hooked up. "Izzy loves you?"

"Naturally." Curtis buffed his nails on his shirt.

"She said that?"

Izzy had, hadn't she? No, wait. He'd told her, but she hadn't said anything. His pause didn't escape Melinda.

"Oh man, you said the 'L' word first and she didn't say anything?" Melinda rocked back in her chair.

"You're making it sound bad. We were *together* together before she left. Women don't do that in those stressful situations unless they're gone on you. She just got confused afterwards. That's all."

"Yeah, *or*, she got freaked out by everything that went on and was looking for whatever stability she could get her hands on and you were the closest, ah, *solid* thing."

Curtis almost dropped the pen. "You know what? Stop talking because you have no idea what you're talking about. Izzy loves me and I love Izzy, and if you love something you let it the fuck go like a fucking butterfly and then it comes back to you and lands on your shoulder."

"Or it jumps in the sack with a new butterfly to forget the old one."

Fists tight, Curtis hunkered down on the sofa. There wouldn't be any new butterflies. Everywhere he'd touched Izzy, kissed her, he'd put up a little Curtis flag claiming her in the name of him. No one could replace him, could they?

Something wet and sticky dribbled onto Curtis's clenched right hand. He'd snapped his pen in half. Red ink stained his fist.

Chapter Twenty-five

Christmas and New Year's came and went. Izzy spent the holidays with her parents and their friends. Her knot had graduated to a canker, fed with the guilt and depression she crammed down along with hors d'oerves and booze. The growth seeped acid and breathing around it hurt. It crowded her lungs and squished her heart. Sometimes it swelled and lodged in her throat and brought tears. Those moments passed.

At her parents' Christmas party, everyone was excited at the prodigal daughter's return. Guests' faces—distant aunts and uncles, people her Mom and Dad knew from their social clubs—zoomed too close to her own, right out of the bumping, companionable crowd like the disembodied and winged heads of vengeful spirits. Their teeth, yellowed with caffeine, nicotine, snapped and chattered at her. Their mouths were traps that snared her in conversations she couldn't follow. On one of her refill trips, she passed her mother, who bumped her playfully with her hip.

"What's that you're drinking, sweetheart, Amaretto? The palette of a five-year-old, I swear," she chided and gave Izzy's cheek a feathery kiss, leaving a waxy stamp of lipstick behind.

A child's palette.

The thought sailed over the mellow tones of jazz, the chink of ice in a swirled glass, the clink of champagne flutes whose bubbling, pale gold liquid caught the soft candle light and refracted it like a ray of sunshine.

That day, the sunlight caught flecks of gold in Alan's hair when he ran ahead of me . . .

Like the man with his back to Izzy just ahead. The man speaking with her father. Was it . . .

Someone jostled her arm and a slap of the deep amber—a flash of Curtis's wolf eyes—liquor in her glass sloshed onto her hand. Time fixed itself.

"Oh, excuse me, dear. You're Delia's daughter, aren't you? What's new with you?"

"Did you know," Izzy slurred to the steely haired woman in the garnet-colored suit, "that Werewolves exist?"

"I'm sorry, dear. Did you say 'Werewolves?'"

Izzy held her prosthetic to her lips, preventing further speech and uproarious laughter. Hearing the word "Werewolves" parroted back at her struck her as absolutely hysterical. What was she? Crazy? Nope. Drunk. Very, very drunk.

Slugging back the rest of her drink, Izzy made a hasty exit, climbing to her old room and throwing the covers from her old bed over her head. She did not sleep. She waited. Waited for the guests' departure and the quiet of the house. Then, she got up, tottered downstairs, poured the rest of the Amaretto into a flask, danced into her coat at the door, and left. A quick trip. No one would know.

The cemetery was four blocks from her parents' house. The low chain link fence boxing in the burial ground was climbable. Izzy vaulted over the gate—there were no passing cars in this neighborhood at three something in the morning—and searched out Alan's place. When she found it among the orderly rows of chalk white crosses and bronze placards, she plopped her drunk self down on the ground covered in a glittering, icy carpet. Grass crunched under her butt. She swigged from the flask and the alcohol, liquid candy, slipped over her tongue and throat like a syrupy glove. She toasted the grave and stared at it a long time— the simple cross, the empty iron vase at its foot, Alan Tunskill beloved son and brother—until a film of tears blurred her vision.

"You know, I always thought you were a better person than me." Izzy didn't bother keeping her voice down and it echoed over the well-kept park. "I thought if I'd been good you'd still be here. And I was angry. Angry you'd died a hero and I was left the helpless damsel. I was angry because I didn't know if the situation had been reversed if I would have had the guts to do what you did and I've had a long, *long* time to think about that." Tears poured like streams of fire down her cold cheeks.

"I never hated you, Alan. But I did hate me. Hated that I wasn't good enough or courageous enough or," she made a dismissive wave with the flask, "you know. Not all the things I thought only you could be. You were one way and I had to be the opposite, right? I could never be as wonderful as you, so I had to be the awful one, which was such a fucking cop out. None of it was true and I know now if it'd been you dragged off by some wolf, I would have come for you. I wouldn't have run because I had the chance to at Keene Lodge and I didn't."

Not until later.

"I got that fucking Wolf King." Izzy sniffed and wiped her nose with the back of her hand, tipping the flask and washing the ground with a sparkling, amber stream. "I'll try to be happy, but I miss you. I miss you so much."

Lying on her stomach, Izzy wailed next to her brother's grave, cried her eyes out until her nose grew so clogged with snot she couldn't breathe and her eyes felt like dried raisins, all the moisture wept right out. She whispered into the sleeping earth, "I love you. I miss you," and then up to the sky when she flopped on her back, "I love you. I miss you." When she closed her eyes, she expected Alan's face imprinted there behind her lids, but she didn't see blue eyes when she shut her own. The eyes she saw were brown, crinkled at their corners with laugh lines. The discarded flask she found with a groping hand and she tilted the rest of its contents through her lips, her fingers and chin already sticky with the drink. The booze was warm like the warm expression reflected in those brown eyes and Izzy felt safe in the frost surrounded by peaceful spirits.

*

In mid-January, Izzy tired of misdirection. Her canker had downgraded back to a knot since her visit to Alan's grave, but the damn knot wouldn't loosen. She had to say something to someone about everything and babbling to a therapist about Werewolves was less likely to get her locked up than if she went off in public. Ignoring Dr. Turner's usual pleasantries, she launched into the tale and went well over time. Dr. Turner didn't stop her. She listened to Izzy, pad and pen cast aside.

"I don't know what to do," Izzy said, choked with emotion. "I shouldn't feel so happy about that, should I? We killed a man."

"Not a man." Dr. Turner fidgeted with the crease of her trousers. "A Werewolf, a creature who would have killed you both if you hadn't defended yourselves." She tossed Izzy the box of tissues from the end table at her right.

Tearing several from the box, Izzy stopped up her eyes and nose. "The whole thing sounds crazy, I know, but the craziest thing is I miss Curtis. Actually *miss* him." Relating her story had conjured a vivid image of Curtis. His large frame, hair in need of a trim, his I've-got-a-secret smile. No doubt about it. She had to be nuts. He was a Werewolf and the Alpha of his pack and one slip up in his speech would compel her to do whatever he pleased. A relationship with him? It would be hard. So much work. Was he even allowed to seriously date outside his species? She supposed the Alpha did what he pleased.

"Unfortunate, but not crazy," Dr. Turner commented.

After a honking blow of her nose, Izzy said, "Isn't that what shrinks say to all the whack jobs?"

Laughing Dr. Turner said, "Probably. You'll have to trust you're not one of them." She raised her palm. "Hand to divinity. Someone in my profession doesn't get this far without learning a lot of the city's secrets. Did you think you were the only one who knew about Werewolves?"

Izzy blinked. "You're serious, aren't you?"

Dr. Turner's chin dipped and she closed her eyes.

"Do you know how many there are?" Izzy asked.

"No. I know they, among other creatures of the *aethervorlde*, exist."

"What other creatures?"

The dark haired woman fiddled with her heavy gold hoop earring and sized up her patient. "None you need to worry about as they're not a threat. You don't do well with surprises and we don't need any more distractions from our work today. We can discuss the supernatural later."

That tone Izzy recognized. Dr. Turner was about to take control of the session. But what was that she'd said? Aether-what?

"Why haven't you called Curtis?" Dr. Turner asked.

Izzy opened her mouth and closed it. Her reason was pitiful.

"I don't want to think about it anymore. Any of it. Alan, Thomas, my arm, none of it. And Curtis is right in the center."

"It hurts thinking about those things."

"It does."

"But it hurts missing Curtis, doesn't it? What good is avoidance? I recognize Keene Lodge is the symbolic source of the largest pains you've ever felt, but aren't there other places of pain for you? Do you avoid all of them? Sooner or later you wouldn't be able to leave your apartment."

Sinking into the cushy armchair, Izzy said, "I don't know that I can go back again."

"That's certainly an option considering past and present circumstance. You'll have to weigh the costs. Which is worse: confronting what happened at Keene Lodge and the baggage accompanying that or leaving what and who you love about that place behind?"

Izzy's head snapped up. "I never said anything about love."

"You didn't have to," Dr. Turner said.

Chapter Twenty-six

Snow crunched under Izzy's boots as she trekked over Keene Lodge's front lawn. Petey burst from the main house's back porch tailed by a, for once, excitable Nook. The Samoyed spun circles when she approached and the husky stuck his head through the wood slats.

"Hi, guys," she said and doled out the pats and behind-the-ear scratches. Hiking up to the enclosed front porch, she entered the cozy lobby.

Seated behind the front desk as always, Melinda sandwiched a phone between her shoulder and ear and a young man—he looked about Melinda's age—used the counter as a leaning post. Melinda's jaw dropped when the redhead saw Izzy and she frowned. The expression quickly melted into a very large grin. She waved and hurried off the line. Body repositioned to face Izzy, the young man squinted at her and slouched back. An air of carelessness surrounded him. On Curtis, this carelessness came across as easygoing, but on this man . . . his lazy stance paired with his sharp green eyes came as a silent challenge that Izzy did her best to shrug off.

"Didn't think I'd see you again." Melinda adjusted her bushy ponytail. "This is Danny."

Eschewing niceties, Danny lifted his chin by way of hello.

"He's our new part-time handyman slash receptionist and full-time pack mate."

Izzy extended her hand. "Nice to meet you. I'm—"

"Yeah, I know," Danny said. "Pack ward."

"Actually, my name's Isabelle." She kept her hand out and, with a minute shrug of one shoulder, Danny slapped his hand into hers, rattling her whole body. Anticipating a death squeeze grip, he surprised her, giving her hand a polite and perfunctory shake.

"Right," Melinda said. "Everyone knows everyone, woop-dee-doo." Taking her bottom lip in her teeth, she shot Izzy a suggestive and excessively eye-lashy upward glance. "Here for the weekend?"

"Don't know yet," Izzy said.

Tires squealed in the parking lot.

"Guess you will soon." Melinda smiled and plucked up the ringing phone, switching the caller over to speakerphone and motioning Danny behind the desk.

Izzy almost smacked Curtis in the head with the front door when she flung it open. Dancing back, he blocked his face with his arm. At the first glimpse of him, the remaining tangle of emotion from her knot pulled loose. All she could do was stare at him.

"Hey," he said breathlessly, eyes bright.

"Hey," she countered. "How'd you know I was here?"

Curtis tapped his nose.

"Right. Right. The scent thing."

"We're not heating all of Colorado!" Melinda shouted from inside.

Izzy shut the door. They lingered for a minute without speaking, mouths opening and closing like mute fishes. She broke the ice.

"Sorry for not calling first. If I didn't just come up here, I don't think I ever would."

"Understandable," Curtis said. It appeared he wanted to do something with his hands, thought better of it, and jammed them in his pockets. "You come for your dog?"

"My dog?"

Curtis nodded. "Nook. He's been mopey since you left. Grouchier than usual."

"Um, no."

Now or never, Izzy.

"I came for grilled cheese," she finished.

Brows lifting, the start of a smile quirked the corner of Curtis's mouth.

"I've got bread and American in the car. Beer, too," she said. A chilly breeze carried his clean scent to her. Soap and detergent and wood chips.

"Trouble with the stove at home?" Curtis asked.

"Yeah." Izzy concentrated on her boots. "You're not anywhere near it."

Curtis didn't say a word to that and Izzy's stomach dropped. Maybe she'd been gone too long. Maybe he thought she'd bolt again. Not that she blamed him. Running was her M.O. Why stop now? She brushed a stray wisp of hair behind her ear. It was senseless stringing out her humiliation. She'd made her valiant effort. It was time to go. Her re-knotted knot twisted and engorged and she made for the screen door. Strong hands caught her mid-stride. She looked up into Curtis's smiling face. His brown eyes crinkled that way she loved.

"I think I can handle a sandwich or two. Come with me?"

A question. Curtis hadn't seen her in months yet he was ever careful not to invoke the Alpha's power. He didn't need it. Izzy wanted nothing more than to go with him. She placed her hand in his and let him lead her down the stairs.

They stopped at Izzy's car for her grocery bags—she hadn't fibbed about the grilled cheese and beer—and packed into Curtis's Jeep. They reached the cabin in record time.

"Looks a bit different than the last time you were here, I know," Curtis said and slung the bread on the counter. The beer he gave an appreciative once over and arranged it and the pack of American single slices in the fridge.

The cabin *was* different. An actual rustic wood dining set, four chairs and everything, replaced the mangled card table and a brand new sofa sat in front of a (also) brand new and significantly larger flat screen. A space-age surround sound system flanked the sofa.

"Still going through the old DVD collection." Curtis ran a finger over the speaker she appraised. "Upgrading to Blue—"

Izzy pounced on him, wrapped her arms around his neck and her legs around his waist. God, she'd missed him, everything about him. His stubble abraded her cheek when she kissed him. Arms locked around her back and he squeezed her so hard she almost squeaked. Laughter puffed out from him like a breath when she reared back.

"So, you've landed back on my shoulder, after all," he murmured.

"What?"

"Nothing."

They abandoned food and drink for other pleasures. The mattress, when he laid her on it, cushioned Izzy's back and Curtis's hands and knees when he came over her. Their clothes—and Izzy's prosthetic—vanished under his deft hands. Not a trace of the wolf marked him as he entered her. She needed to see that, needed to see the human side of him stronger than the spirit animal he hosted. If she'd seen even a trace of the beast during their voluntary frenzy, she couldn't have stayed. No amount of love could justify risking her life each time emotions ran high. He was fully Curtis Keene straining above her, eyes closed, mouth open to snatch gasps of air. Her breasts bounced with his steady thrusts. Bringing up her left hand, Izzy cupped his rough cheek. His eyes popped open and he gave her a lazy smile before he bent to kiss her.

As his lips brushed hers, Izzy said, "I love you," and his brown eyes crinkled again.

"I love you too, Izzy."

They came together, faces close, breaths mingling. After that, they lay together, side by side, Curtis's arm cradling Izzy's head, his fingers tickling her shoulder. For hours, they talked, Curtis telling Izzy about the pack and the lodge and Izzy telling him about the successful production and her rather maudlin holidays.

"Amaretto?" Curtis chuckled and his Adam's apple bobbed up and down.

"I like Amaretto."

"Izzy, you're probably the sweetest drunk that ever got soused in a graveyard." He tucked her hair back over her ear and asked seriously, "You all right?"

"Yeah," she said, then turned her head to him. The pillow sighed with the weight of her cheek. "But I don't think the grass by Alan's spot will make it to spring."

"Why's that?"

"I kind of watered a bunch of it with the Amaretto."

With a flash of his white teeth, Curtis filled the room with his booming laughter and, soon after, Izzy's delicate voice joined his. They laughed together for a long time.

Bonus Material

Take a sneak peek at the next story in the Keene Lodge pack trilogy!

ON A ROCKY SPIT OF LAND STRETCHING OUT INTO THE OCEAN, Darial coalesced out of the *aethervorlde*. But three times had he done so since he'd escaped his prison deep in the spirit realm.

Gray-green waters crested over the rocks on which he perched, leaving them slick and slivery under the overcast sky, the cloud veil so low and thick that the physical world seemed but a sliver of a place. Intuition told him the water was cold. He could not feel the icy spray on his face nor the wind whistling over the cavern pocked cliffs at his back. A powerful spirit he was to materialize in the physical plane, but not powerful enough to feel, to affect.

To conquer.

Darial clenched and unclenched his fists, drank in the glassy quality of his spirit flesh, black and shiny as obsidian. A desert he'd visited first, then a weed choked marsh. Searching. Searching for his jailer. Hunting the one with the power to free the rest of the Black Dogs of the Hunt.

Where are you, brother?

Darial knew his treacherous brother hid himself in this world. Vadriel had accomplished what no great spirit since Yahweh—and the pacifist had squandered his physical shell—had: become flesh. An immortal not made of the cold elements of the Earth, but of bone, muscle, and sinew. No scent of Vadriel carried on these winds. None dwelled here, not even the wolves. The soldiers, wolf spirits housed within mortal hosts, he'd caught whiff of in the sun blasted desert and in the swamps. Did they remember their purpose after left so long to fallow? Would Darial's presence call them to arms? He prayed so. For, when he found his brother, and find him he would, the Black Dogs of the Hunt would run free and wild again and Hell would follow at their heels.

About the Author

Envy Augustine's crammed in a one-bedroom apartment with an obligatory crotchety writer's cat and a non-obligatory grouchy husband. She can be found scrunched in the left-hand corner of the sofa scribbling on yellow legal pads. Come say "hey" at *www.envyaugustine.blogspot.com* or on Facebook (where she hangs out regularly) at *www.facebook.com/envy.augustine*.

In the mood for more Crimson Romance? Check out *Witch's Soulmate* by Denyse Cohen at *CrimsonRomance.com*.

www.ingramcontent.com/pod-product-compliance
Lightning Source LLC
Chambersburg PA
CBHW010637100726
47900CB00011B/2865

* 9 7 8 1 4 4 0 5 5 8 9 3 1 *